Praise for AARON ELKINS and
SKELETON DANCE

"Aaron Elkins always tells a story that keeps readers turning pages."
Denver Post

"A terrific follow-up to *Old Bones*. . . . Mischievous wit, fascinating erudition, juicy (but never mean-spirited) academic gossip, and a gorgeous setting redolent with Gitanes and goose liver combine to make this mystery an especially delectable treat. . . . Every suspect is a full-blown comic creation capable of surprise."
Publishers Weekly

"Aaron Elkins is that most cherished of authors, one who leaves you feeling you've absorbed important knowledge you never knew you lacked. . . . The essential key to unlocking the mystery . . . is a forensic tidbit no reader will ever forget."
Chicago Sun-Times

"Enthralling. . . . Gideon is just about as likable as a golden retriever. . . . Combining his natural curiosity with an encyclopedic knowledge of anthropology and forensics, Gideon is quickly on a trail that ends in surprises, double reverses and danger."
Dallas Morning News

"*Skeleton Dance* is an informative and enjoyable look at our collective family tree, nuts and all."
San Francisco Chronicle

Other Avon Books by
Aaron Elkins

LOOT

AARON ELKINS

SKELETON DANCE

AVON BOOKS
An Imprint of HarperCollinsPublishers

AVON BOOKS
An Imprint of HarperCollins*Publishers*
10 East 53rd Street
New York, New York 10022-5299

Copyright © 2000 by Aaron Elkins
ISBN: 0-380-73163-0
www.avonbooks.com

First Avon Books paperback printing: March 2001
First Morrow hardcover printing: April 2000

Avon Trademark Reg. U.S. Pat. Off. and in Other Countries, Marca Registrada, Hecho en U.S.A.
HarperCollins® is a trademark of HarperCollins Publishers Inc.

Printed in the U.S.A.

ACKNOWLEDGMENTS

As usual, Gideon Oliver has borrowed widely from his real-life colleagues. In *Skeleton Dance*, he owes particular thanks to Dr. Marc S. Micozzi, director of the College of Physicians in Philadelphia, for getting him out of his various forensic dilemmas.

Help in Neanderthal matters came from two French scientists, Dr. Bruno Maureille of the University of Bordeau and M. Stephan Madeleine of the National Museum of Prehistory, and in this country from Dr. Susan Foster McCarter of Johns Hopkins University, all of whom willingly took the time and trouble to share their expertise. Captain Norm Hapke of America West Airlines patiently educated me on matters related to flying, and Mark Jenkins of Monterey Peninsula Day School and Dominique Paterne-Jenkins of All Saints' Day School in Carmel provided the necessary French lessons.

Finally, my thanks go to the proprietor of the Hotel Cro-Magnon in Les Eyzies, M. Leyssales, for his friendly help, his permission to use the hotel, and his stories of the good old days.

CHAPTER
1

Once, the thing in the cave had been a man, but that had been long ago. As the years passed it had lain buried in the rich, red-brown humus, slowly decomposing, its nourishing organic wastes feeding successive generations of flatworms and beetle grubs. Then, as the soil settled and fissured, the blowfly larvae had come, followed inevitably by streams of ants and earwigs, and, later still, by the busy rodents of the valley: wood rats, field mice, and squirrels. Over time the protective covering of soil had been largely scratched and worn away, allowing most of the bones to be pulled apart and many of them hustled off to forest dens and lairs, there to be gnawed at leisure.

But now the sounds of deep-chested snuffling and of strong claws scrabbling just beyond the entrance indicated that something more formidable than field mice or squirrels had found its way to the cave. A moment later a squarish, black head with glistening, excited eyes and a mouth filled with shearing, crushing teeth thrust itself into the entrance, low to the

*ground. The creature went for one of the largest
bones, a partially buried femur, worrying it free of the
soil with teeth and claws. It bent its head sideways to
get its powerful jaws around the narrow part of the
shaft, just below the lesser trochanter, where long ago
the Quadriceps femoris had attached, the massive set
of muscles that had once taken the living man striding upright along the valley paths.*

*With a final jerk of its head to set the bone more
firmly in its mouth, the creature turned back to the
opening and loped out of the dimness and into the sun.
The next day it was back, and the next, and the next
after that....*

Dr. Émile Grize, the longtime holder of the Chair
of Paleopathology at the Institut de Préhistoire,
scanned the meager assemblage of bones with a
sniff of disapproval. "You've brought me very
little to work with."

"It's all that we have," said Auguste Marielle,
prefect of police of the village of Les Eyzies. He
said it with a self-deprecating smile, but in truth
he didn't care for Grize's attitude at all, for the
implication that Marielle himself, or his department, was somehow at fault. What was he supposed to do, bring bones that didn't exist?

"They look like something my dog might
bring home," Grize added, in case Marielle had
failed to grasp the point.

"That is the case, in fact," said Marielle. "Ha,
ha, you've hit the nail on the head there, Professor."

The bones, he explained, with his plump shoulders jiggling in a show of good humor, were from an untended patch of weeds and dirt behind the cottage of a stonemason and his wife, where they had been buried by the family dog, which had been returning with them from its solitary outings for several days. The mason, a reclusive malcontent well known in the village, had belatedly notified the police at the urging of his uneasy wife, and the bones had been dug out of the Peyrauds' backyard by Marielle's people only an hour or two earlier. The dog had watched the unearthing of his treasures with indignation and amazement, and Peyraud himself, beginning to regret that he had done his duty in contacting the police, had threatened legal action unless he was compensated for the ruin of his "vegetable garden," whereupon Marielle had told him in no uncertain terms—

"Yes, very interesting," said Grize. "Now this may take some time. You can wait here if you wish, or I can have you notified."

Marielle chose to wait, drinking wretched coffee from a plastic cup and twiddling his thumbs while Grize fingered the materials, leaning over them like a monkey lost in the mysteries of a length of knotted string or a pair of spectacles. And at last, at long last, he straightened up and delivered his pronouncement.

"Yes, they're human, there's no question about that. Right ulna, right femur, right fibula..." He arranged each as he named it, so they lay in a perfect row. "…right first and third metacarpals, rib, rib, partial navicular…"

Marielle put down his watery coffee while Grize rambled on. *If there was no question about it,* he thought sourly, *what took you all morning to tell me?*

"Except for these tiny ones, of course," the paleopathologist concluded, "which I believe to be *Apodemus sylvaticus.*"

"Apo…Apo…?"

"Mouse bones. You see, here is a tibia, here a little scapula, here a—"

"But these others are human—you're positive?"

Grize's chin came up. "If you're not satisfied, you can always get another opinion."

"No, no, sir, I assure you, I'm satisfied, extremely satisfied."

"Dr. Beaupierre, perhaps, or Dr. Montfort might be—"

"No, Professor, believe me, if you say these bones are human, that's certainly good enough for me, oh, more than good enough."

"Umf," said Dr. Grize.

That's the way it was with Grize, Marielle thought, you were always walking on eggshells with him; Marielle had dealt with him before and had known what to expect. He was a little man, that was his problem. Like Napoleon, it made him quarrelsome. And since he was unmarried, he wasn't used to losing arguments every day, which didn't help either; no doubt it also explained why he was so used to hearing himself talk. Difficult as he might be, however, Grize was a scientist of repute, and he knew his bones.

"And is it possible to say anything about the manner of death?" Marielle asked.

"From these? Impossible. As you see, they have been thoroughly gnawed. Any possible indicators of disease or trauma have been eradicated. However, speaking as a trained paleopathologist, I can state with assurance that they are probably male—the general robusticity strongly supports this; they are adult—in those few places where it can be detected, symphyseal union is complete; and they are possibly—I repeat, *possibly*—from the same person."

"And that's all you can tell me?"

Crunch, there went another eggshell. Grize's mouth compressed into a tight little bud. "As a paleopathologist, my area of expertise is ancient disease," he said. "It may be that one of your modern 'forensic' specialists"—the quotation marks were practically audible—"could do better, but I doubt it very much. You are welcome to consult one, however." He placed the bones, including the mouse bones, back in the typing-paper box in which Marielle had brought them and pushed it across his desk.

"Good day, sir."

Marielle spent the rest of the morning pondering his situation. Under the French system of criminal justice, rural police departments did not perform important criminal investigations; these were left to higher levels of authority. Thus, should these bones turn out to be linked to some old murder, which seemed not unlikely, the responsibility would fall to the regional *police judiciaire*, headquartered in Périgueux. This being the case, his obvious course of action would be to notify Inspector Joly in that city at once and let him take charge.

Yes, but suppose that no foul play was involved? Suppose that the reason for the sudden appearance of human bones in old Peyraud's backyard were to prove innocent—the result, for example, of graveyard remains exposed by the early rains, as had happened more than once in the past? What then?

Then, of course, the great Inspector Joly would have been put to inconvenience over nothing, and, as Marielle knew all too well from previous experience, he would not bother to hide his vexation. Joly was, in fact, famous for not bothering to hide his vexation. And the thought of that stiff-necked, long-faced prig treating him to an hour or two of oh-so-forbearing sighs was too much to bear. No, Joly was not to be called in, not yet.

By noon he had come up with a plan. With luck, he might never need to bring in the *police judiciaire* at all.

"Now, Noyon," he said to the crisply uniformed young *officier de la paix* whom he had summoned to his office, "having determined that the bones in question are human, what is needed is to establish whether or not we are dealing with a case of homicide, wouldn't you agree?"

"Yes, sir!" said Noyon. Freshly graduated from the national police academy at Nice and newly assigned to Les Eyzies for his field training, he was grateful for this early opportunity to show his mettle.

"And to do that it is necessary first of all to locate the place from which the dog has been bringing the bones, so that the scene can be properly examined, wouldn't you say?"

"Yes, sir, exactly!"

"And to accomplish *that*, it would seem logical to let the animal lead us to it, no?"

"Yes, sir," Noyon said a little less eagerly, beginning to have some reservations.

"What I want you to do, then, Noyon, is to find an unobtrusive spot within sight of the Peyraud backyard, keeping your eye on the dog. It's brought home bones before. It will bring them home again. See if you can find out from where. That's your assignment. Are there any questions?"

"You want me to...to stake out the *dog*?"

Marielle eyed him frigidly. "Unless you have an objection?"

"No, sir, no objection at all! I think it's a fine

plan. I'm sure it'll work. I'll do my best. Thank you, sir, I appreciate your confidence. I'll get over there right now."

Damn, Noyon thought, *you sure know when you're the new man on the team.*

Three days later, a dusty and bramble-scarred Officer Noyon was back at his commander's desk with discouraging results. The dog was cunning, devious, two-faced, malicious, he said, with a tremor of real hatred in his voice. "He tricked me. He wouldn't let me follow him. He left by different routes, and he never came home the same way twice. When he brought bones back, I swear he laughed at me! I know when a dog's laughing."

Marielle listened with narrowed eyes. "So after three days we're no closer to finding out where they're coming from than we were when we started, is that the substance of your report?"

"Well, yes," Noyon replied, scrambling for a good side to things, "but we do have several more bones than we started with."

Marielle lifted his eyes to the ceiling and resigned himself to the inevitable; he'd come to the end of the line and he knew it. To wait still longer without notifying the judicial police would be disastrous.

And turning to his secretary with a heavy heart, he said: "Get me Périgueux."

CHAPTER
2

The Peyraud "vegetable garden" was scarcely large enough to hold the four men, one woman, and one dog that stood in it. Lucien Anatole Joly, *inspecteur principal* of the Police Nationale's Directorate of Judicial Police, Department of Dordogne, had been looking steadily at Marielle for some time without speaking.

"You are telling me, then," he said without expression, "that since the matter has been in your charge, no action has been taken other than to observe the animal? For three days?"

He wasn't really surprised. He had had dealings with Marielle before: a puffed-up functionary better suited to have been the village postmaster, where he could have known everybody's business even better, and without having to exert himself.

Under his stiff blue uniform collar the back of Marielle's neck burned, but he wasn't about to let this bloodless dandy in his fine Paris suit get on his nerves, especially not in front of Noyon and that old crank Peyraud. He smiled knowledgeably at Joly, colleague to colleague. "Well, it's not as if the bones were going to go bad in three days, you know, Inspector."

"The bones?" Joly replied without returning the smile. "No, the bones won't have been harmed by the passage of a few days. The site from which they come, however, is a different matter. Three days, we may add, during which an active and inquisitive dog has been permitted—encouraged—to disturb the scene to its heart's content."

The superior tone was too much for Marielle. "And you would have done it differently, Inspector?"

Joly, his head tipped back, eyed the shorter, stubbier Marielle down his nose. The man was forever arguing, forever questioning. In themselves, these were commendable traits in Joly's eyes, but only when they went along with listening and learning, which Marielle, for all his quibbling, rarely did.

"To begin with," Joly said crisply, "I would not have permitted the animal to continue to disrupt the site."

"Very true," old Peyraud contributed from the sidelines. "There you have it. Not permit the animal to continue to disrupt the site." He scratched at the gray stubble on his jaw.

Marielle threw him a scalding glance but addressed Joly. "Oh? And how then would you propose to find this 'site'?"

"Yes, that's the question, isn't it?" Joly said, speaking mostly to himself. There wasn't any point, and certainly no pleasure, in quarreling with Marielle. "What is the dog's name?" he asked Peyraud.

"He doesn't have a name."

"Sometimes we call him Toutou," offered Madame Peyraud.

Joly turned to the dog and bent from the waist so that his hands were on his knees. "Come here, Toutou, come on now." Smiling, he held out one hand.

To Marielle's amazement, the cur came, sniffing at the inspector's fingers. Did it think it was going to get its bones back? Ha, good luck to it. When Joly scratched it behind a flea-bitten ear, the dog licked his wrist. Well, they said Hitler had gotten along with dogs too.

"Now, Toutou," Joly said, his tone friendlier than the one he'd been using with Marielle, "now, old fellow, we'll need to find out where you've been getting those bones. Are you going to help us?"

Toutou grinned and wagged his tail.

"Good dog." Joly straightened up. "You won't mind," he said to Peyraud, "if these gentlemen and I take Toutou out for an hour and look about the countryside? You have something we can use as a leash, perhaps?"

Marielle stifled his irritation. How like Joly that was. That smug assumption that the great and wise *inspecteur principal* could accomplish in an hour or two what the poor, benighted police force of Les Eyzies couldn't manage in three days.

"Any particular direction you'd care to go in, Inspector?" he asked lightly as Joly was knotting a length of rope around the dog's collar.

"I was hoping you might help me with that, Marielle."

"I? If I knew—"

"The wind, does it usually come from this direction?"

Marielle gawked at him. "What?"

Peyraud cut in. "Yes, almost always from the northeast. It rides up the valley."

"Well, then, Marielle," said Joly, "I suggest we stroll northeast with a good hold on Toutou, permit him to follow his nose, and see what we find."

"Now *that's* a good idea!" cried Officer Noyon, who instantly made himself as small as possible.

"All set, Toutou?" Joly asked, coiling the end of the seven-foot rope around his hand. "Lead away, then."

It was as if the dog had been waiting all along to be asked. Straining at the rope, his narrow red tongue lolling between stretched black lips, he led the three men along the sloping shelf at the base of the limestone cliffs that backed up against the village, into a copse of stunted oak and juniper and out again, still skirting the undulating, cave-riddled foot of the cliffs as they curved into the forest, away from the village and the river. Never once did he stop to mark a bush, investigate an intriguing hole, or chase a rabbit, real or imaginary. Without deviating he led them to a fall of jumbled boulders that had dropped away from the face of the overhanging cliffs not so many years before—one could still look up and see the whitish patch near the top from which a vast block of the limestone had sheared off and slid down to fracture into huge pieces below.

Once there, the eager Toutou dragged them among the rocks, then sidled into a narrow crevice that had been invisible until they were almost on it. Pulling the panting, excited dog back and keeping it still with a handhold on the rope leash, Joly squatted on his haunches to peer into the opening. The crevice was an irregular, waist-high space between the base of the concave wall of the cliff and the lower part of one of the big boulders that leaned against it, forming a constricted corridor, narrowing toward the top, about four meters long and less than a meter high. At the far end, dim and shadowed, was what appeared to be a shallow, low-ceilinged cave in the base of the cliff; what the locals called an *abri*—the sort of place that little boys were forever stumbling into and turning up one prehistoric find or another, bringing real and would-be archaeologists out in droves.

Just over his shoulder, Marielle laughed aloud. "It's an *abri*. Those bones are ten thousand years old. We've been on a wild-goose chase, looking for what's left of some Stone Age man, what do you think of that?"

It was clear that the prefect regarded this as a personal victory. In the rear, the dutiful Noyon chuckled wanly.

"We'll see soon enough," Joly said. "I'll go first." He handed the rope to Noyon. "Officer, you stay here with the dog."

"It's the story of my life," Noyon murmured.

With a resigned glance, first at the dirt floor of the crevice and then at his crisply creased trousers—what immutable law was it that ordained that he would have to be wearing the new suit from Arnys today?—Joly settled to his knees and began to crawl through the corridor. Behind him, the amazed, deeply offended Toutou yapped loudly away.

"Marielle," Joly called back as he neared the end, "it gets quite narrow in here. If it's too difficult—"

"Don't worry about me, I can make it fine," Marielle snapped, and by dint of a few contortions, a torn epaulet, and an iron determination not to be outdone, he did.

By the time Marielle reached the cave, Joly was sitting on a rounded boulder near the entrance, trying to make sense of the jumbled bones and disturbed earth around him. Obviously, the body had originally been buried in the center of the space, where some of it—the pelvis, the lower part of the vertebral column, and at least one of the upper leg bones—was still partially interred. As for the rest—as much as was still there—it was clear that Toutou had been busy, and probably some of his friends as well. Dozens of bones had been wrenched out of the ground and scattered around the cave. There were a shoulder blade and some hand and foot bones in a little heap at the rear, a rib practically at the inspector's feet, vertebrae here and there, and half of an upside-down human jawbone near the cave entrance. All had been heavily gnawed, with edges and bone ends virtually chewed away. Many, if not most, of the bones were missing altogether; possibly they were in the cardboard box at the Les Eyzies *mairie*, courtesy of Toutou.

Marielle, on his hands and knees, emerged huffing and red-faced from the crevice into the *abri*. "Ha," he said jovially, getting to his feet. "What do we have here?"

Joly held up his hand. "Stop there, please. We don't wish to disturb the site any further until it's been processed."

Marielle smiled at him. "Inspector, I hope you won't think it impertinent of me," he said, "but I find myself wondering what process you are referring to. This is a Cro-Magnon *abri*, many thousands of years old. I assure you, I'm familiar with these things. You see those bits of flint scattered about? They are tool flakes."

"I believe so, yes."

"And the black deposits up there? The result of centuries of fires."

"Yes, I thought as much."

"The cave opening, as you observe, is oriented toward the south to take advantage of the sun, as was typical of the Stone Age; the rock fall which now blocks it is clearly recent. And this"—he gestured at the skeleton—"is without doubt a Cro-Magnon burial."

"There I have to disagree. I'm afraid we have a homicide investigation on our hands."

"If so, I fear the perpetrator may be somewhat beyond our reach by now."

Joly was astonished. Was the man capable of humor then? "No, I don't think so. I believe this is a recent burial."

"Recent!" Marielle shook his head. "Everything here bespeaks antiquity. Believe me, I've studied these things. Observe the placement of the body, the flexed position, the orientation relative to the cave opening. Observe the fact that the skeleton is without any sign of clothing. Observe—"

"I'm not a student of these things myself, Marielle," Joly said shortly, standing up and coming within a couple of inches of striking his head on the stony roof. The smug and gassy Marielle had finally gotten his goat, as he usually managed to do after an hour or so. "Do you suppose that's why I wasn't aware that the Cro-Magnon people went in for dentistry?"

"Dentistry?..." Marielle took a harder look at the broken jawbone, where he was dismayed to see the dull sheen of a gold crown on one of the rear teeth. He felt himself flush, hoping that Joly couldn't see it in the dimness of the cave. "It's, ah, possible that I was mistaken about the age...."

"Highly possible, I should say. Now then, Marielle—"

"But on the other hand," the stung Marielle interrupted, "with all due respect, it seems possible that *you* are mistaken as to the immediate need for a homicide investigation. Where is the evidence of a crime? Many people—villagers, campers, tourists—explore these caves. People have died in them before. They slip and fall, they are crushed by loosened rocks, they die of natural causes—"

Joly looked at him, only barely managing to keep from shaking his head at the man's never-ending obtuseness.

"And do they bury themselves as well?" he asked.

CHAPTER
3

"All right, then, how does this one sound?" Julie said, talking through a ballpoint pen clenched like a pirate's dagger between her teeth. "It's just a few miles from Piltdown." She smoothed the copy of "Holiday Rentals in Southeast England" that lay open on her lap, took the pen from her mouth, circled an entry, and read aloud.

"'Huffield Manor. Surrounded by flagstone terraces and overlooking its own six acres of wooded hillside near the handsome medieval village of Horsted Keynes, this beguiling eighteenth-century stone priory has been converted to a luxurious six-room manor house, completely renovated in 1997. Original beamed ceilings throughout. Large, marble-tiled entry hall with sweeping oak staircase and oak-balustraded minstrel gallery—'"

Gideon looked up from the fresh-from-the-printer sheets that were spread over his own lap.

18

"Hey, hold it, I think you're getting confused. I get half pay while I'm on sabbatical, not double pay. What does this place rent for?"

"I haven't gotten to that yet. Ummm...yikes, scratch that!" She went back to turning pages while Gideon returned to his own reading. "Okay, here's one. 'Cozy stone cottage, a rustic, romantic little charmer...' "

"That sounds more like it," Gideon said.

They had been sitting in their living room for an hour, unwinding over wine and cheese, listening to Mozart, and savoring the view that ran from Puget Sound and the pearly Seattle skyline, a few miles to the east, to cozy Eagle Harbor closer at hand, where one of the big green-and-white ferries from the city was amiably lumbering up to settle against the Bainbridge Island ferry dock, only two blocks away from where they sat and no more than a five-minute walk. The easy access to downtown Seattle—in effect, one could walk to it from semirural Bainbridge—was one of the big selling points of their recently purchased house, set higgledy-piggledy with its neighbors on the hillside above the dock.

The next ferry would be leaving at ten minutes after five, and they planned to be on it for a Friday-night dinner with friends and then a Mariner game at the new ballpark. In the meantime Gideon browsed through the day's output of the book he was working on and Julie fine-tuned their upcoming travel schedule—a four-week jaunt to Germany's Neander Valley, to Oxford and Sussex in England, and to the Dordogne in France, in that order, scheduled to begin the following week. The itinerary had been determined by Gideon's research needs. Julie, a supervisory park ranger at Olympic National Park's administrative headquarters in Port Angeles, would be visiting one or two parks while they were overseas, but was basically going along, as she freely put it, for the ride, and to provide much-needed "logistical support" for the notoriously absentminded Gideon.

"'...situated in a small, rural village on the banks of the Ouse, within easy driving distance of Sheffield Park, Cuckfield, Piltdown, etc. Sitting room with river view, one bedroom, one bath, small but modern kitchen with fridge...'" She stopped reading and waved the brochure at him. "Hello? Anybody there?"

"Hm? Oh, sorry. Sure, that sounds fine."

"What sounds fine?"

He cleared his throat. "What you said."

She put down the brochure. "What are you working on, anyway—the book?"

The Book. *Bones to Pick: Wrong Turns, Dead Ends, and Popular Misconceptions in the Study of Humankind.* It had grown out of a public lecture he'd given a year earlier at the university, part of a survey-of-the-sciences extension series. His presentation, "Error, Gullibility, and Self-Deception in the Social Sciences," had been at-

tended by Lester Rizzo, the executive editor of
Javelin Press, who had approached Gideon afterward to ask if he would be interested in ex-
panding the subject and turning it into a book
for publication under Javelin's "Frontiers of Science" imprint.

Gideon had agreed, partly because he was
flattered at the idea of joining the roster of distinguished scientists who had already contributed
to the series, partly because he was looking for
something different to do on his upcoming sabbatical, and partly because almost anything that
was still ten months away from doing was likely
to seem like a pretty doable idea, whatever it
was. The fifteen-thousand-dollar advance—
ready money, up front; a startlingly original concept to anyone accustomed to writing for the
academic presses—hadn't hurt either. Even
Lester's first editorial suggestion, the first of
many ("You're writing for the masses here. What
do you say we dumb down the title a little?"),
hadn't put him seriously off; surely Lester knew
more about selling books than he did. So, stifling
his natural reservations, he'd gone along with it,
although not as far as Lester would have liked
(*Bungles, Blunders, and Bloopers*). Hence *Bones to
Pick*, a reasonable compromise.

He nodded, filling their glasses from the bottle of merlot. "Yeah, the book. I've been stuck on
the same section for two days. I can't figure out
how to get into it."

"What section is it?"

"You want Lester's title or mine?"

"Yours."

"'The Case of the Neologistically Prolix Hyperboreans.'" He smiled. "What do you think?"

She made a face. "Well, to tell the truth..."

"Julie, it's meant to be amusing, for Christ's sake."

"Oh. And Lester's version?"

"'The Myth of the Eskimos' Two Dozen Words for Snow,'" he said testily. "Something like that." He cut a few more slices from the loaf of French bread, loaded them with wedges of Gorgonzola, and arranged them on the plate.

"Well, don't get mad, but I have to admit that I like Lester's version better. Not," she added quickly, "that it's as amusing as yours, of course, but— Hey, wait a minute—the *myth* of the Eskimos' two dozen words for snow? You mean they *don't* have them? Separate words for dry snow, and wet snow, and slushy snow—"

"Not two dozen, not fifty, not nine, not forty-eight, and not two hundred and two—each of which has been reported by 'authorities,' most of whom probably know as much Eskimo as I do."

"But...well, how many *do* they have?"

"Ah, you see, that's the hard part. Maybe two, maybe a hundred, depending on whether you're thinking of Inuit or Yupak, or whether you're counting lexemes, or morphemes, or derived—"

"Careful, you're losing me. To say nothing of the waiting masses."

"Look, the important thing is, it doesn't matter, it doesn't prove anything. However many they have, it's no big deal. Look at it this way: how many words do we have for water?"

"Well, I was going to say one, but now I think I'd better wait and see."

"Good move. What about 'ice'? 'Fog'? 'Mist'? 'Snow,' for that matter?"

"Yes, I guess if you want to stretch a point—"

"But it's not stretching a point. They all stand for water in different forms. And what about 'river,' 'stream,' 'brook,' 'creek,' 'eddy'? They all mean water—water moving at different rates in different conditions."

"And you're saying that's the kind of thing the Eskimos do for snow?"

"Sure. And if some Eskimo linguist studied us, he'd probably say English is amazing: separate, completely independent words for standing-water-in-large-quantities, standing-water-in-medium- sized-quantities, standing-water-in-small-quantities—"

She wrinkled her nose. "Hold on now..."

"'Ocean,' 'lake,' and 'pond,'" he said. "We even have one for standing-water-in-teeny-weeny-quantities."

"Mmm..." Thinking, she stared out the window. "Puddle?"

"Now you're catching on. See?"

"Yes, I'm starting to. It's interesting. Now, what's your problem, exactly?"

"I can't seem to come up with a simple way of starting."

"Why don't you write what you just said? The whole bit, from the beginning?"

He looked at her. "That's a good idea. I will." But his face, which had momentarily cleared, fell. "What did I say?"

"Sorry," she said. "If I'd realized you weren't paying attention I'd have taken notes."

"God help me," he wailed, but he was laughing.

He was laughing more these days, she noted with pleasure. Not that he'd ever been ill-humored; far from it. But over the last year or so she'd begun to sense a lessening of verve, of the essential liveliness and interest in everything that had always been such a big part of him. She'd pondered on the possibilities of midlife crisis (he was forty-four), of career dissatisfaction (he was a full professor at the University of Washington's Port Angeles campus; where did he go from there?), and even—but only briefly and when she was in one of her own rare periods of insecurity—of boredom with their marriage.

It had taken her a while, but in the end she'd put her finger on it: it was Port Angeles itself, the remote onetime lumbering town on the far side of the Olympic Peninsula, where the university, in an effort to be ready for the sure-to-come population expansion from Seattle, had built a well-endowed full-scale campus. The problem was that they had gotten there a bit too early. Port Angeles was a lively, attractive town in a glorious location, but a cultural center—a city—it

wasn't, not yet. And Gideon, she had belatedly
realized after five years of marriage, was a city
person through and through, born and bred in
Los Angeles. He had taken the Port Angeles position, an associate professorship at the time,
largely for her sake, so that she could continue
working with ease at Olympic National Park.

He'd never once complained; indeed, in
many ways it was obvious that he loved the
place—the clean air, the nearby Olympic Moun-
tains, the startlingly beautiful alpine lakes
tucked into pristine green valleys, the laid-back
atmosphere of the university campus. But no
opera, no real theater or museums, no fine
restaurants, no Mariner games. To get to any of
those meant a four-hour round-trip by highway,
bridge, and ferryboat, and when the weather
was bad, a pretty common occurrence in these
parts, it meant a night spent in a Seattle hotel
and a predawn start home the next day if it happened to be a workday. And so, little by little,
they'd pretty much stopped going, except for
the occasional university event at the main campus. That had suited her fine; she was a country
girl at heart, never at her best in cities. But, she
had only recently come to realize, it hadn't
suited him.

And so when the opportunity had been offered him to join the faculty at the main campus
in Seattle—he'd turned down a similar chance
once before—she had encouraged him to accept,
and this time he had, and they had moved to

Bainbridge Island, still on the Olympic Peninsula side of Puget Sound but only six miles from downtown Seattle, a comfortable thirty-five-minute ferry ride. She had pushed for the move in an openhearted spirit of self-sacrifice—it would mean a ninety-minute drive to work for her each way instead of her former ten-minute walk—but she'd found that it was a good thing for her too. Her drive was beautiful and uncrowded, a relaxing, mind-clearing ramble over the Hood Canal bridge, through grand, fragrant forests of Douglas fir, and along the lush flanks of the Olympics all the way to Port Angeles. With a new flextime arrangement, she went in only four days a week now. And she and Gideon were now getting into the city a couple of times a week for one thing or another—and, except for the one night the ferries had stopped running because of the high seas, they had been getting home the same night regardless of the weather.

Things were good. It had been a smart move.

"Going to have any more wine?" she asked, reaching for the bottle.

"I don't think so, thanks," he said, smiling, just as the telephone in the kitchen rang. "Oh, jeez," he said, "that has to be Lester. Would you mind taking it? Tell him I'm anywhere but here, and you don't know when I'll be back."

"I'll do what I can," she said, getting up, "but you know, you'll have to talk to him sometime."

"Not if I can help it. Tell him I went out for a

quart of milk last Monday," he called after her, "and you haven't seen me since."

For over a week his editor had been pestering him about the title page. Lester wanted the author listed as "Gideon Oliver, the Skeleton Detective," making use of the irksome nickname that had been applied to him years before by a reporter and had stuck to him like a bloodsucking leech ever since. Lester thought it might sell a few extra books. After all, he had pointed out in his straightforward way, a lot of people had heard of the skeleton detective, even if they couldn't say exactly where, but who the hell had ever heard of Gideon Oliver?

Gideon could hardly argue with that, but he'd put his foot down anyway. His academic colleagues, who were a lot more important to his daily happiness than Lester was, would never have let him live it down.

Julie was back in a few seconds with the telephone. "It's not Lester, unless Lester pronounces your name 'Geedyong Ohleevaire.'" She handed him the phone and went back to her chair and her brochures.

"Gideon? This is...ahum..."

"Lucien?"

"Yes, that's right. I'm pleased that you recognize my voice."

"Well, of course I would."

Actually, it wasn't the voice, or even the accent; it was that "ahum." Lucien Joly, a formal type, wasn't all that comfortable referring to himself by his first name. Gideon had considered it a major accomplishment, that afternoon in the little French village of Dinan, when the inspector had first done it. At the time, Joly had been attending a forensic sciences seminar in Saint-Malo a few miles away, where Gideon had been one of the speakers. Afterward they'd worked together on a case and had become friends of a sort. Later Joly had been transferred to Périgueux, the capital city of the *département* of the Dordogne, and when Gideon had made his current plans to go to nearby Les Eyzies to research the celebrated archaeological hoax known as the Old Man of Tayac, he had telephoned him to suggest that they get together. They had agreed to meet for dinner in Les Eyzies at the restaurant Au Vieux Moulin, one of Joly's favorites, on October 7. That was still five weeks away.

"Is there a problem with the seventh?" Gideon asked. "Need to change our date?"

"Change the date?" Julie said from the sofa. "No way. It's taken me a week to work everything out as it is. Besides, I'm only halfway through my French lessons."

"Not a problem, exactly, no," said Joly. "But do you suppose you might come a little earlier?"

"Could be. When did you have in mind?"

"The sooner the better. I was thinking of next week."

"Next week?"

"Next *week*?" echoed Julie. "Absolutely not! Gideon, I'm warning you, you're in very dangerous territory here."

"Yes," said Joly. "I was hoping you could make France your first stop instead of your last."

"I don't think so, Lucien," Gideon said. "We've been working on our itinerary for weeks—"

"*We've* been working?" said Julie to the ceiling. "I really love that."

"—making reservations, arranging flights, and so forth. We already have room reservations in Les Eyzies next month, at the Hôtel Cro-Magnon. That's where I stayed the last time I was there, and I really like it. I wouldn't want to lose—"

"I'm sure I would have no trouble changing your reservation for you. The thing is, you see, these rather intriguing bones have just turned up here—"

"But we don't even arrive in France until—" He stopped. "Um…bones, did you say?"

"Yes, it's a curious case. They've been found in what seems to be a Paleolithic cave, oddly enough—by a dog, as it happens—and although I have no doubt that it's a homicide, I can't prove it. I was hoping that if you came earlier you might look them over while they're still there and see what you can turn up. It would be a great service to me, but, of course, if it's impossible…"

"Well, no, I wouldn't say it's *impossible*..."

Up into the air in a fountain of glossy colored paper went the brochures. "I knew it," Julie muttered. "The minute I heard that 'Um... bones?' I knew it. Les Eyzies, here we come. Honestly—"

"Lucien, it seems to be a little noisy at this end. Could you speak up a bit?"

CHAPTER
4

Paris may well be the most beautiful city in the world, but its outskirts are nothing to brag about. Leaving the Gare d'Austerlitz by train and rolling south toward the Dordogne, one travels first through what seems like tens of miles of railroad yards, empty of people but dotted with grimy, isolated freight cars and passenger coaches that stand like tombstones on spurs that lead nowhere. Then come block on block of drab apartment houses, followed by grubby gray suburbs that are succeeded in turn by grubby gray villages (relieved by an occasional glorious church), all set in flat, featureless countryside.

"Every time I take a train out of Paris," Gideon mused, "I wonder if the landscape is really this ugly, or does it just look that way after you've had your eyes dazzled by Paris itself?"

"It has to be the former," Julie said. "We didn't see enough of Paris to get dazzled."

"That's a good point," Gideon said, nodding.

"And what we did see wasn't that dazzling."

"Very true."

They had begun the fourteen-hour, eight-time-zone flight from Seattle early the day before, arrived jet-lagged and seedy at six-fifteen this morning, showered and changed at the airport, taken the Air France bus to the city, had a disappointingly so-so breakfast in a glassed-in streetside brasserie, managed to get in a morning walk around the Tuileries, and then caught a taxi to the train station, where a two-day-old garbagemen's strike had left the place looking as if it had been hit by a tornado. All in all, not a wildly successful Paris visit, and their moods reflected it.

After an hour or so on the rails, however, during much of which Julie slept, the land developed some character, the fields becoming more contoured, the villages a little prettier and more individual; about on a par, say, with what you'd see driving through southern New Jersey. But then, as the train moved deeper into the rural heart of France, eventually crossing into the *département* of the Dordogne—or the Périgord, as most Frenchmen still referred to it—there were increasingly frequent glimpses of deep-green forests of chestnut and oak, smooth-flowing rivers, and wonderful outcroppings of limestone, brilliant against the darkness of the green.

Gideon too tried sleeping, but, although he was relaxed and comfortable enough, it came only in drifting patches, and most of the time he simply looked dumbly and contentedly at the scenes sliding by the window, or equally dumbly and contentedly at Julie, sound asleep in the chair opposite in their otherwise empty compartment, a single misplaced tendril of her glossy, curly black hair quivering back and forth on her cheek with every quiet breath.

"You're not watching me sleep, are you?" she asked with her eyes closed.

"Yeah, you caught me. I can't help it. You're sure pretty. I keep meaning to tell you that."

She smiled, brushed away the tendril, opened her eyes, and straightened up, looking surprisingly rested. "Oh—it's beautiful out there."

"We're in the Dordogne. You've been asleep for a couple of hours."

"Those hollows in the cliffs—those are the famous *abris*?"

"Uh-huh. You're looking at what was the most crowded place in Europe thirty-five thousand years ago, a real population center. The Cro-Magnons had just arrived, and the Neanderthals hadn't quite died out yet, or evolved, or whatever happened to them. Every one of those hollows—the ones you could reach, anyway—probably had a few tenants at one time or another. The Old Man of Tayac came from one just like that long, low one at the foot of that double cleft."

Julie, still a little sleepy, watched it go by. "You know, you've only talked about the Tayac hoax in snippets now and then. I wouldn't mind having a better idea of what it was all about."

"Sure, what do you want to know?"

"Well, I know you know the people who were involved, the people from that institute—"

"The Institute of Prehistory...l'Institut de Préhistoire."

"—but you weren't actually here at the time it happened, were you?"

"No, a little before, unfortunately. I missed it by a couple of months. And the reason I knew them was that I was putting in a few weeks on that middle-Neanderthal dig up the road near Le Moustier. It didn't have anything to do with the institute, but I was staying right there in Les Eyzies—at the Hôtel Cro-Magnon, in fact—and of course anthropologists like to talk to other anthropologists—"

Julie smiled. "To argue, you mean."

"That too," Gideon said equably. "Anyway, I made a courtesy call when I arrived, and eventually I got to know them fairly well. But I was long gone by the time the ruckus over the Old Man started, and pretty much out of touch. I followed it in the journals, like everyone else."

"And what was that about, exactly—the ruckus?"

"Julie, are you sure I never told you about it?"

"Well, you might have. It's possible my mind wandered—kind of like yours does sometimes when I tell you about the National Park five-year plan. But now I'm here; it seems more relevant."

"Fair enough," he said, laughing. "Okay, it all goes back almost ten years, to when the institute first dug this Neanderthal site—the Tayac site. They found two burials, a mature adult male and a child of about three, along with a few stone tools, and that was it. The dig was wrapped up six or seven years ago and closed down. The burials and most of the stone tools and things are in the Museum of Man in Paris."

"And the mature adult, that was the Old Man of Tayac?"

"In person."

"And what was so special about him?"

"About him, per se? Nothing; just one more Neanderthal old geezer—arthritic, toothless, bent over with age—probably all of thirty-five years old. An authentic, fairly typical burial. It was what was dug up later on that made him special."

"Later on? But you said the dig was closed."

"Yes, but you see, the director of the institute, Ely Carpenter, was convinced—obsessed is more like it—that there was more to be found in the *abri*, and even though there wasn't any more funding to keep the dig going, he kept at it on his own, poking around the cave in his spare time, and damned if he didn't eventually hit the jackpot." He looked up. "Here comes the coffee cart. Interested?"

"Desperately."

As usual on European trains the coffee came in a flimsy plastic double cup with a packet of grounds in the upper part, over which the vendor poured hot water; a gimcrack affair, to put it mildly. But also as usual, it was delicious: deeply aromatic, hearty, and soul-satisfying, especially to a couple of coffee lovers whose biological clocks were under the unhappy impression that it was four o'clock in the morning. For a minute they paused in the narrative and sipped, letting the rich stuff flow like heated wine through their systems.

"Where was I?" Gideon asked after he'd downed half of it.

"Umm...'hit the jackpot.'"

"Right. On second thought, make that 'won the booby prize.' What Ely came up with, you see, was this small cache of grave goods that were part of the old man's burial but had apparently been overlooked during the official excavation."

"Overlooked?" said Julie, surprised. "Sounds a little careless."

"Well, some of the ceiling had collapsed at least once during the last thirty-five thousand years or so, you see, and it'd confused the strata quite a bit, so I guess it was excusable. Anyway, it was what Ely found in the cache that was so important."

"Which was?"

"Four small, brownish bones about an inch long, metapodials—foot bones, tarsal bones— from a prehistoric cave lynx. And what made them unique..." Gideon, no mean storyteller, paused for a couple of beats for the desired dramatic effect. "...was that three of them had oval holes cleanly drilled through one end. The fourth was perforated partway through."

Julie frowned at him over the rim of her cup. "So?"

"So they constituted, or seemed to constitute at the time, the very first concrete evidence that Neanderthals were advanced enough to produce any kind of art. You see, those bones were surely part of a necklace or bracelet that would have been strung together and worn. Plenty of things like that have shown up at Cro-Magnon sites, sure, but this was the first time they'd found any in a Neanderthal setting—in fact, they were the first Neanderthal decorative objects of *any* kind, or at least the first ones that weren't ambiguous."

Julie thought for a moment. "I can see why that would be important, but how could anyone say for sure that the Neanderthals *made* them? You said the Cro-Magnons were here at the same time. So who's to say *they* didn't make them? How do you know that this Old Man didn't steal them, or find them, or trade for them, or—"

"Ah, that's the part that was so slick, Julie. It was that fourth bone, the one that was only partway drilled through. The fact that one of them was unfinished was proof—well, as close as you can come to proof in this kind of thing—that it was in the act of being made right there, on the spot. The natural assumption was that the Old

Man of Tayac was a craftsman, and that he was buried with the products of his labor—maybe accidentally, maybe not."

"Ah, I see," she said, sitting back and gazing at the countryside again. "Yes, that was clever." She finished her coffee and put the cup on the tiny folding table below the window. "How did they find out it was a hoax?"

"It was an anonymous letter. It showed up at a Paris newspaper—*Paris-Match*, I think it was—about a month later, claiming that those four bones had been taken from some dusty little paleontology museum not far from Les Eyzies, perforated, and then planted in the *abri*, waiting to be found." He hunched his shoulders. "They did an investigation, the claim turned out to be accurate, and that was that. The whole thing was discredited as a fraud."

"Wow. I can see how that would have made a few waves."

"More than a few. Anyhow, the question of whether Ely actually perpetrated the whole thing or just innocently fell for it has never been settled, and I'm hoping I can come up with some answers, or at least some credible possibilities. So the very first thing I want to do is sit down and see what the institute people have to say about it now, almost three years later."

"After you look at Inspector Joly's bones for him, you mean."

"Oh, that," said Gideon carelessly. "How much time can that take?"

CHAPTER
5

If all his forensic cases were like this, he would be a happy man.

Dry. No gore, no brains, no guts, nothing greasy, nothing putrid, nothing nasty. Just clean, dry bones. The only smell, aside from the not unpleasant fustiness of the bones themselves—not so very different from that of old books or decaying leather—was the damp, woodsy fragrance of the mosses and lichens that had managed to gain a foothold in the dim rocky crevices at the base of the walls. It was almost like working at an early-man site.

Well, why wouldn't it be, it *was* an early-man site, an *abri;* maybe Cro-Magnon as Joly thought, but probably Neanderthal. The sloping roof of the cave, a few inches higher than Gideon was tall, was black with the soot of hundreds of fires, and embedded here and there in the earthen floor he could see small shards of chert and flint, dozens of them—not the scrapers or choppers or hand axes that you saw in museums, but the waste material, the discarded flakes that had been chipped away to form the stone tools. Long ago, some ancient fur-wrapped flintknapper, possibly more than one, had squatted there by the fire, patiently hunched over his work, slowly shaping household implements or crude weapons from the smooth, dark stones of the nearby valley.

Much later, millennia later, others had come. A pair of archaeological test trenches, only faintly perceptible now, had been sunk at right angles to each other. It had been some time ago, perhaps thirty years, perhaps fifty. Whoever had dug them had apparently found nothing to encourage a full-scale excavation; the trenches had been filled in again and the excavators had gone elsewhere.

Later still, another visitor had found his way there, but this one had never left, or at least some of him hadn't, and Gideon had spent part of the morning and most of the afternoon working over what remained, using trowel, toothbrush, paintbrush, tongue depressors, and fingers in roughly that order. Gradually, he had freed the reddish-tinged bones from the dirt floor of the cave, where the body had been buried in the backfill at the intersection of the trenches. In the relatively soft, loose soil, and with most of what was left of the skeleton already disturbed by rodents or carnivores, it was an easy job and a quick one—or it would have been had not Joly insisted on having his people draw charts, take photographs, bag insect remains, put the dug-up dirt through a sieve, and generally get in the way after each couple of millimeters of earth had been scraped away. Well, it was nobody's fault but Gideon's; it was at his forensic seminar in Saint-Malo that Joly had learned the proper techniques of retrieving skeletal material, and Joly, as Gideon well knew, was nothing if not a stickler.

Moreover, with the inspector watching his every move, he'd been forced to do everything by the book himself. At first he'd tried to justify a little judicious corner-cutting, but his argument ("*You* have to do it the way I taught you because the rules are there for a reason, but *I* can do it this way because I'm an expert and I know when it's all right to break them") had met with the contempt it deserved.

And so what should have been an hour's work had ended up taking almost four, but now the grubwork was done. All of the bones that had remained in place were exposed. The body had been buried on its left side, and so the right side, being uppermost, had suffered the greatest depredation. Much of the left half was still intact. In total, Gideon estimated that a little more than half the bones, the skull among them, had been carried off or consumed, but the official count could wait until later, when the remains were in the morgue, where the light would be better and he wouldn't have to work kneeling on a kneepad (provided by a considerate Joly) and balancing a clipboard on his thigh. For the moment he was after information of the most basic sort, much of which had already come to light and which he was now presenting to the inspector.

First things first: the remains appeared to be those of a single individual—they matched in general size and appearance and there were no duplicates—but even that conclusion would have to be checked in the lab. Until you placed each bone against its apposite member to see if they fit together, you couldn't be sure; joints were as individual as fingerprints. Second, it was a male; half a dozen hard-to-miss indicators on the pelvis told him that. Race was trickier, not only because race was always trickier than sex (in sex, you only had two choices—flipping a coin would give you the right answer half the time—but when it came to races, anthropologists were still arguing about how many there were, or even if the concept of race had any usable meaning), but because most of the better racial criteria were in the skull, and there wasn't any skull. For the moment he was guessing Caucasian, but later he would do a set of metric analyses and run discriminant function coefficients on the long bones to see if he could come up with something definitive.

As to age, the one pubic symphysis that was relatively ungnawed was rimmed and moderately hollowed, putting it at an advanced phase

five on the Suchey-Brooks scale, which suggested a man somewhere around fifty, give or
take a decade. The only sign of pathology that
had jumped out so far was an interesting area of
thickening and callus formation on the top half
of the left ulna, just below the elbow, an indicator of inflammation that might have been the result of skin ulceration, or part of a disease
syndrome such as syphilis, or perhaps the effect
of an injury, although he was fairly sure there
hadn't been a fracture. Unfortunately, the right
forearm wasn't present, so it was impossible to
say if the hypertrophy was bilateral or—

"Yes, yes," Joly said tartly. He'd been either
perched uncomfortably on a rounded boulder
near the cave entrance, one well-creased trouser
leg crossed over the other and lighting up an occasional Gitane, or else leaning over Gideon's
shoulder, for the whole time, and his patience,
never one of his strong points, was beginning to
fray. "And how long would you say he's been
here?"

Gideon leaned back on his haunches. "Hard
to say with any precision, Lucien. All there is in
the way of soft tissue, aside from some dried
goop, are a few shreds of ligament and some
cartilage from the joint capsules, so at least we
know he's been here awhile." He reached
around behind him for one of the scattered
bones, the right tibia, held one end of it to his
nostrils, and inhaled, first gently, then deeply.
Joly made a face.

"Well, now, wait a second," Gideon said. "I can still pick up some candle-wax odor."

"Candle wax? I don't understand."

Gideon looked up. "I thought I talked about bone smells at the seminar. Where were you?"

"Very possibly you did," Joly said. "I may have disregarded it as being irrelevant to any activity in which I might conceivably find myself engaged in the future."

Completely understandable, Gideon thought, smiling. He couldn't picture the refined and elegant Joly sniffing bones either. "Well, the smell is the odor of the fat in the bone marrow. After it passes through the rancid stage—and you don't have to hold it anywhere near your nose to recognize that—it develops this characteristic waxy smell that lasts for a few years. At a guess, I'd say these have been here a minimum of two or three years, but fewer than ten. Less than I thought at first."

He sniffed at the tibia again. "Let's say between two and five years, right around there. The skeletonization is a little more advanced than you might expect for that amount of time, but that's probably because it's such a shallow burial and the soil was already disturbed by these trenches, which made it easy for bugs and things to get in. Two to five years, that's my guess."

Joly looked pleased. "Excellent. I've had our chemist analyze the what-is-it-called, the level of acidity—"

"The pH level?"

"Yes, the pH level of some of the soil that was adhering to the bones. His conclusion was that it was consistent with a time since death of three to six years. Putting the two estimates together we arrive at a range of three to five years."

"Approximately," Gideon warned. "I don't know about your chemist, but speaking for myself, I'm not talking high science here. This stuff is variable as hell—the composition of the soil, the amount of moisture, the temperature, all kinds of things. If you have any unsolved missing-person cases from *anywhere* around that time, I wouldn't rule them out. We're probably looking at one of them."

"But we don't," Joly said. "There are no records of missing persons, of males at any rate, from this or the neighboring communes that could possibly fit the time of which we're speaking."

"Mm. So he's probably from out of the area."

"It would seem so." Joly lit up another cigarette and sat watching as Gideon continued examining the remains. "And what else?"

"Well, he's got a couple of old, healed fractures. A broken rib and a crushed calcaneus—that's the heel bone, in case you missed that part of the session too. The second might be a help in identifying him, because he may have walked with a limp."

"Yes?" said Joly, writing in his notebook with a slim silver ballpoint pen.

"Or then again, he may not. No way to tell."

"Ah," said Joly with a sigh. He closed the notebook, retrieved his cigarette from the small foil ashtray he'd brought with him, and continued to smoke. "And what else?" he said again after a while.

"Hmm?" Gideon said, prodding a vertebra. "What makes you think there's anything else?"

"Because I know you, my friend. You like to save the best morsels for last, the better to dazzle the brain of the poor, plodding policeman."

Gideon laughed. It wasn't the first time he'd been called a hot dog by a cop, and he was willing to admit to it. As engrossing as it could be, there weren't many aspects of forensic anthropology that could properly be called "fun," but pulling unexpected rabbits out of hats to the bogglement of various police sergeants, lieutenants, and inspectors was surely one of them.

"Well, I'm sorry, I don't know what else there is that I can tell you," he said. "Or would you be interested in things like...oh, cause of death, bullet holes, that kind of thing?"

Joly mutely rolled his eyes, stubbed his cigarette out in the ashtray, and came and hunkered down beside Gideon, first carefully (and characteristically) pulling up his trouser legs to preserve the creases. "Can you really establish a probable cause of death, then?"

"I can do better than that," Gideon said. "I can establish a definite cause of death. Unless, of

course, you want to assume he survived being
shot through the heart."

"Shot through the heart?" Joly's eyes moved
rapidly over what was left of the skeleton's thorax. "But there's no—"

"Look at the body of the eighth thoracic vertebra."

"Gideon, your excellent instruction notwithstanding, I wouldn't know a thoracic vertebra
from a left toe bone, let alone how many of them
there are or which one is the eighth, or where the
'body' is to be found."

"Sorry. Here, let me free it—it'll be easier to
see." He gently worked it out of the soil with his
fingers, laid it on a square of butcher paper, and
pointed at the vertebral body, the thick, cylindri-
cal center of the vertebra, where a rough, irregular gutter had been gouged out along the upper
left edge. He tapped it with a chopstick. "Gunshot wound."

Joly scowled at it, and then at Gideon. "Am I
not correct in thinking that a bullet hole in bone
is generally round, at least at its point of entry?"

"Yes, you're correct."

"But this—this isn't round at all. It might just
as well have been made by an ax, a knife, even a
hammer. I find myself wondering how you can
state with such confidence that it was made by a
bullet and nothing else but a bullet."

Gideon had learned over the years that police-
men were about evenly divided between those

who regarded him as a snake-oil salesman and those who expected miracles. (Once an Idaho county sheriff had handed him a murder victim's tibia, confidently waiting for him to determine height, weight, nationality, and hair color from it, on the grounds that he'd seen it done on *Quincy*, so he knew it was possible.) Inspector Joly, who had started out in the snake-oil camp, had soon converted, if not to the expectation of wonders, then at least to a solid respect for what could be gleaned by a professional from a few old bones; this despite a certain reserve and an ironic manner that was more a matter of constitution than of criticism.

"Actually, you're right and you're not right," Gideon said. "Entry holes in the skull mostly look like bullet holes, yes—they're usually round; not always, by any means, but usually—but when you're talking about the long bones, or the ribs, or especially the vertebrae, they can shatter or crumble in a hundred different ways. You never know what you're going to get. A lot of times you can't make any determination of cause from them."

"But in this case you can?"

"From the broken edges themselves, no, but look at this." He bent the battery-operated gooseneck lamp, also provided by the police, down to six inches from the vertebra, flooding the pitted surface with white light. "Now. Look here where I'm pointing: the rim of the broken part...right here. Use the magnifying glass. See anything?"

Joly examined the area silently, then leaned closer. "Do you mean this bit of grayish discoloration?"

"That's what I mean. That's a deposit left by the bullet."

Joly put down the lens and looked doubtfully at him. "On the *bone*? Are you sure? In my experience, bullet wipe is found only on the skin or on the outer clothing—whatever the bullet first strikes wipes it clean, isn't that so?"

"Yes, but this isn't bullet wipe. Bullet wipe is from the dirt and lubricant that the slug picks up on its way out of the gun barrel."

"I'm aware of that. And this?"

"This is different, or at least I think it is. I think this is from the body of the bullet itself. It's lead that gets scraped off when the bullet breaks through something hard, like bone. And since you find it at the point of *entry* into the bone—when you do find it, that is, which isn't always—it tells you what direction the shot came from, in this case from almost straight in front of him, or rather just a shade to the left of center, because the sternum wasn't perforated first, which it would have been if the bullet had come through the middle of his chest. As you can see, the left transverse process on the vertebra has been broken off too, which goes along with that scenario. So I'd say it entered his body an inch or two to the left of the sternum, probably through the fourth intercostal space."

"And a bullet entering through the fourth intercostal space on the left side, and penetrating the eighth thoracic vertebra in this manner, would necessarily have passed through the heart?"

"Smack through the middle of the left ventricle, no possible way of avoiding it. Death within seconds."

"Yes?" Joly once again scrutinized the thin gray edging, no more a quarter of an inch long and a sixteenth of an inch wide. "It's not very much to look at, to provide such extensive information," he said doubtfully. A faint residue of the old snake-oil look gleamed in his eyes. "I don't look forward to having to convince a judge."

"Well, I could be wrong," Gideon said agreeably. "But all you have to do is have your lab check it with a dissection microscope. I'm betting they'll find it's made up of tiny flakes of lead."

"I shall," Joly said. "We'll see."

Gideon got to his feet, knowing from the resistance of his knees to straightening that he'd been at it too long. "Lucien, I'm bushed. I'm ready for some fresh air, and I think we've done about all we can here. How about getting this stuff bagged and sent over to the lab? We're supposed to be meeting Julie at six."

With the help of one of the two *officiers de la*

paix that Joly had brought with him, the fragile bones were individually wrapped in newspaper to prevent their grinding against each other and then placed in evidence bags—simple brown paper bags stamped with the case number 99-4, indicating that it was Dordogne's fourth homicide of the year. That was nice, Gideon thought. In Seattle, they got to their fourth murder a long time before September.

Working alphabetically down the body, each bag was also individually labeled, a simple system that Gideon had been using since his graduate school days: the broken mandible in Bag A, the one remaining clavicle and scapula in Bag B, the vertebrae—except for the eighth thoracic, which Joly was taking back to Périgueux with him—in Bag C, and so on. The result was a group of sacks that fit comfortably into a cardboard carton originally used to pack four dozen cans of *macaroni au fromage*.

Gideon shook his head as he gently fitted in the last of the sacks. Macaroni and cheese. Now there was a hell of a way to end up.

While Gideon worked, Joly had gone back to sit on his boulder, jotting down notes and thinking aloud. "No clothing, no personal possessions whatever—you wouldn't say that there was any possibility of their having completely rotted away, would you?"

"No, not a chance. Someone took them—to keep him from being identified, I suppose."

"Mm. I don't imagine there's any way to tell if

he was killed here on the spot or carried here from somewhere else after he was murdered?"

Gideon shook his head. "You're right, there isn't. I can tell you about half of him has been carried *out* of the cave since he's been here, but that's about all. Either carried out or chomped down right here."

"And are you able to tell me anything about his appearance? His height, for example?"

"There I can help. I'll give you a stature estimate later, when I run some measurements, but it looks as if he'll turn out to be around average, not real tall, not real short. For France, I mean—say about five-eight, give or take an inch or two."

Joly, who was extraordinarily tall for a Frenchman, topping Gideon's six feet one by an inch, wrote it down. "And what about weight?"

"If you mean was he fat or thin, there's no way to tell that from the bones, but his body type—his build—was probably average too, not particularly muscular, not particularly slight. Your average Frenchman, in other words."

"Average, average, and average," Joly said, sighing as he wrote. "I grow discouraged."

"I can't give you what isn't there, Lucien. I wish I could tell you he was seven feet one and weighed a hundred and thirty pounds and had six fingers on his left hand."

"Yes, that would help narrow things down," Joly agreed.

"But, unfortunately, I haven't come across a

single thing that could conceivably be used for individual identification. No useful dental abnormalities, other than that crown you spotted and a filling in one of the bicuspids....Wait a second. Come to think of it..."

He opened Bag A again and took out the broken mandible—it was the right side, from the first bicuspid back—to reexamine the teeth. Four of the five were still present, the third molar having fallen out (after death, judging from the sharp, deep, well-defined socket). He held the bone on a level with his eyes and ran his finger over the teeth. "Yes, I should have realized it before. Something else for you to jot down: I think he might have been missing one of his upper right molars."

Joly looked up from his notebook with a sympathetic smile. "I think you mean one of his *lower* right molars. I've been working you too hard. You *are* getting tired."

"No, I mean upper."

"But there are no—"

"Look at this tooth, the first molar. See how it sticks out beyond the other teeth?"

Joly squinted at it. "Ah...no."

"Well, it does, or at least I think it does. And see how there's less wear on it than on the others?"

"Not really, no."

"Well, there is—or at least I think there is—and that's what happens to a tooth when its opposite member—the tooth it abuts—isn't there to keep it in place and wear it down. Teeth have a way of floating around unless they're held down. And the tooth that the lower first molar abuts is the upper first molar. So my conclusion is that it's missing, and in fact that it'd been missing for a while before he died, because it takes some time before it gets noticeable."

Joly scratched something out with his pen and slipped the notebook into his pocket. "And to think I doubted you."

"Well, I'm not positive, you understand. I'm a little out on a limb here, so if it doesn't turn out that way don't be too—"

"Inspecteur?" said the second of the two officers, who had been combing through the dirt directly under where the skeleton had been buried. He pointed to a dull, misshapen nugget in the red soil. *"Une balle."* A bullet.

With Joly, Gideon hurried over for a closer look. What he saw was a small, squat cylinder of what looked like lead with a bluntly pointed conical head, something like a .22-caliber slug from a cheap Saturday-night special, of which Gideon had seen more than he wished. But this one was different, with a hollowed-out base and an oddly constricted middle—as if a wire had been wound around it and pulled tight—so that the whole thing was shaped like a squat hourglass. And that was something he couldn't remember having run into before.

"What kind of bullet is that, Lucien?"

"It's not a bullet," Joly said, bending over to peer at it, his hands on his knees. "I believe it's an air-rifle pellet."

"An *air*-gun pellet?" Gideon said incredulously. "I've never heard of anyone killed by an air gun." Actually, he had, a teenager accidentally shot through the eye so that the pellet had lodged in his brain, but in this case they were dealing with penetration of skin, of muscle, of *bone*. "I didn't think it was possible."

"No, no, not an air *gun*, an air *rifle*. This is not from one of your—what is it, your toys that shoot, what are they called..."

"BB's."

"Yes, BB's. No, my friend, an air rifle is a different matter—a weapon, not a toy. Equipped with a sophisticated gas-compression system and the proper ammunition, it can be quite powerful, quite accurate—as a hunting weapon, for example."

"I didn't know that," Gideon said, happy to give Joly a chance to do some showing off of his own.

The pellet having been duly photographed *in situ*, Joly stooped, picked it up, and placed it on his palm. "I believe this is what is called a magnum, probably a six-point-three-five-millimeter pellet, or perhaps only a five-millimeter. Larger and heavier than most pellets, but of course quite light compared to your average firearm bullet." He closed his eyes while he hefted it. "I doubt if it weighs even fifty grains," he said with a significant look at Gideon.

"Oh?" Gideon said, completely out of his element by now.

"That would suggest," Joly explained, "that he was shot from close range, certainly less than twenty meters and probably a great deal less, considering that bone was penetrated. Such a light projectile would lose energy very quickly, regardless of the initial muzzle velocity, you see."

"I see," Gideon said. "That would also explain why it didn't make it all the way through."

Joly nodded his agreement. "Very good, Durand," he said with satisfaction, giving the strange pellet to the officer to bag.

He brushed invisible dirt from spotless hands and smiled, pleased with the day's efforts. "Come, shall we go and meet your Julie?"

CHAPTER
6

"Julie, this is my old friend and valued colleague Inspector Joly. Lucien, allow me to present my wife."

Joly bowed, straight-backed and stiff. "A great pleasure, madame."

"Please, call me Julie."

"Yes? Thank you, and please call me..."

Ahum, thought Gideon.

"...*ahum,* Lucien."

The soft gurgle of the nearby river floated through the open French windows of the restaurant Au Vieux Moulin, set, as its name implied, in an ancient stone mill at the entrance to the village of Les Eyzies. At the table nearest the window the second course, *risotto aux truffes,* had been cleared away, the silverware removed and replaced for the third time, and the *ravioles de langoustine aux jus de crustacés* announced and presented in a ceramic tureen from which the

waiter deftly whipped the cover with a practiced flourish.

The conversation, easy and pleasantly unfo-
cused to this point, flagged as they worked their
way attentively through the ravioli, and the
plates and silver had been removed once again
before Joly spoke, introducing a new subject.
"Gideon, I would like to know a little more
about this notorious scandal that has so plagued
the Institut de Préhistoire—the Old Gentleman
of Tayac. Tayac—that is the name of an *abri*, I
presume?"

"Yes, a Neanderthal *abri* just north of here,
probably no more than a quarter of a mile from
the one we were working in today. The institute
ran a summer dig there for a few seasons in the
early nineties. The habitation level was carbon-
dated at around thirty-five thousand years B.P."

"B.P.?"

"Sorry—'before the present.'"

Joly poured them all a little more of the local
white wine, a fruity Montravel. "I see. And what
of this hoax, this argument?"

"Well, first you have to understand—as Julie
pointed out yesterday—that anthropologists
love to argue—"

"Is that so?" Joly murmured.

"—and nowhere is that more true than in Neanderthal research." He leaned back out of the
way as the waiter laid the gleaming arsenal of
utensils for the next course. "Right from the beginning—and the original Neanderthal Man

was found in 1856—there's been a continuing, usually noisy fight over where to put him."

Joly showed his surprise; one of his eyebrows went up a millimeter. "Where to put him? He's not in a museum?"

"What I meant," Gideon said, laughing, "was where to put him taxonomically."

The issue, he explained, was the place of the Neanderthals in the long progression of human evolution. Were these muscular, beetle-browed creatures our ancestors—that is, the ancestors of modern Europeans—or were they evolutionary dead ends, crowded off the branches of the human tree like so many withered fruits when our true ancestors, the Cro-Magnons, arrived in Europe from Africa, bringing with them the technological marvels and cultural advances of the Upper Paleolithic age? Was Neanderthal Man the shambling, grunting, bent-kneed brute of the comics, dragging his woman along by the hair, or was he a sensitive being with language, culture, and an appreciation of beauty and art? Were the Neanderthals, in fact, human beings at all, or did they belong somewhere lower in the evolutionary scale, down with the monkeys and the apes?

"I see," Joly said. "And what is the position of the Institut de Préhistoire on these questions?"

"They don't have a position. They're divided just like everyone else. Half of them are staunch defenders of the Neanderthals as card-carrying *Homo sapiens*, and the other half think they should be frog-marched out of the human line altogether, right into the trash pile with *Giganto-pithecus*, *Australopithecus boisei*, and all the other evolutionary wriggles that didn't go anywhere." That, at least, had been the way they'd all felt back then, and knowing them, Gideon couldn't imagine they'd changed their views very much.

Julie took over at that point, telling Joly, with considerable zest, about the finding of the four perforated bones and their subsequent exposure as a fraud. By the time she finished the *magret de canard* had been brought, demolished, and re-moved; likewise the *salade verte*, and the three of them were doing their seriously diminished best with the cheese course.

After a long, meditative lull in the conversa-tion, Joly, first asking Julie's permission, lit his first Gitane of the evening. "And this is so very important?" he finally said as smoke swirled from his mouth and nostrils. "The making of a necklace?"

Gideon washed down a sliver of cheese—Gérôme, according to Joly—with a sip from his wineglass, now filled with a dry red Bergerac. "You better believe it. To put it simply, the mak-ing of decorative objects is one of the things that make us unique, a convenient dividing line be-tween human beings and everything else that's ever lived. Apes don't do it, monkeys don't do it, *Homo erectus* didn't do it. Only *Homo sapiens* does it. So if you can establish that the Nean-derthals did it too, that pretty much means you have to classify them as one of us—not *Homo neanderthalensis*, a separate species of their own, but *Homo sapiens neanderthalensis*, a fully human subspecies, a kind of race."

"I see," Joly said. "Then I assume these bones caused a considerable uproar among those interested in such things?"

"Are you kidding? Once the news got out, it split the whole world of Middle and Upper Paleolithic anthropologists—"

"All eleven of them," Julie said, then quickly held up her hands. "I apologize, I couldn't help myself."

"—into two warring camps. The institute staff themselves were split right down the middle. Some people flat out refused to believe it, some even came pretty close to calling Ely Carpenter a faker, but his defenders were just as adamant, and the Old Man of Tayac—le Vieux de Tayac—carried the day."

"Carpenter," Joly said, tipping his head back to expel a lungful of smoke. "Not 'Carpentier'? He wasn't a Frenchman?"

"No, he was an American, but he'd lived in France for a long time, a decade or more."

"And he himself was the perpetrator?" Joly asked.

"Nobody knows," Gideon said. "He denied it, of course, but he came in for a lot of abuse and ridicule. So did the institute, even though they didn't really have any part in it. Even today some people think Carpenter was responsible, some people think he was duped. Either way, he was thoroughly disgraced."

"Which do *you* think he was," Julie asked, "duper or dupee? You haven't said."

"I think he was duped. Sure, he might have *wanted* something like this to be true, but from what I know about him he wasn't the kind of guy to try to falsify the archaeological record. Besides, it was such a primitive kind of fake. Someone with Carpenter's credentials would've been able to pull off something a lot more sophisticated, a lot harder to detect."

"How was it done?" Joly asked.

"The holes in the bones were made with an electric drill bit—which, I should point out, was not found in your standard Middle Paleolithic tool kit—and then stained with something so that they didn't look freshly made. That was it. Somebody like Carpenter would have *known* it was only a question of time before someone saw through it."

"And afterward," Joly asked, "what happened to him?"

"Oh, about what you'd expect. His reputation was in shreds, of course, and from what I understand he got a little paranoid about it, kind of wacky. In the end, he had to resign, of course."

"And now where is he?"

"No place he can be reached, I'm afraid. He was an amateur pilot, he had his own plane, and he crashed it not too long afterward, up in Brittany."

Joly gazed at the beamed ceiling for a while, smoking placidly. "If he was so good a scientist," he said, watching the blue-gray tendrils spiral slowly up to be torn apart in the breeze, "and if the hoax was so primitive, how was it that he was taken in?"

"That's the question, all right. It's one of the things I'll be tackling in the book."

"And who did the taking in?" Julie added.

Gideon nodded. "Yup, that's also the question. A man named Jacques Beaupierre's the director now, and he's given me his blessing to talk to the whole staff and ask them anything I want. I'm hoping I can come up with some answers."

"I would also be interested to know—" Joly began.

"Lucien, let me ask *you* something. What's with all this interest in the Old Man of Tayac? You don't think—or do you think—there's some connection between the institute and Mr. X back there in the cave?"

Joly plucked a shred of tobacco from his lips and leaned back in his chair. "Let me show you something." From the inside pocket of his suit jacket he took an unsealed white envelope. Inside were three black-and-white photographs, all of the same object, that he laid out side by side on the tablecloth. He waited for their response.

"A rusty trowel," Julie said after a moment.

"Lying on the ground," said Gideon.

"Keenly observed," said Joly. "It was found by one of my officers in the brush about twenty-five meters from the entrance to the *abri* in which we were this afternoon. Now look at this one, the enlargement. What do you see burned into the handle?"

Gideon turned the photo to read the letters. "Initials...I.P." He glanced back up at Joly. "Meaning?"

"Institut de Préhistoire!" Julie said.

"Very good, madame—ah, Julie. So I also concluded. And when I took it there, Monsieur Beaupierre took one look at it and identified it as having originally come from their tool bin." He turned to Gideon. "There's your connection, my friend."

Gideon let this sink in for a moment. "Twenty-five meters away. You can't exactly call that the scene of the crime."

"Approximately eighty feet," Joly said. "About as far, wouldn't you say, as a man might be expected to throw it, if he had just come out of the cave and wished to get rid of it at once?"

Gideon shook his head. "Sorry, Lucien, I think you're reaching. These people have run digs all over the place around here. Archaeologists are always leaving stuff like this behind, or having it ripped off, or just losing it." He gathered up the photographs and handed them back to the inspector. "My guess is that what you've got here is a simple coincidence."

"Good," said Joly, pocketing the envelope. "Excellent. I love simple coincidences. I delight in simple coincidences. Whenever I see a simple coincidence I smell a commendation in the offing."

For a few minutes they all digested quietly, Joly smoking and Julie and Gideon sipping wine, all three ruminating over their thoughts. The tray of cheeses was removed, the demitasse cups brought.

"I've been thinking about the issues we were discussing earlier," Joly said. "*Was* Neanderthal a human being? Was he *not* a human being?" He followed this with one of his elaborate Gallic shrugs—eyebrows, chin, and shoulders all going up at the same time, mouth going down. "Forgive me, but there have been no Neanderthals for tens of thousands of years, so what does it matter?" He ground out his cigarette, already smoked two-thirds of the way down. "To speak frankly, it hardly seems something that sensible people would quarrel over."

"Sensible people, no," Julie said, "but we're talking about Paleolithic archaeologists. It's against their principles to agree with each other."

Gideon laughed along with her. "She's right—they get nervous when everybody has the same theory. They haven't even agreed on whether 'Neanderthal' should have an 'h' in it or not; there are the old-guard pro-'h' and the radical anti-'h' camps. You know, the institute's holding a public symposium at the community lecture hall tomorrow, Lucien. Why don't you come to it? You'll get some idea."

"What is the subject?"

"It's called 'Neanderthal and Cro-Magnon: Differences and Similarities.' Could get pretty lively."

Joly pursed his narrow lips. "'Neanderthal' with or without the 'h'?"

"With, I think. They're traditionalists on that point."

"Even so, I'm sorry to say I have other business." His eyes lit up. "Ah, dessert. Prepare yourselves."

The market town of Les Eyzies winds for half a mile along the east bank of the green, slow-flowing river Vézère, prettily situated at the base of an undulating three-hundred-foot-high wall of honey-colored limestone cliffs. In the Middle Ages it had been little more than an unwelcoming cluster of mean stone houses huddled beneath the great, brooding chateau of the barons of Beynac, built into the very face of the cliffside, but today, with the lords long gone, the village hums with activity. Visitors come because of the region's celebrated prehistoric finds, the local gourmet shops and restaurants, and the refreshing mixture of commercial bustle and open-faced country simplicity that is the essence of village life.

Charming in the daytime, it is spine-tinglingly evocative at night, when the modern shops and cafés are dark, but the ancient cobbled streets are lamplit, and strategically placed floodlights illuminate the bony ruins of the chateau on its rock-cut terrace, the medieval stone houses that still remain around it, and, above all, the dramatic cliffs themselves that rear up only a few yards from the main street, brilliantly lit at their base but disappearing into blackness above.

It had been light when they went into the restaurant; it was dark when they came out, and for a few minutes the three of them stood in the parking lot without speaking, their faces turned up to the light-bathed curves and hollows of the cliffs. Gideon and Julie turned down Joly's offer of a lift back to the Hôtel Cro-Magnon, preferring to walk the quarter mile, and started slowly on their way.

"Lucien speaks better English than I do," Julie said after a while. "It hardly seems fair."

"Well, his father worked for the Ministry of Foreign Affairs. Lucien spent most of his adolescence in London."

"Ah."

"He sure knows how to order a meal too, doesn't he?"

"It was *wonderful*, but my God, I don't think I'll ever be able to eat again. Look at me, I'm waddling, not walking. You know, this answers a question I've had for years."

Gideon cocked an eyebrow. "Oh?"

"Well, I couldn't help wondering why your on-site research has always focused on early man in Europe, especially here in the south of

France, rather than in Africa, where the remains are so much more ancient. I think I'm finally beginning to see why."

"Well, of course," Gideon said. "It's pretty tough finding a three-star restaurant in the Rift Valley. I thought you'd figured that out a long time ago." He reached an arm around her shoulder and pulled her close to kiss her soft, fragrant hair, and then they fell silent, walking hand in hand through the near-deserted streets.

When they came to the hotel, Julie started in, but Gideon tugged her along. "Not yet. I want to show you something."

"In the dark?"

"I'm equipped," he said, taking out a pocket flashlight and flicking it on.

He led her to an unlit, nondescript alley that turned toward the cliffside half a block beyond the hotel, at the end of which, aided by the flashlight, they threaded their way between a couple of parked cars and pushed through a rusted, unlocked, waist-high metal gate, ducking their heads—or at least Gideon had to duck his—to enter a small, shallow *abri*, one of several that dimpled the base of the cliffs here, one beside the other. The next one over held a propane tank; the one after that, considerably larger, formed the rear wall of the Hôtel Cro-Magnon. The one in which they stood, however, the smallest of the three, held nothing at all.

Julie looked around, puzzled. "This is what you wanted to show me?"

Gideon smiled. "Yes." He shone the flashlight onto a weathered marble plaque bolted to the stone immediately above the opening.

Ici furent découverts en 1868
les hommes de Cro-Magnon
par François Berthoumeyrou.

Julie's lips moved as she worked her way through the French. "Here...something...discovered in..." Her eyes widened. "Gideon, is this actually the original Cro-Magnon Man cave? This little place?"

That was exactly what it was, he told her, pleased with her reaction. They were on hallowed historic (or prehistoric) ground. It had been right there, right beneath their feet in that unremarkable, little-visited cavelet, that three thirty-millennia-old skeletons of a type never before seen in prehistoric burials had been uncovered by workmen during the construction of the Les Eyzies railway station across the road; the very place, so to speak, where modern humankind had made its entrance onto the anthropological stage.

"Wow," said Julie with something gratifyingly close to awe. "It sends goose bumps down your back, doesn't it?" She smiled at him. "Did you bring that flashlight all the way from home just so you could show me this place in the dark?"

He shrugged. "It doesn't weigh anything."

"You're a romantic, you know that?"

"Of course. I thought that was why you married me."

"You know, maybe it was at that."

"Gideon," she said on the short walk back to the hotel, "do you think my French is good enough to let me get anything out of that Neanderthal–Cro-Magnon symposium you were telling Lucien about?"

"You don't need French. It's in English."

"English? How come?"

The Institut de Préhistoire, he explained, was funded jointly by the Université du Périgord and the Chicago-based Horizon Foundation, and was by charter composed of both French and American scholars. Bilingual fluency was required for appointment, and papers and symposia might be in either language. This particular one was to be videotaped for use in American universities and would therefore be conducted in English.

"That's great," she said. "I'll plan on going, then."

"Good, but I have to tell you, if it's more goose bumps you're after, forget it. It's likely to be pretty dry stuff."

"That's okay," she said, standing on tiptoe to nuzzle at his earlobe as he turned the key to their room. "I have other sources for goose bumps."

CHAPTER
7

Inasmuch as the session wasn't scheduled until two in the afternoon, they decided to take the morning off and relax. In the afternoon, while Julie attended the symposium, Gideon would finish up with the bones.

So for a few hours they acted like tourists. They had a leisurely breakfast in their room in the ivy-covered Hôtel Cro-Magnon, which was every bit as rustic and pretty an inn as Gideon had remembered. Afterward, they strolled along the street, chatting about nothing in particular and looking in shop windows, but mostly simply passing the time together, peacefully, pleasantly, without event or object. A sort of jet-lag-decompression time.

They were heading into a café for a coffee stop when Gideon spotted a familiar figure coming diagonally across the street toward them, somewhat in the manner of a soft-bodied sea creature undulating over the ocean floor.

"Here comes Jacques Beaupierre," Gideon said.

Julie stared. "*That's* the director of the Périgord Institute of Prehistory? The old gentleman who just walked right in front of that truck?"

It was true, and it was typical. The plump, balding Beaupierre had just ambled directly across the path of a flatbed truck loaded with baskets of walnuts, which had been forced to pull up to a sudden stop. One of the baskets had tipped over, spilling nuts onto the truck's bed and into the road, and the driver was leaning out of the window vigorously making his objections known. Beaupierre, equally oblivious to truck, driver, and nuts, was placidly continuing his crossing, an amiably dreamy look in his blue, bespectacled eyes. He was, if the movements of his lips were any indication, deep in consultation with himself. Gideon guessed that if he were to be suddenly stopped and asked where he was or where he was going, it would take a while for him to come up with the answers.

"Well, it's true, he's not the most focused guy in the world," Gideon said, "but"—searching for something good to say—"but he does know his Middle Paleolithic stone-tool technology."

"Oh, well, then."

Archaeology had been Beaupierre's whole life, Gideon knew. He had been born and raised in Les Eyzies, the son and grandson of local amateur antiquarians, and he had been immersed in local prehistory since the age of nine. At the same time, he was a man whose native keenness of mind had never been his forte, and it was common knowledge, or at least common belief, that his ascendance to the directorship after Carpenter's humiliating resignation had been based more on seniority than merit; the seventy-four-year-old Beaupierre had been with the institute since the day of its inception almost forty years before. He had already been passed over three times, most recently when he'd competed for it against Carpenter himself, and to the general surprise of the archaeological establishment, Carpenter, the new kid on the block, had been appointed. But with the all-too-colorful Ely Carpenter soon gone in a cloud of scandal, it was felt that the prudent, industrious Beaupierre's day had come. Besides, there wasn't much risk in it; by that time the directorship had become little more than an honorary post with a few routine administrative duties.

"Bonjour, Jacques," Gideon called, when the unseeing Beaupierre, lost in thought, or at any rate lost in something, came abreast of them.

Beaupierre stopped. "Eh? Mm?" He peered blinking at Gideon through his glasses—rectangular-lensed and framed in thick black plastic, a style last in vogue in the 1950s—and broke into a sweet smile. "Ah, it's Gideon, isn't it? You've arrived! Is it Tuesday then, or am I…"

"We got here yesterday," Gideon said, shaking Beaupierre's offered hand. "This is my wife, Julie."

"How delightful! *Enchanté, madame.* Gideon, these interviews of yours—when would you wish to begin them?"

"As soon as I can. I have this case I'm working on with the police, but I can fit them in whenever it's convenient for you and your people."

Beaupierre put his finger to his rounded chin. "I wonder, could you join us later this morning at our staff meeting? You could make your arrangements with them individually."

"Well…"

"Go ahead," Julie said. "I'll be fine, there's plenty to do. Besides, I've already gotten more quality time out of you than I was expecting for the whole trip."

"Excellent, most kind, madame," said Beaupierre. "Our meeting is at eleven, Gideon. Perhaps you could describe your purposes in coming in a little more detail. I've told them, of course, but it would be an opportunity for you to orient all of them yourself at a single sitting, and, mm…well."

"Sure, I'd like to."

"In the afternoon, however, we are taken up. There is a symposium at two." He turned to Julie. "Madame, if you have some interest in the Middle Paleolithic era, perhaps you would care to honor us by attending? It will be in English, you know."

"Yes, thank you, I'm planning to be there."

Beaupierre seemed genuinely delighted. "I look forward to seeing you and to introducing you to our fellows. And you, Gideon—we'll see you at eleven? You remember where we meet?"

"Is it still that café just down from the institute, on the square—"

"The Café du Centre, yes, that's the place. But only until next week," he added, beaming joyfully at them, "when we finally move into our new quarters, our wonderful new quarters, with our own full-size conference room at last, and a reception area, and the most modern storage facilities, and...and so forth. The dedication ceremony will be Monday morning. Will you still be here then? Can you come?"

"If we're here, we'll certainly come," Gideon said.

"We'd love to," Julie said.

"You have no idea how long it's been in coming, or what a difference it will make. Oh, the difficulties...ah, well, mm..." He bobbed to them individually and shook hands with Gideon. "Good day to you both. A great pleasure, madame."

"Actually, he seemed pretty focused to me," Julie said as the director continued on his way. "Once he got started."

"He did, didn't he? Maybe I've been giving him a bum rap. He's sharper than I remembered."

"Oh, Gideon!" Beaupierre had gone about ten paces and turned. "Which way was I going when we met?"

"Uh...the same way you are now."

"Ah, good," said Beaupierre, patting his belly. "Then I've had my breakfast."

When he stopped off at the Hôtel Cro-Magnon before going to the staff meeting, Gideon was told by the clerk at the desk that an Inspector Joly from Périgueux had telephoned, asking him to call.

"Lucien, what's up?"

"Ah, Gideon, a little news. I've been speaking with the prefect in Les Eyzies about a fellow named Jean Bousquet, who disappeared from the village three years ago—"

"Wait a minute—I thought you told me there weren't any unclosed cases."

"This is a little different. Bousquet was never reported to the police as missing, he was reported as a thief."

By his landlady, Madame Renouard, according to whom Bousquet had fled after removing from a secret drawer in her cupboard 60 francs in cash, an antique lapel watch valued at 180 francs, and a treasured cameo brooch, one of a pair that had belonged to her grandmother. He had also left with his rent four weeks in arrears, a matter of some 600 francs. The municipal police, under Prefect Marielle, had mounted an unsuccessful search for him, concluding after a week that he had permanently left the area, and there the matter had lain. A few months later there was a brief flurry of speculation that he might have returned; Madame Renouard, discovering that her grandmother's *other* cameo brooch was missing, was convinced that the rapacious Bousquet must have slunk back to complete the heist. But there was no other evidence to support this, and it had come to nothing. Bousquet, having disappeared once, was not seen again.

"And so you think that might have been him in the cave?"

"I offer it as a possibility," said Joly. "He seems to have had no shortage of enemies. Apparently he was a drifter who had come to the area not long before and had found a job plying a shovel. He had had bad relations with several townspeople, and there are reports of some unpleasantness with a coworker at his place of employment. I lack the details, but would you agree that it sounds worth looking into?"

"Yes, it does. Well, I'll be back at the bones this afternoon, Lucien. I'll give you a call and let you know what I have. You find out what you can about his physical characteristics and, who knows, maybe we can come up with a match."

"Very good. Oh, by the way, our police pathologist, Dr. Roussillot, is nominally in charge of the remains, so he is required to certify your findings. He may choose to join you at the morgue. I hope you don't mind?"

"Mind, why should I mind?"

"Well, I'm afraid Dr. Roussillot may be somewhat stiff-necked for your taste. A nice enough fellow to be sure, but fairly new on the job—he was a professor until last year, you see, and as a result has an inclination to be somewhat fussy and punctilious, as well as an unfortunate tendency toward tedious speeches. Ah, not, that is to say, that professors necessarily—"

"That's okay, Lucien, don't worry about it."

"You will try to get along with him, won't you?"

Gideon laughed. "I get along with you, don't I?"

"He spent two years at Cambridge, speaks a wonderful English."

"Lucien, don't worry about it, I'll get along fine with the guy."

"Excellent," Joly said, sounding relieved. "Oh, and perhaps you could also do me the service of seeing if there is anything to the story of this Bousquet's 'unpleasantness' with a co-worker? I'm sure that you could do it more smoothly, more in the natural course of events, than I could."

"I appreciate the compliment," Gideon said in all sincerity, "but how in the hell am I supposed to do that?"

"His place of employment," said Joly, "was the Institut de Préhistoire."

CHAPTER
8

Some things never changed.

So Gideon thought with a smile as he stood unnoticed in the doorway of the Café du Centre's small, plain back room. It was a few minutes before eleven o'clock and the institute's fellows had gathered early for their meeting. There they were at the same scarred round table, the only table in the room, coffee cups and frosted carafes of water at hand, going at it hammer and tongs, just as they'd been doing three years ago, two of them stalwartly standing up for the Neanderthals as brothers, or at least cousins (despite the recent DNA evidence to the contrary), and the other three just as vigorously (and more accurately, in Gideon's view) in favor of demoting them to distant in-laws, no closer to humans than they were to the great apes.

Leading the anti-Neanderthal charge, as before, was the diminutive but formidable Audrey Godwin-Pope, one of the two Americans on the staff, and at sixty-eight its second-oldest member, after Beaupierre; a forthright, free-spoken woman with iron-gray hair done up in a bun, author of over a hundred monographs, and president of Sisters in Time, the feminist caucus of the International Archaeological Society. Audrey was on her second—or was it her third?—four-year appointment to the institute. (According to the charter the American fellows received four-year renewable appointments; the French fellows were appointed to indefinite terms.) Three years earlier, the last time the directorship had been open, she too had been a competitor, along with Beaupierre and Carpenter, but of course Carpenter had been selected and then a few months later Beaupierre had been appointed to replace him. Now it was widely and approvingly understood that Audrey was next in line in the unlikely event that Beaupierre left any time soon.

Supporting her against the pro-Neanderthalers was the vinegary, pedantic Émile Grize, the staff paleopathologist, the only Frenchman Gideon knew who affected bow ties, generally oversized and usually with a gaudy multicolored pattern, both of which sadly accentuated his own meager frame and vaguely reptilian features. Today it was flying yellow egrets on a field of mauve, not a happy choice for a man with the complexion of an over-the-hill Roquefort cheese.

The third and final member of the Neanderthal-as-poor-relation group was the other American, and the other woman, on the staff, Prudence McGinnis, her flyaway red hair more or less held back by a couple of barrettes. Sitting within easy reach of a plate of chocolate brioches, Pru was big, jolly, and irrepressible, with a washerwoman's thick red wrists and forearms and a body like an only slightly gone-to-seed female Russian shot-putter's. Gideon and Pru's friendship went back to his days at Northern California State, when Pru, only three years younger than Gideon, had been a student in the very first graduate course he had taught. With her cocky, funny, shoot-from-the-hip New York manner she had struck many on the faculty as insufficiently reverent, but Gideon had taken to her from the first. Irreverence had been in short supply in the anthro department at Northern Cal, and from Gideon's perspective Pru had been a breath of fresh air.

At odds with them on almost every point was the smaller pro-Neanderthal contingent, composed, as before, of Jacques Beaupierre, the affable, constitutionally absentminded director; and the gruff, bearlike Michel Montfort, distinguished Paleolithic archaeologist, diplomate of the French Académie des Sciences, and generally acknowledged to be the institute's most distinguished scholar if not its most diplomatic member. As befitting his status, he had been offered the directorship several times, offered it on a silver platter, but having no interest in or patience with administrative matters, he had consistently declined—to the relief of all concerned.

Although outnumbered three to two and on the less generally accepted side of the argument, Beaupierre and Montfort more than managed to hold their own, thanks mostly to Montfort's imposing persona and acknowledged preeminence.

It was amazing, really, that they never got tired of haranguing each other, or that they'd never physically attacked one another in sheer frustration. (Or maybe they had, who knew?) Probably the explanation lay in the fact that they were out of each other's sight for seven months out of every twelve. According to the terms of its charter, the institute was in session only five months a year, from late June to the end of November, typically allowing them a three-month digging season followed by a two-month "data consolidation" period. Except for Jacques Beaupierre, whose administrative duties were year-round, and Pru McGinnis, who held no outside faculty position, the staff members spent the rest of the year away from the institute and each other on half- or three-quarter-time appointments at their home universities.

But whatever the reason, their endless debate had never been in danger of growing stale. "Ridiculous!" Montfort was declaring in his blunt Alsatian French at the moment. "Do you really think that if we could take a typical Nean-

derthal, give him a shave, dress him up in a jog-
ging suit, and sit him down in a New York subway train, the other passengers would even look
twice at him?"

Pru received this with a hearty laugh. "You're
absolutely right, and you want to know why?
Because people who ride the New York subways
know better than to notice *anybody*. Believe me, I
know what I'm talking about here."

Watching from the doorway, Gideon smiled.
It was nice to see that Pru was still Pru.

"As to the New York subway," said Émile
Grize dryly, the egrets bobbing under his chin,
"that is a subject on which, happily, I am unable
to speak with conviction. However, as a trained
paleopathologist"—as Gideon remembered,
Émile began a lot of sentences with "As a trained
paleopathologist"; in his own mind he was the
one real scientist in this band of rock-hunters—
"as a trained paleopathologist I can assure you
that a Neanderthal would *not* pass unnoticed in
the Paris Métro, however well-shaven."

He sounded positively offended at the idea, as
if, were poor Charlie Caveperson to shamble
unassumingly aboard at the Étoile Métro station, he, Émile Grize, would personally boot
him off at the next stop.

"Be that as it may," said Audrey Godwin-
Pope in her usual no-nonsense manner, "I
would think we might agree that the outward
appearance of these beings is beside the point."

"*Does* this interminable discussion actually have a point?" Montfort asked. "It continues to elude me."

"It was my impression," Audrey said, standing up to him (no surprise there), "that it was their social organization that was under discussion, and there even you, Michel, have to admit the evidence is unambiguous. They had none— at least not on a human level. Everything we know about Neanderthal society tells us that it was on a par with that of a wandering troop of mountain gorillas, nothing more."

"Is that so?" Montfort snorted, leaning combatively forward. "Suppose you tell me then: when was the last time you encountered a wandering troop of mountain gorillas that made a practice of burying their grandfathers?"

Touché, Gideon thought. Montfort was on the wrong side of the argument, but *touché* all the same.

"I saw a study recently," Jacques Beaupierre piped up, "that suggests there is now good reason to believe that the morphological differences between Neanderthal Man—"

"Neanderthals," said Audrey with the stoic demeanor of someone who was making the same correction for the thousandth time and had no hope that it was going to take this time any more than it had before. Nice to see that she hadn't changed either. "Or Neanderthalers, if you prefer."

"—differences between Neanderthals," said

Beaupierre without missing a beat—he was used to it too, "and modern humans are not evolutionary at all, but nothing more than the result of an iodine-deficient diet, due to their distance from the seacoast."

"Iodine deficiency is well known to result in thyroid dysfunction and eventually, if severe and protracted enough, in cretinism," Émile observed in his surgical but long-winded fashion. "Are we therefore to assume that the position of this study is that the Neanderthal population is not a separate race or species at all, but simply an assemblage of cretins?"

Beaupierre's brow furrowed. "Ah...well, yes, I suppose that *would* follow, yes."

It was enough to make people sigh, and shake their heads, and glance around the room, finally becoming aware of Gideon. Pru at once jumped up and strode to the door to welcome him, her hand outstretched and her lively gray eyes almost on a level with his own. He smiled, equally glad to see her, although he could have done without her bone-cracking gorilla handshake, which he saw coming but couldn't in decency avoid. Audrey, more restrained, merely said, "Hello, Gideon, it's nice to see you again," but her stern mouth softened and even curved upward a little at the corners. These, fellow Americans, were the two people he knew best and liked most. Montfort, whom he knew less well, was his usual crusty self but went so far as to rise halfway, grunt, and shake hands somewhat absently (a relief after Pru's knuckle-grinder). Only Émile Grize limited himself to no more than a frugal nod, which Gideon accepted as a cordial welcome, considering the source.

Audrey and Pru made room for him between them, a *café crème* was brought for him, and the business part of the meeting was attended to. With the institute in its annual data-consolidation mode, archaeological digs had been suspended while members concentrated on interpreting the season's findings. Thus, the discussion concerned little more than the publication schedules of various institute proceedings and monographs, and these were quickly, almost cursorily, dealt with. The language of discussion was then mercifully switched to English as a kindness to the newcomer, and Beaupierre turned the floor over to "our old friend Gideon Oliver, the Skeleton Detective of America."

Ignoring the raised hairs on the nape of his neck that this hated phrase invariably produced, Gideon began: "As you all know, I'm here in connection with the book I'm doing on errors and fallacies in the social sciences, anthropology in particular. The Old Man of Tayac—"

But the sudden sensation of wary, quivering antennae all about him produced by these few words told him that they did not all know—in fact that none of them, apart from Beaupierre, had known—anything about it. Surprised,

Gideon turned inquiringly to the director. "I thought you said...?"

"Ah, I've told everyone that you would be coming here to interview them," Beaupierre said nervously. "But it may be, now that I think of it, that perhaps I neglected to mention, ah, the exact subject matter of your, ah, interest in, mm..." He closed his mouth, took a sip of coffee, and apparently lost interest, gazing tranquilly out the window, an earnest, cogitative look on his face. Beaupierre had a way of doing that—simply quitting in the middle of a sentence, giving the impression that it was still going on somewhere in the ether, only not out loud. It was as if a radio had been switched off in the middle of a sentence. Sometimes he'd flip the switch back on again in the middle of another sentence, which was equally disconcerting.

There was a polite interval, apparently to permit the director to continue if he wished, which he didn't, and then Audrey filled her water glass and looked at Gideon. "Is this a serious academic work, Gideon?"

Oh, boy; not a question he'd been looking forward to answering. His throat began to get a little dry, and he too filled his glass from one of the carafes. "Well, not exactly, no, Audrey. It's intended for a popular audience, but I do mean to treat the subject in a serious, scholarly way." Well, in as serious and scholarly a way as Lester would let him get away with.

"And what, may I ask," said Émile Grize, "is the title of this popular yet scholarly book?" As it often was with Émile, it was a toss-up as to whether or not he meant to be sarcastic.

"*Wrong Turns, Dead Ends, and Popular Misconceptions in the Study of Humankind,*" Gideon said, figuring he was better off ignoring for the moment the less scholarly sounding *Bones to Pick* part. Even so, it didn't do much to tone down the general air of mistrust. (Thank God he had held out against Lester's *Bungles, Blunders, and Bloopers.*) Still, what could he expect? How happy could they be about dusting off a farce that had made them a public laughingstock only a few years earlier? The Tayac hoopla had even made it to the Jay Leno show for four nights running, surely a first for the field of Middle Paleolithic decorative technology.

"I *do* mean this to be as serious and scholarly a piece of work as I can make it," he said truthfully. "I've been over this with my publisher a hundred times. I'm not interested in cheap laughs or in making our field look as if it's full of charlatans and fools. Scientists have made mistakes plenty of times, sure, and sometimes—but not very often—they've been plain dishonest—villains, even."

Pru's hand flew to her heart. She gasped. "Good God, sir, surely you jest."

"And I don't intend to cover any of that up," Gideon went on. "But the story of almost every hoax and every mistake has a scientist as hero too, and it's the heroes that I mean to concentrate on."

The eminent Michel Montfort had had little to say since Gideon's arrival, preferring instead to sit staring out the window in one of his well-remembered scowling silences, tapping his fingernails on the table, making inroads into the chocolate brioches, and presumably thinking great thoughts. Now his snuffling bass broke in again.

"And who is the 'hero' in the saga of the Old Man of Tayac?"

Gideon hesitated. "You are, sir."

Montfort was visibly startled. "*I* am! Thank you very much, no! You can leave me out of your damned book."

"But you are." Gideon leaned earnestly toward him. "Professor Montfort, in my view the whole structure of anthropology—of any science—depends on the moral integrity of individual scientists who put the extension of knowledge ahead of any personal stake, however great, in the outcome of research. And you did that."

Gideon's forehead was suddenly warm. What he'd said had come across as painfully stuffy and pretentious, even to him, but it had come from the heart; Montfort *was* the hero of the story. Decades earlier, he had been one of the first to propound the idea of the essential humanity of the Neanderthals—their sensitivity, their intelligence, their cultural development.

He had written eloquently and spoken—less eloquently but just as fervently—on the subject for two decades, presenting papers at one conference after another, eventually becoming its acknowledged spokesman. Ely Carpenter, taking up archaeology late in life, had been his student, a protégé—although younger by only a few years—who wholeheartedly embraced his views and in whose subsequent success his mentor had taken enormous pride.

When Carpenter, by that time the director of the institute, had come up with those four perforated bones, Montfort had been ecstatic too. He had trumpeted the find as the long-hoped-for confirmation of his own theories and had stood shoulder to shoulder with Carpenter, zestfully fending off the doubters and the attackers.

But when evidence began mounting that the bones had actually been pilfered from a nearby museum, then doctored and "planted" in the Tayac *abri,* the scholarly abuse (and scholars were in a class of their own when it came to abuse) rained down on Carpenter, on Montfort, and even on the blameless institute. It must have felt to Montfort as if his life's work had been made ludicrous, and yet, in the best tradition of science, he had calmly, objectively reexamined the now-discredited bones on his own and had eventually published the definitive paper, a landmark piece of scientific detective work showing exactly how the bones had been treated to make them look authentic. He had stoutly continued to maintain that Carpenter was the victim, not the perpetrator, but at the same time he had unshrinkingly established for good and all that he and his protégé had been in the wrong, gullible dupes at best; his enemies had been right all the while. And that, as far as Gideon was concerned, was enough to make him a hero.

"Permit me to offer a small but significant semantic correction, Gideon," Émile said into the silence. "I submit that what you're describing is nothing more than simple scholarly disinterestedness—commendable, certainly, but hardly heroic. Now, speaking as a—"

Trained paleopathologist, Gideon thought.

"—trained scientist," Émile said, "I have to assume that disinterestedness is the foundation on which we—that is, all of us who call ourselves scientists—guide all of our actions. To accord it 'heroic' status is to make the error of implying that it is singular rather than customary and expected. I mean no disrespect, Michel."

But Montfort had been visibly moved by Gideon's speech. He slowly massaged his forehead, one hand at each temple, and grunted something about the desirability of leaving sleeping dogs to themselves, but said that if Gideon cared to interview him about Tayac he would make himself available. That turned the tide. There was a little grumbling, but in the end, much to Gideon's relief, everyone came around and agreed to talk to him.

Once the schedule was settled, the subject turned immediately and surprisingly to the new skeleton from the *abri*. They had been following the story all week, they said. It had been well covered from the start in *Sud Ouest*, the local newspaper, and even more so when Inspector Joly was brought in, and this morning there had been an interview with Prefect of Police Marielle in which Gideon was mentioned by name. Questions flew: Did he know whose body it was? Was it true that the individual had been shot, murdered? Had he completed his analysis? Could he tell how long the body had been there? Did the police have a suspect? Was—

No, he said, he didn't know whose body it was; and yes, he had been shot to death; and no, his analysis wasn't complete, he'd be going to the Saint-Cyprien morgue that afternoon to clean the bones and examine them further; and yes— He paused. "Wait, hold it, why is everyone so interested in this?"

"And why wouldn't we be interested?" Beaupierre asked; the first time he'd been heard from since introducing Gideon. "A murdered man found in one of our own rock shelters."

"Your own—? I don't—you mean those were *your* test trenches?"

"Certainly," Beaupierre said, laughing. "I dug them myself. They were sunk more than thirty years ago, one of the institute's early endeavors. You'll find the site in the archaeological record as PN-119. Unfortunately, it held nothing of interest."

Maybe not, Gideon thought, but the coincidences—the kind of coincidences that Joly liked so much—were beginning to pile up. First it turns out that the murdered man might have been a former institute employee, and now it seems that the body was buried in an old institute site. And what about that trowel, don't forget about that. There was something going on behind the scenes here, but what?

"Unless, of course," Pru said to the director, "you accidentally overlooked a body buried in the middle of the floor."

But the unswervingly literal-minded Jacques Beaupierre was the wrong man for such banter. Confounded, he stared at her. "Are you joking?"

"Yes, Jacques."

Beaupierre didn't get it. "I'm sure I would *never* have overlooked such a thing."

"You didn't overlook anything, Jacques," Gideon assured him. "He wasn't buried there until much later, in the backfill from the trenches. He's only been there three years or so."

There was a sudden shift in mood around him, nothing so obvious as darting eyes or pregnant glances, but a sort of ripple, a fraction of a second that was out of kilter, as if a movie film had skittered over a torn sprocket hole. The discontinuity wasn't lost on Gideon, but what did it mean? Three years ago—that was when the commotion over the Old Man of Tayac had erupted. Was there a connection *there*?

Pru cleared her throat. "We had no idea it was so recent."

"The newspaper implied it'd been there for decades," Audrey said.

Gideon shook his head. "No, nowhere near that. Right around three years, that's all." Well, two to five, to be honest, but he'd clearly struck a chord of some kind with three, and if ever there was a time to do what Joly had asked him to, this was it. "You know, I was talking to the inspector this morning, and he wanted me to check something with you. He seems to think he might know who those bones belonged to: a man by the name of Jean Bousquet. I understand he worked here."

It was Audrey who answered after a barely perceptible general pause. "Bousquet? Yes, he was a temporary laborer, a hard man to get along with. It was a mistake to hire him—I don't think anyone here would argue with that—but temporary help isn't easy to find. It's hard, dirty work; they have to dig on their knees, or even on their bellies, half the time."

Pru laughed. "What, and we don't?"

"...really be Bousquet?" Beaupierre mumbled, coming in from his private wavelength. "But I don't see how, ah, mm..." And off he went again.

This time Gideon stayed with him. "You don't see what, Jacques?"

Beaupierre absently ran his fingers over his scalp, assuring himself that the few dozen heavily sprayed strands of hair that he combed over the top were still in place. "Well, only that it would mean that he must have returned from Corsica afterward, and why would he—"

"From Corsica?" Gideon exclaimed. "He went to Corsica? Do you mean, after he disappeared from here?"

"After he left, yes."

"But how do you know that?"

"Why, because he telephoned us. It was a few weeks afterward."

"Maybe even longer than that," Pru said.

"It was a month, perhaps even more," said Montfort.

"Are you sure?" Gideon asked.

"Certainly I'm sure," Montfort told him. "I spoke to him myself. He was after a reference, a character reference." Montfort was one of those rare individuals who could successfully bring off a "harrumph," and he did so now, adding: "Which, I need hardly say, he was unsuccessful in procuring."

"I see," Gideon said thoughtfully. "Huh."

"I'm not tracking here, Gideon," Pru said. "Why is this important?"

"Well, it means he didn't really 'disappear' after all—he just took off for Corsica. So there goes our reason for assuming those were his bones in the cave."

"I see," Pru said with a shrug. "Yeah, I guess that's so."

Others nodded noncommittally. That would seem to have been that, and yet something queer was in the air. *Something...*

"The idea," said Jacques, continuing roughly from where he'd left off, "that that man would have the nerve to come back to Les Eyzies after all the—"

Audrey cut in. "I don't know about you, but I'm all in favor of changing the subject. Do we really want to burden Gideon with old gossip, Jacques?"

"Quite right," Beaupierre agreed, busying himself with his coffee. "No, we don't, quite right."

"I understand," Gideon said, increasingly certain that he didn't. Corsica or no Corsica, he couldn't get away from the feeling—the conviction—that those bones were Bousquet's and that most of the other people in the room thought so too. "It's only that Inspector Joly mentioned that he'd had some kind of unpleasantness here, with one of his coworkers. I was wondering what that was about." This was hardly the smooth and subtle approach he was supposed to be taking, but he had hold of something and he didn't want to let go until he had at least some idea of what it was.

"Oh, well," said Beaupierre, "that's a long story—"

"A long story and a pointless one," Montfort muttered bluntly. Beaupierre might be the director, but it was clear where the fount of moral authority lay.

"Perhaps so," Beaupierre responded. "I only thought—that is well, won't the police be prowling about soon in any case, asking their questions? But then again, of course, mm, it might be best, after all..." He subsided, fumbling with the heavy black temples of his glasses.

"If the police want to ask us about our views on Jean Bousquet's relationships with others, I'm sure we'll all answer as honestly as we can," Audrey said, "but for the time being, I think we'd all agree—I hope we'd all agree—that it would be premature—premature and unfair—for us to engage in speculation?"

The others did agree, but it seemed to Gideon there was something furtive, even shamefaced, in their nods.

"Besides," Pru said, "if nothing else, it'd put Gideon in an uncomfortable position."

But Gideon was already in an uncomfortable position. When he'd raised the subject of Jean Bousquet with them, he'd done it under the impression that Joly's "unpleasantness with a fellow worker" had referred to a problem Bousquet had had with another laborer. But now a less palatable idea had slowly taken root: Bousquet's dispute had been with one of *them*. Why else were they banding together to prevent any discussion of it in front of him?

It was an extremely strong impression, something he felt bound to pass on to Joly, and it went against his instincts. Asking questions openly, getting open answers, and passing them along was one thing. Catching them off-guard and surreptitiously gauging their reactions was another, and it felt too damn close to informing on his friends. Not, of course, that he thought for a moment that one of these people—one of his fellow anthropologists, after all—was guilty of murdering the unfortunate Bousquet (if it *was* Bousquet). Still, it made him feel like a rat.

To his surprise he found that he'd emptied his water glass, and he refilled it while he framed his words. "I'd like to set something straight. The basic reason I'm here is to work on my book, to fill in the gaps in my understanding of the Tayac affair. I hope everybody understands that. On the other hand, I *am* also helping Inspector Joly with those remains."

When he glanced up from the glass, he found them looking at him somewhat uncomprehendingly.

"What I'm trying to tell you is that I just want you to know that—well, that I *am* working with him..."

"Which means," Émile said, the egrets jiggling, "that anything we say may be used against us?"

"Not used against you, no—"

"But passed on to the stalwart inspector."

"Well...yes," Gideon said miserably. "If it's relevant. I think I have to."

"That's completely as it should be, Gideon," said Beaupierre. "It's only that, mm..."

Audrey picked up the ball. "It's only that we'd all be better served if we stayed away from gossip and stuck to facts. Is there anything we can do to assist that doesn't involve speculation, Gideon? I know we'd all like to help."

Gideon wished he were more sure of that himself, but in any case it was the chance he was looking for, and before anyone could disagree he said: "Yes, there is. You could tell me what Bousquet looked like."

They did, but nothing they said was useful. Brown eyes, brown hair, balding at the crown. An average guy, nothing special, not particularly tall, or short, or fat, or thin.

It fit the body in the cave, all right, but so did every other average white guy in France. "Does anybody remember his having any sort of serious infection?" he asked after a moment, thinking of the inflammation he'd found on the left ulna. "Skin ulcers that wouldn't heal, maybe?"

"Skin ulcers where?" asked Beaupierre.

"No, it works better if you tell me."

"No, no skin ulcers," Beaupierre said.

Then why did you ask where? thought Gideon. But of course with Beaupierre, you couldn't necessarily assume he had anything logical in mind when he spoke. Or anything at all.

Thoughtfully, Audrey lifted a hand. "Do you mean an infection that he had while he was here, or are you also interested in earlier ones?"

"Either," Gideon said. He wasn't sure how old the bone inflammation was.

"Well, he had TB when he was a boy, I know that. He told me about it once. He got it in West Africa—his father was a well driller when Jean was in his teens, and the family lived in Mali for a while. Afterward, he had to spend some time at a government sanatorium in Menton."

"Do you mean skeletal TB?" Gideon asked with interest. He hadn't spotted any signs of it in his earlier examination—whatever the inflammation on the ulna was, it wasn't tubercular—but then he hadn't been looking for it, and the bones hadn't been cleaned yet, and if it had been a slight case he might easily have missed it. In the morgue, with good lighting and cleaned bones, it would be different.

"No, I don't think so," she said uncertainly. "The other kind, that affects the lungs."

"Pulmonary tuberculosis," Émile said professorially. "Consumption, in the vernacular. That will be no help to you, Gideon. As a trained paleopathologist I'm well aware—as I'm sure you are—that it leaves no evidence whatever on the bones."

"Actually it does sometimes," Gideon said. He knew he was stepping on Émile's ultrasensitive toes, but science was science. "It turns out there are some characteristic skeletal lesions that show up about half the time. It's a new finding. There was a paper in the *AJPA* a few years ago. You might have missed it."

"Apparently I did," Émile said, tight-mouthed. "And what sort of lesions would these be?"

"Extremely subtle ones," Gideon said diplomatically. "That's why no one's noticed them until now. What you find is this diffuse periostitis on the internal aspects of some of the ribs—generally four through eight, on the left side. They're faint, but they can be seen if you know to look for them."

"Is that so?" said Émile, growing interested. He might not like being taught anything by the younger Gideon, but he *was* a paleopathologist (a trained paleopathologist)—one of the best there was, Gideon was ready to admit—and this was new data. "And this would presumably be a by-product of chronic pulmonary tubercular infection of the subjacent pleural tissue?"

"Exactly. The—"

"Chronic pulmonary tubercular infection of the subjacent pleural tissue," said Beaupierre. "My, my, the waters are growing deep for us mere archaeologists. Well, well, Gideon, it's been most interesting, but I think we ought to conclude now. It's almost noon, and I'm sure we all have some final preparations to make for the symposium."

"One thing more," Montfort said, reemerging from the solitary, superior plane to which he'd retreated again. "In regard to your book, Dr. Oliver: I don't want—I'm sure none of us want—to see Professor Carpenter made to look ridiculous."

There were murmurs of assent around the table; heartfelt, as far as Gideon could tell. Carpenter had been a popular and—until the debacle that had ended his career—a respected director.

"I won't make him look ridiculous," Gideon said.

"Nor his scholarship either," added Beaupierre.

But that was a trickier proposition. "I'm not trying to make anything look ridiculous, Jacques, but I don't see how I can get around the fact that his scholarship *is* suspect. How else could he have been—"

Montfort interrupted. "Dr. Beaupierre refers not to the unfortunate episode of the Old Man of Tayac, but to the entire body of Professor Carpenter's work, the total thrust of his research. And mine," he added with unmistakable emphasis. "As unfortunate as his lapse of judgment in this case was, I hope you will make it clear that it has no bearing on the fact that other Neanderthals in other places *do* demonstrate beyond any possible doubt the existence of artistic proclivities."

"They do, do they?" said Audrey, her hackles rising. "Beyond *any* possible doubt?"

"Better duck," Pru breathed in Gideon's ear. "We're off again."

She was right. Montfort rounded on Audrey, his eyes glittering with the zeal of battle. "Doctor, I am at a loss to understand how you can continue to dispute the existence of art, legitimate art, in the Middle Paleolithic. We now have evidence of pigment traces—yellow, red, black, brown—applied to stone at well over two dozen Neanderthal sites. Are you seriously suggesting that this was all unintentional, the result of some kind of repeated accident?"

"Of course not," said Audrey, taking up the challenge, "but I hope you're not suggesting that the application of coloring materials to a surface is necessarily an artistic act."

"Not an artistic act?" put in Beaupierre. "But...but of course it's an artistic act. What else would you call it?"

"Any one of a hundred things: simple curiosity, or a primitive enjoyment of novel effects, or an instinct for play. In all these sites you mention, can you point to a single application of color that could be called a pattern, a meaningful design?"

"Oh...pouf," said Beaupierre weakly.

"Go ahead and pouf all you like, Jacques,"

Émile said, "but Audrey is clearly in the right. All these pigment traces of yours are no more than smears or formless dabs. Oh, at best I suppose they might represent a naïve form of aesthetic appreciation on the part of Neanderthal Man—"

"Neanderthals," Audrey said automatically.

"On the part of Neanderthals, but nothing to be confused with artistic intent as we use the term."

"Oh, yes?" said Montfort, warming to the debate. "And just how do you propose to separate the two? Is there really so obvious a difference between artistic appreciation and aesthetic appreciation—even 'naïve' aesthetic appreciation, as you choose to call it?"

"That's right," said Beaupierre. "Yes, very true. We all know, mm, ah…"

"Oh, come on, people, give me a break," Pru said. "Babies play with crayons. Give a chimp some finger paints and he's happy for hours. So what? Does that make him an artist?"

"But what about the incised stone, the worked bone?" said Montfort. "Do chimpanzees carve crosses in stone?"

Several voices responded, but Audrey's was the most penetrating. "For heaven's sake, Michel, are you back on that nummulite fossil from Hungary? One of the lines on that 'cross' is a natural crack, you know that as well as I do."

"And the other?"

"The other," said Émile, "is an ambiguous

mark that could easily have been caused by skinning, butchering, or any one of a thousand utilitarian, totally unaesthetic activities."

Montfort looked sadly at him. "Always and forever the ready answer."

"I may not be an archaeologist—" Émile said.

Montfort muttered something inaudible.

"—but it hardly takes an archaeologist to see it's just a *scratch*, that's all, a simple scratch on a stone. To refer to it as an 'incision,' a term connoting human agency, is spurious and misleading. I don't mean this in a personal sense, of course, Michel."

Montfort snorted. "And do you also have an answer for the complexly incised—pardon me, the *scratched*—bone fragment from Pêche de l'Azé?" He thumped the table, making empty coffee cups rattle in their saucers.

"Natural erosion," said Émile, uncowed, with his chin thrust out.

"The perforated reindeer phalanges from La Quina—"

"Carnivore activity."

Montfort, shaking his head, gazed sadly at him.

"But...but the perforated wolf metacarpal from Böcksteinschmiede?" said Beaupierre, taking up the argument as well as he could. "What about that?"

"Not proven to be Middle Paleolithic, as opposed to Upper Paleolithic!" cried Audrey, partway to her feet.

Beaupierre and Montfort let fly at the same time. Oh, yes? How did she explain the artifacts from Bilzingsleben? What about Repolusthöhle? Arcy-sur-Cure? Cueva Morín in Spain?

Gideon had been long forgotten. All of them, including even the usually mellow Pru, were talking at once, or rather shouting; banging the table and waving their arms for emphasis. Through the open door of the room Gideon saw the café's proprietor, standing behind the bar, exchange smiles and wags of the head with a couple of his customers. These scientists!

"I guess I'll be going," he announced. "Thanks very much for your help."

He thought no one had heard him over the din, but as he rose from his chair Pru touched his elbow, smiled, and said in her fluent French:

"Bienvenue chez les fous."

Welcome back to the madhouse.

CHAPTER
9

Because Les Eyzies had neither a morgue nor a hospital, the bagged bones from the cave had been taken to the morgue room of the hospital at Saint-Cyprien, another ancient Périgord town five miles from Les Eyzies, this one clustered at the foot of an imposing twelfth-century abbey on the banks of the Dordogne. Having driven there in the compact olive-green Peugeot that Julie had rented for them by E-mail from the United States, Gideon was told by the front-desk receptionist, a friendly, chatty woman who laughed at the end of every sentence, that he would find the morgue in the basement—right down those stairs, in the room at the end of the corridor.

"Will I need a key, madame?" he asked in French.

She chuckled good-naturedly. "No, you won't need one, monsieur, we don't usually lock the morgue. Not too many people try to get in—or out, for that matter. And besides, the other gentleman is there."

"Other gentleman?" he said, surprised. And then: "Oh, would that be Dr. Roussillot, the police pathologist?"

"I don't know, I didn't ask his name."

She didn't ask Gideon's name either, he reflected critically as he went down the stairs. Joly himself might run a tight ship, but this sort of evidence storage would never pass muster under American chain-of-evidence requirements. Gideon was the second—at least the second—person to have access to the bones without having to provide identification. Aside from that, they'd been left unattended for who knew how long; that left a huge chink into which a defense attorney or a judge could toss a monkey wrench on the grounds that it could no longer be proved beyond a doubt that these bones really were the selfsame bones that had been removed from the cave. And it was on just such objections that many an otherwise solid case could—indeed, had—come apart at the seams.

The basement corridor's main purpose seemed to be to serve as a storage area for conveyances. Gideon had to thread his way around gurneys, wheelchairs, and walkers to get to the double doors at the end of the hallway. Once there, he pushed them open to enter a small, immaculate, white-tiled room furnished with a desk along one wall, a rack with clean rubber aprons and white coats, a barred, glass-fronted

cabinet holding the usual blood-freezing assortment of autopsy tools, and, in the center, a single
old-fashioned porcelain-topped autopsy table at
which a heavily built man in a white coat was
removing one of the paper bags of bones from
the macaroni carton.

At Gideon's entrance, he looked up sharply,
the point of his fastidiously shaped Van Dyke
bristling. "What do you want? This is a re-
stricted area. I'm extremely busy. Do you have
permission to be here?"

Dr. Roussillot, I presume, Gideon thought. "I'm
Gideon Oliver," he said in French, cautiously
advancing. "You must be Dr. Roussillot."

He received a wary nod in reply.

"Well, I'm the anthropologist who's been
working with Inspector Joly. I'm supposed—"

"Of course, forgive me, the *anthropologist*," he
said, not really rudely, but making it amply clear
whose turf this was, who was encroaching on
whom, and who'd better not try getting away
with any snake oil. He leaned over to shake
hands, briefly and formally—one businesslike
flap down, one up—then made room for Gideon
at the table, shoving to one side the marred
leather satchel at his feet. "Be so good as to bring
me up to date, please, Professor."

Gideon did, resorting to shaky Latin when his
French didn't extend to the diffuse periosteal lesions that he would be hunting for on the ribs.

"How interesting. Shall we examine the ribs,
then?"

"If you don't mind, I'd rather set everything out in anatomical order first. It'll only take a minute. Will you give me a hand?"

"Certainly," said Roussillot.

Gideon started at the head end. Roussillot, beginning with the lower body, removed the left femur from its sack and grasped it firmly around the shaft. "I'm sorry about this," he said. "I don't see any other way."

"Hm?" Gideon said absently, absorbed in scraping a bit of dirt from a clavicle. "Sorry about—"

He was sitting on the floor.

His legs were crumpled in front of him. His head hung loosely forward with his chin digging into his sternum. He was staring dully at his hands, one of which lay, palm down, flat against the cool smoothness of the linoleum floor; the other was loosely curled in his lap. A hard, sharp vertical edge, a corner of something, cut into his spine. When he shifted to ease the discomfort, the sudden loss of support sent him flopping bonelessly over backward, banging his head on the floor and wrenching a grunt of pain out of him.

Whooh!

The sound startled, then steadied him. His body and his mind began to come together. He waited for the white flash of pain to dim and for the billows of nausea to recede, then gingerly reopened his eyes. He was looking at a ceiling bank of blue-white neon lights shielded by metal grilles. When they began a slow, circling tilt from left to right he shut his eyes again and kept them shut while strength and consciousness flowed—trickled—back into him.

Where was he? What had happened to him? He'd had a quick lunch with Julie in Les Eyzies, he remembered that. They'd taken marinated roast beef and tomato sandwiches, bottles of Orangina, and paper cones of French fries to a bench near the river and he'd told her about the unexpected direction the staff meeting had taken. Then, while she went back to the hotel to put her feet up for an hour before going off to her symposium, he'd driven to Saint-Cyprien to finish his examination of the bones, and there he'd met—

The bones! His eyes flew open. The ceiling started its tilt again, but this time he stuck it out, staring hard at the lights and willing them to be still. When they settled down to no more than a shimmering wobble, he gathered himself together and pulled himself slowly up with the aid of the autopsy table. For the first time he was aware of a jackhammer pain behind his left ear, just above the mastoid process. He put his fingers on the spot and winced when they touched a tender walnut-sized knot. At least he now knew what had put him on the floor in the first place.

He also knew, even before he'd made it to his feet, what he would find, and find it he did. The bones were gone, the satchel was gone, Dr. Roussillot—the so-called Dr. Roussillot—was gone.

But the *macaroni au fromage* carton was still there. Grasping the table hard for support, he stared at the empty box until his blurry vision cleared a little more. And in one of its corners, caught under a flap of cardboard, he saw a single tooth, a familiar one with a dull gray filling, a first bicuspid that had come loose from the mandible; all that was left of the skeleton from the *abri*.

As he got his fingers clumsily around it, the walls began their slow wheeling again, the edges of his sight to grow dark. Clutching the table, Gideon let himself back down to the floor, making it just as the black, sick void reared up and engulfed him again.

"I talked to the doctor," Julie said. "The tests were all negative—nothing broken. It was just a simple concussion. He was really happy with the results."

"Oh, just a simple concussion, is that right?" Gideon said, slumped in an armchair, with his head leaning back and a damp towel thrown across his eyes. "Just a little neuroaxonic fragmentation? Merely some cortical ischemic necrosis, is that all? Just some trifling disintegration of the midline reticular nuclei here and there? Oh, I'm delighted to hear he's happy."

"Something tells me you're not in a very good mood."

"No? Well, you wouldn't be either. What else did he say?"

"He said you'd probably be feeling worse before you felt better—"

"He got that right."

"—but a good night's sleep should take care

of it. He left you some sleeping pills. If you still feel funny tomorrow, he wants you to go back and see him again."

"Right, sure." He took the towel from his eyes and threw it ill-humoredly onto the high-backed sofa, squinting at the bright afternoon light streaming into the room.

"He gave you some pain pills too; want them?"

"No, I don't want to get dopey. God."

"Gideon, are you sure you wouldn't rather be in bed?"

He shook his head, a mistake.

"Should I have some food sent up? Or we could go downstairs if you feel up to it."

"No, I just want to sit here and whine."

She was quiet for a while. Then she said: "I think I know what your problem is. It goes back to your college days, when you used to box. You got knocked out four times, after all—"

"Three," Gideon growled. "Two, if you don't count TKOs."

"—and you're probably just wondering how many more brain cells you can afford to lose. Am I warm?"

She said it lightly, a throwaway pleasantry accompanied by a smile, but her voice was taut, and Gideon was abruptly aware of how drawn her face was, how anxious her eyes, how flat and yellowish the area under them. Until now he'd been too wrapped up in his own misery to notice, but he noticed now. He'd taken a knock on the head, yes, but it was Julie who'd gotten the telephone call that told her her husband had apparently had some sort of seizure and was in the hospital undergoing head X-rays, Julie who'd had to make the frightened taxi ride to Saint-Cyprien, Julie who'd held his hand and made small jokes while he lay with his head immobilized in a metal cage, waiting to be slid into the ominous, clanking MRI machine. And since then it had been Julie who'd continued to make small jokes and small talk in that strange, tight little voice, jollying him along while he'd sat ungratefully around, first in the hospital and now in their hotel room, doing little more than grumbling that he felt rotten.

My God, he thought, ashamed and guilty, what if the situation had been reversed? What would he be feeling if it had been Julie who'd been hurt and he who'd received the call?

He waited for the thickening in his throat to ease, and then he gave her a smile of his own, his first in a long time. "Don't you worry about it, I have brain cells you wouldn't believe; plenty to spare, enough for two people."

It was a pleasure to see her eyes come snapping alive again. "Now that," she said, "sounds more like the modest fellow I know and love."

She leaned over to kiss him, and as she did, they heard the sound of a car pulling up to the curb below. Julie went to the window, came back, and kissed him again. "Maybe you ought to get some shoes on. *L'inspecteur est arrivé.*"

* * *

The Cro-Magnon's upstairs lounge was situated on a stairway landing in a corner just big enough for three comfortable armchairs and a coffee table. Being at the rear of the building, directly against the cliffside, it lacked, as did many of the other houses and shops, a conventional back wall. Instead, the smooth, curving limestone of the cliff itself served as the wall. The effect, especially when coupled with the subdued lighting from two low-wattage table lamps, was of a cave, an *abri* with modern conveniences.

It was in this pleasant, restful niche—easy on Gideon's throbbing eyes—that they met with Joly over a pot of tea and a plate of fruit tarts brought upstairs by Monsieur Leyssales, the hotel's proprietor.

"The man you describe," said Joly, gravely stirring a second teaspoon of sugar into his second cup of tea, "is not Dr. Roussillot."

Gideon smiled, or tried to. "Gee, why am I not surprised?"

"He was completely unfamiliar to you?"

"Absolutely."

"You have no idea who he might be or why he was there?"

"Who, no. Why...well, *why* seems pretty obvious. To get the bones out of there."

"Gideon," Julie said tentatively, "don't get upset now, but *who* seems pretty obvious too—or rather who was behind it. It had to be somebody from the institute—somebody who was at the staff meeting."

"Well, no, I wouldn't say—"

"Yes, you would. There wasn't time for the word to get around to anybody else. You walked into that morgue just one hour after the end of that meeting, and this fake Roussillot was already there."

"Yes, but he wasn't at the meeting," Gideon said doggedly. "Or anywhere in the café. I would have remembered."

"Well, of course not. But whoever it was must have been afraid someone might recognize him if he showed up at the hospital himself, so he got somebody else—maybe a friend, maybe somebody he hired, who knows—to get rid of the bones for him. How hard would it have been—"

"All right, okay," Gideon said dejectedly, "you're right, I agree with you. I guess I just don't like to say it, even to myself."

"But what I find myself wondering," Joly said, "is how this person knew enough to pretend to be Dr. Roussillot. How would he know who Dr. Roussillot is?"

"Oh, that wasn't hard," Gideon said. "I walked right up to him and told him that's who he was: 'You must be Dr. Roussillot.' He was happy to go along."

"Ah." Pause. "And he struck you with the leg bone, the femur? There, behind the left ear, where that remarkable protuberance is?"

"I assume so. The last I remember, he had the bone in his hand. And that's where the lump is, so I suppose that's where he hit me—twice. There are actually two remarkable protuberances, not one."

Joly frowned at him. "What do you mean, you assume so? Don't you remember being struck?"

"No."

"But it may be important. Perhaps if you try to reconstruct—"

"Lucien, let me explain something to you. When people say they remember the blow that knocked them out, they're either making it up or kidding themselves. A knockout blow is a concussion, and a concussion is an interruption of cortical electric activity that induces a retrograde amnesia which ninety-nine times out of a hundred obliterates any memory of the precipitating trauma and more often than not the events immediately preceding. Period, *fini*, end of discussion, subject closed, all right?"

"I..."

Julie smiled at the startled Joly. "He's a little touchy on the subject of concussions today."

"I don't wonder," Joly said peaceably. "All right, then, let's go over the rest of what we know, or think we know, one more time." He crossed his long, thin legs, first adjusting the trouser crease, and propped his gold-rimmed cup and saucer on his knee. "Now. As Julie points out, we can tentatively assume that the person who attacked you and removed the bones learned where they were from someone who was present at the staff meeting when you announced their location."

"I didn't *announce* it, I just—"

"Second, I think we can proceed on the assumption that the bones were taken—and taken so quickly—in order to prevent your examining them, inasmuch as you yourself told them you would be doing so this afternoon."

Gideon was stretched out nearly supine in his chair, staring at his shoes. "This is really making me feel great, Lucien." He tapped his temple with a finger. "Really smart, you know?"

"Third, we can probably assume that the purpose of removing them was to prevent the possibility of your finding evidence of tuberculosis on the ribs and thus provisionally identifying the remains as Jean Bousquet's. We can assume this because you yourself told—"

Gideon waved a hand at him. "I know, I know. Boy, you really like to rub it in, don't you?"

"All right, then," Joly said, "given that much—"

Julie put down her tea. "May I say something, Lucien? Wouldn't it make just as much sense to assume that whoever took the bones did it to prevent Gideon from finding out it *wasn't* Bousquet?"

Joly frowned at her over the rim of his cup. "Wasn't Bousquet?"

"Well, say Gideon had looked at them and those marks on the ribs *weren't* there, it would mean—or at least it might mean—that it wasn't Bousquet at all, but someone else. And maybe somebody didn't want you to know *that*. Isn't that possible?"

"I suppose—"

"Possible but not probable," Gideon said. "I know these people; they think like scientists. They know perfectly well that whereas *finding* periostitis would be a positive sign of the disease and therefore a strong indicator that the bones are Bousquet's, *not* finding it wouldn't prove anything one way or the other—particularly because TB is a rare disease nowadays, and almost half of the very few people who do get it never develop those lesions anyway."

"Yes," Julie said, "but do the people at the institute know that?"

"They do now," Gideon said miserably. "That's another thing I happened to mention this morning."

"Considering that you spent only forty minutes with them," Joly observed, "you managed to impart a great deal of useful information."

Gideon slouched deeper into the armchair.

Julie poured more tea for the three of them, adding the sugar that Gideon asked for to settle his uneasy stomach. "Gideon, which one do you think was behind it? Any idea?"

"Not a clue."

"But obviously, one of them must know something about Bousquet's history that he wasn't telling."

"I think they *all* know something they weren't telling. Beaupierre almost gave it away at one point, but they jumped all over him, and he shut up like a clam, and so did everybody else."

"And you believe they were protecting a member of the group, one of their own," Joly said.

Gideon nodded. "Yes. Unless I'm way off base, I think the 'coworker' you told me about, the one that Bousquet had his 'unpleasantness' with, is one of them. And they all banded together to protect whoever it is."

"Which inescapably leads us to wonder if this unnamed person may have murdered Bousquet over this unnamed unpleasantness?"

It was, of course, the question that had been on Gideon's mind all afternoon, ever since he'd come to on the floor of the morgue, and he'd yet to reach an answer. "Lucien, I just don't know. Anything I'd say would be a guess."

"Then guess."

"All right, my guess is no. Or if one of them actually did—which is hard for me to make myself take seriously—I don't think that's what it is that the others know. I got the feeling that what they know is merely that he or she had some kind of trouble with Bousquet and they're worried that it's going to make difficulties for him, or her, with the police. With you. That's all."

"If that's all," Julie said hotly, "why did they steal the bones and almost kill you doing it? Is that supposed to make things less difficult with the police?"

"I don't know that either."

There was a long silence, and then Joly said: "I have something interesting to tell you. I had an informative conversation with Madame Renouard a little while ago."

"Madame Renouard," Gideon repeated, searching his mind. "That's...?"

"Bousquet's landlady, who was able to enlighten me in the matter of his relations at the institute. If we assume that her account is reliable, Bousquet did indeed have difficulties—I mean to say, extreme difficulties—with one particular member of the staff." He broke a plum tart in two, delicately inserted one piece into his mouth, and used a napkin to carefully wipe powdered sugar from his lips and fingers.

Gideon fidgeted. "So, who?"

Joly disposed of the rest of the tart and swabbed down his lips and fingers again while he chewed and swallowed. "As a matter of fact, it was Ely Carpenter."

"Carpenter!" Gideon exclaimed unwisely, cringing at the bright flash of pain behind his eyes.

"Carpenter," said Julie more softly. "Now that raises some interesting questions."

"For example," Gideon said, thinking aloud, "was Bousquet somehow tied in with the hoax?"

He was indeed, said Joly. According to Madame Renouard, Carpenter had somehow come to the conclusion that Jean Bousquet was the writer of the anonymous letter to *Paris-Match* that had first exposed the Tayac fraud. In what had apparently been an intense public scene at the institute, Carpenter had accused Bousquet to his face, and Bousquet had hotly denied that he'd had anything to do with it. Carpenter had gone further, suggesting that Bousquet had somehow been involved with the scheme from the beginning—the planting of the bones, followed by the subsequent exposé—all with the intention of humiliating him, Carpenter.

"But what reason could he have?" Julie asked. "Bousquet was just a temporary workman, wasn't he? Why would he want to humiliate the director?"

There again, the all-knowing Madame Renouard claimed to have the inside story. Not long before, it had been discovered that one or two Paleolithic stone implements had disappeared from the institute's storage area. On investigating, Carpenter had concluded that Bousquet had sold them to tourists—another accusation that Bousquet had angrily rejected—and issued Bousquet a formal reprimand and warning. The injured Bousquet had made no secret, at least not to his landlady and his fellow boarders, of his resentment.

"I've seen the letter to *Paris-Match*," Joly said. "It is not the language of an educated man, and certainly not that of a professional archaeologist."

"So you think it might be true—that Bousquet wrote it?" Gideon asked.

"I think it shouldn't be dismissed as a possibility. Nor should the possibility that he was behind the hoax."

Julie shook her head. "I don't know. Could somebody like that know enough to really take in an expert, a genuine archaeologist? It's hard to believe."

"It is," Gideon agreed. "On the other hand, if you think about it, that's exactly what *Bones to Pick* is about: the amazing capacity of even the most learned experts to turn into gullible chumps if they *want* to believe something."

"That's so, but whether Bousquet was or wasn't the perpetrator is irrelevant to our purposes," Joly said. "The fact that Carpenter *thought* it was true still remains." He paused to let this sink in. "You see what it means, don't you?"

Gideon slowly nodded. "It means I probably got it wrong. They're not protecting one of themselves, they're protecting Carpenter, or rather his memory. They're afraid he's going to be accused of killing Bousquet."

"Well, maybe he did kill Bousquet," Julie said. "He's dead. Somebody killed him."

"Yes, that's the point I was about to make," Joly said. From a pocket of his suit coat he took the small leather-bound notebook he carried and with the aid of a moistened forefinger turned to one of its pages. "Consider these facts. The hoax was first exposed by means of the letter on the first of September. On the twenty-fifth,

Carpenter suddenly submitted his resignation and, without waiting to learn if it was accepted, flew off into the night sky toward Brest, a journey he didn't live to complete. On the twenty-eighth of the same month, Madame Renouard notified the police that Bousquet had not been seen for three days—since the twenty-fifth of September, to be exact. Do you not find it suggestive that—"

"Forget it, Lucien," said Gideon. "You're definitely on the wrong track there. Bousquet was still alive long after Carpenter died. Ely couldn't have killed him."

Joly's eyebrows went up; his mouth pursed. He waited for Gideon to continue.

"He called the institute a month or so later to ask for a job reference. They told me this morning. From Corsica, they thought."

"And how would they know where he was calling from?"

"Well, that's what he said, I suppose. But wherever he was calling from, he was definitely alive, so that lets Ely out."

"Unless," Joly said after a moment's thought, "the account was concocted for your benefit."

"Why would they do that?"

"For the reason you suggested: to prevent suspicion from attaching to Carpenter."

"I really don't think so," said Gideon, but with something less than total conviction, "but—anyhow, aren't we getting a little ahead of ourselves? Let's not jump—"

Julie interrupted. "No, it's a point. You told us they all obviously liked Carpenter and would've wanted to protect him, right? So isn't it at least possible—"

"Look," Gideon said, "we don't even know for sure that those bones *are* Bousquet's. I mean, I think they are too—we sure don't have any other candidates, do we?—but unless we get them back, which seems pretty unlikely, there's no possible way to prove it."

"But isn't there?" Julie said through a mouthful of plum tart, then paused to gulp some tea to get it down. "What about that tooth that was left in the box? It has some dental work on it, doesn't it? I can remember a dozen cases where that was all you needed for a positive identification."

"Right," Gideon said. "All we had to do was ask the right dentist to see whether they matched the files of one of his patients. But to find the right dentist you have to have a pretty good idea of who the victim is so that—"

"Which we do. Jean Bousquet."

"Sure, but who was Jean Bousquet's dentist?"

"Why should that be so difficult to find out? He must have had a dentist. Someone did that work. And you said there was a crown too, on another tooth."

"But not somebody from around here," Gideon said. "The crown had a lot of wear on it; it was in his mouth a good ten years, probably more. And Bousquet was a drifter—who knows where he was ten years ago?"

"Not I," Joly agreed sadly.

"Oh," said Julie.

"Of course, it's always possible he did go to a dentist while he was here," Gideon said, "and that dentist might be able to help."

"Yes, I'll see," Joly said, but they all knew there wasn't much hope of that. Drifters, whether French or American, didn't typically make regular visits to the dentist, and Bousquet had spent only three months in Les Eyzies.

"So," Julie said brightly after a solemn pause during which the only sound was the clinking of china cups on china saucers, "where to from here?"

"I was thinking," Gideon said. "Tomorrow I start my interviews on the hoax. I ought to be able to pry a little more out of them about what was going on at the time without too much trouble."

Julie stared at him and then at Joly. "He's got to be kidding."

"Thank you, Gideon," Joly said politely, "but I have my own resources."

"Sure you do, but you said I could do it more subtly than you could before. Why not now?"

"Why not..." Julie put down her cup with a bang. "Because they've already fragmented your...your stupid neuroaxons, haven't they? What do you expect them to do next? Politely ask if you wouldn't be good enough, old chap, to stay out of it?"

"Julie makes a good—" Joly began.

"Now be reasonable, people," Gideon said. "Let's look at this objectively. No one had any intention of killing me or even injuring me—"

"No? What was it then?" Julie asked. "Some form of ritual greeting known only to Middle Paleolithic archaeologists? 'Salutations, O fellow archaeologist.' Bop!"

What he'd meant, he explained, was that it was obvious that no one had gone to the Saint-Cyprien morgue with the objective of doing him harm. The purpose had clearly been to remove the bones so that they couldn't be identified, nothing more. Gideon had had the misfortune to walk in at the wrong time. The tap on the head he'd received—

"Tap on the head!" Julie exclaimed to Joly. "That wasn't what he was calling it an hour ago."

—had been a desperation measure, nothing more. "And if the guy had wanted me dead, why didn't he finish the job then, instead of leaving me on the floor unconscious?"

"Maybe he thought you *were* dead."

"No, he wouldn't have thought I was dead. And anyway, I'm not any kind of a threat to anybody anymore. With the bones gone, what could they have to worry about from me? Besides, my asking everybody questions is perfectly natural. They're all expecting it. That's what I'm here for, remember?"

Pretty impeccable logic, he thought, but Joly seemed doubtful and Julie wasn't buying it at all. "I'd say the issue is moot," she said. "How do you expect to interview anybody tomorrow? You can't even blink your eyes without wincing."

"Granted, but tomorrow, if I'm feeling better—"

"I'll tell you what," Joly said thoughtfully. "I expect to be busy with other things tomorrow in any case—I want to chat with some of Bousquet's acquaintances, and with the receptionist at the Saint-Cyprien hospital, and so on. Assuming that you're physically able, I don't think it would be a bad thing at all if you went ahead with your scheduled interviews."

"Fine."

"But only on the condition that you don't play at detective. You're to stick to the subject of your book and not raise questions about Bousquet and his troubles with Carpenter or anyone else, or about the missing bones. That's my job. On the other hand, if information presents itself without provocation on your part, well and good—I'll be interested to hear."

"Deal."

"And it would be wise to make no mention of the episode at Saint-Cyprien. Only the guilty party is likely to know of it, and it might be that he would say something to give himself away."

"Good point, I agree. Julie, what about you? If you'd really feel better if I didn't—"

"Do you *really* promise to do what Lucien asked you to? Stick to the Old Man of Tayac?"

He raised his hand. "Word of honor."

"Okay, good, I'll go along with it as long as you promise not to do anything dumb. *You* might have brain cells to spare, but I only have one husband, and I'm not interested in being in the market for another."

"I'm relieved to hear it."

She stirred her tea and laid down her spoon. "On the other hand, another day like today and I just might change my mind."

11

"Mmm," Julie said luxuriously, "what a lovely way to start the day."

Gideon smiled. "Not bad."

He moved his face, only six inches from hers, even closer, to brush his lips along the warm, velvet curve of her cheek. "I'm sorry I was such a miserable grouch yesterday. I sure love you."

"Mmm," she said again with her eyes closed, arching her neck to press her face against his.

"You have the world's most absolutely gorgeous submaxillary triangle, did I ever tell you that?" he murmured into her throat.

"Yes, many times," she said sleepily. "It never fails to take my breath away."

His fingertips glided over the tender flesh beneath her chin. "The soft swell of your digastricus—"

"Thank you. Now, shh." With a practiced motion that was all the more affecting because of its easy, familiar intimacy, she pushed on his shoulder to let him know she wanted him on his back. Having arranged him to her satisfaction, she patted his chest as if she were plumping a pillow, worked her head into the hollow of his shoulder, threw one round, sturdy leg over him, sighed, and fell back asleep. Gideon remained awake but was content—much more than content—to lie without moving, his arm under the weight of her and his fingers curled loosely in her dark hair, utterly relaxed and empty of mind, conscious of little more than her closeness and the clean, sweet, warm smell of her. The window was open; dappled morning sunshine filtered through the slats of the wooden shutters, making patterns on the floor and paler, shifting, green-tinged reflections on the ceiling. Time passed.

"I hope," he said, when she began to move and stretch, "that in addition to being pleasant, this morning's, um, activity proved to you that I am back in command of my capacities."

She opened her eyes and smiled at him. "I was worried about your head, not—"

"My head is fine too," he said. "Everything is fine." It was too, or very nearly. "Tell me, what can I do to convince you?"

"Well…" She rolled onto her back, yawning. "Maybe if you went downstairs and came back with a couple of *cafés au lait*, that might do it."

He kissed her one more time and climbed out of bed. "Give me five minutes."

Julie snuggled back under the covers and

closed her eyes again. "You might want to put on some clothes first," she said, snickered quietly to herself, and went back to sleep.

At one side of the Hôtel Cro-Magnon, enclosed by crumbling stone walls covered by trailing ivy, was a private breakfast garden with a few round tables of filigreed metal, a sheltered oasis of shade trees, bright flowers, and potted plants no more than ten yards from the main street. It was here, at an umbrellaed table, with the last droplets of morning dew still shimmering on the leaves around them, that they sat awaiting their breakfasts half an hour later.

"What's your schedule this morning?" Julie asked. "Do you see Jacques Beaupierre first?"

"Yes, that seemed like the right protocol. He's on for ten o'clock, followed at ten-thirty by Pru, who's probably going to be the most informative, then Montfort and the rest of them."

"You're just doing half-hour interviews? You could have done that over the phone from home. Not that I'm complaining," she said, taking in the scene around them.

"These are just the introductory sessions, to give me an overview. I'm sure I'll have follow-up questions for them later."

"M'sieu-m'dame," said Madame Leyssales, the proprietress, bearing a tray heavily loaded with their *cafés complets*—big stoneware pitchers of coffee and hot milk, little ceramic pots of jam and butter, and heaped baskets of warm rolls and croissants. Each of the empty coffee cups had a third of a baguette standing upright in it, wrapped in a napkin.

Julie's eyes widened. "Wow, things have changed in France. I seem to remember rather small breakfasts, by and large."

"It's not that," Madame Leyssales said as she set the tray down. "It's only that I remember the gentleman and his appetite from the last time he was here."

"And bless you for it, madame," Gideon said, tucking in at once. "I haven't had anything since lunch yesterday."

"*Bon appétit*," she said unnecessarily and retired.

It wasn't until the coffee was half gone, the baskets half emptied, and the table littered with flakes of croissant that Gideon sat back with a sigh. "Now, where were we?"

"You were telling me your schedule."

"Right—Julie, aren't you having any croissants at all? You can't get them like this in the States."

"I was afraid I'd get my hand stabbed if I reached for one. Is it safe now?"

He laughed. "I'm reasonably sated, yes. Anyway, I should be free at noon or a little after. How about joining me for lunch?"

"Rats, I can't. I have a ticket for the eleven-thirty Font de Gaume cave tour. It was the only opening they had all day. But I'm meeting Pru McGinnis for lunch at one—she introduced herself at the session yesterday, and I really liked her. Why don't you join us?"

"No good. At one I'm due at the *mairie* to give a deposition."

"About that 'tap on the head,' you mean?"

"Right. Joly's going to meet me there and help me through it."

"And then what? Back to the institute for more interviews?"

"No, they'll have to wait for tomorrow. All the institute people are going to be at part two of that symposium this afternoon. I should probably finish up at the *mairie* by two or two-thirty, and then I'm free. What about you? Are you going to sit in on the symposium again?"

She tore off a piece of croissant, applied cherry jam, and chewed away. "Mm, you're right; good. No, I don't want to go to the symposium." She hesitated, chewing. "Can I ask you something? Do these institute people really have a good reputation? They all seemed...well, frankly, like a bunch of...of quibbling eccentrics to me."

"That's because they do quibble and they're mostly pretty eccentric. But yes, you bet they have a good reputation—a terrific reputation—and they deserve it. That little outfit has been right at the forefront of Paleolithic scholarship for almost thirty years. A guy like Beaupierre may live in his own world most of the time, but nobody can match him for Mesolithic tool technology, and Montfort is a giant in European archaeology—even the Tayac mess couldn't change that—and Émile can be kind of a jerk, but he's done some wonderful stuff on ancient disease demographics, and Audrey's contributed more to the understanding of Cro-Magnon social structure than almost anyone, and even Pru—"

"Okay, okay, I believe you," Julie said. "Just the same, I think I'll give it a skip." She gave him a little grin with just the corners of her mouth. "But you know what would be fun? I heard there's a kind of reconstructed early-man cave village up the road a little, near Tursac, with scenes of Neanderthals and Cro-Magnons hunting woolly mammoths, and fighting saber-toothed tigers, and so on. It's called Préhistoparc. How about going up there?"

"Julie, saber-toothed tigers were extinct in the Old World by the end of the Pliocene. They didn't coexist with Neanderthals or Cro-Magnons, so they could hardly have been hunted by them."

Julie rolled her eyes. "How did I wind up with such a pedant? Come on, what do you say?"

"What, you'd rather spend two hours walking around some phony-baloney Paleolithic Disneyland than hear some of the world's premier authorities, people who really know what they're talking about, discuss the latest ideas on Mousterian stone-tool typology?"

"Sure, wouldn't you?"

"Definitely," Gideon said.

"Besides," said Julie, laughing, "I've had all the Châtelperronian side scrapers, bifacial Acheulian hand axes, and Levalloisian flake cores I can stand for some time to come."

"Wow, that sounded great."

She grinned at him. "Just don't ask me what any of it means."

The offices of the Institut de Préhistoire were on the second floor of one of the few two-story buildings on Les Eyzies's main street, at the other end of the village (i.e., four blocks away) from the Hôtel Cro-Magnon. Sturdily built of rough-cut limestone blocks in the traditional Périgord style, with a steeply pitched stone-tiled roof, it was owned by a cooperative society of canned *foie gras* producers. The society occupied the ground floor, a single spacious chamber furnished in the grand style of an 1880s bank, with dark mahogany railings around the sides, Turkish carpets underfoot, claw-footed mahogany desks for its officers, and a hushed air of profitable, discreetly conducted commerce. A spotlit display of its members' products, in the form of a gleaming pyramid of gold and silver cans of goose liver, occupied pride of place on an ornate stand at the center of the room. The prosperous-looking men at the desks eyed Gideon expectantly when he entered but lost interest when he nodded and went to the stairwell that led to the upper floor; evidently he was merely another archaeologist.

Once having climbed the stairs into what seemed to be a general-use area, part archaeological storeroom, part break room, and part copy center, Gideon found himself thoroughly at home: scuffed thirty-year-old steel-and-Naugahyde office furniture, a photocopy machine, an ancient but apparently functioning mimeograph machine, a glass pot of brown sludge—coffee?—that looked as if it had been on the warmer for a week, two tables littered with journals, primitive stone tools, and Coke cans, and the mixed smells of millennia-old stone dust, wooden floorboards, and stale coffee—all the familiar, user-friendly sights, scents, and clutter of scholarly inquiry.

On the table nearest him were a dozen or so pieces of worked stone, rounded chunks of quartzite four or five inches across, one end of which had been crudely chipped from both sides into a rough but usable cutting edge. These were the bifacial Acheulian hand axes that Julie had referred to. He picked one up almost automatically and hefted it, grasping the smooth, rounded portion. This was one of the deep, one of the near-mystical, pleasures of anthropology, at least as far as Gideon was concerned. He had in his hand a tool that had been made and used perhaps 100,000 years ago. Just as he now grasped it, a strange, primitive creature, not quite human as we understand the term, languageless, naked or perhaps clothed in animal skins, had once clutched it—this very same stone—in a filthy hand to hammer bloodily away at living bone or horn. One could almost feel, or at least imagine that one could feel, a connection, an affinity, across that unimaginable gulf of time and essence—

"Puis-je vous aider?" The voice was icy, female, proprietary, and suspicious. *"Je m'appelle Madame Lacouture."*

Gideon jumped guiltily and practically flung the tool back on the table. "Excuse me, madame," he stammered in French. "I have an appointment with Dr. Beaupierre."

Madame Lacouture, a sharp-faced, peremptory woman in a mannish suit, reminded him of a dozen academic department-head secretaries he had known (and trembled before). He had often wondered if it was an international type, perhaps genetically determined, transcending all cultural barriers. In any case, this particular one was plainly skeptical. "Professor Beaupierre has informed me of no appointments. Your name and your affiliation, please?"

"Gideon Oliver. I'm from the University of Washington. Uh, *Professor* Oliver," he added, in hopes that it might impress her a little more.

It didn't come close. "Come with me, please," she said briskly, throwing him a we'll-soon-see-about-this look over one padded shoulder.

She marched him past a flimsy wallboard partition to a narrow hallway off which a row of offices, constructed from the same cheap wallboard, opened. The first was Beaupierre's, as cluttered and utilitarian as the outer area, with nothing on the walls but a marked-up scheduling calendar, and with piles of open books and journals teetering on tables and even on the floor. The director, seated at his desk, didn't hear them coming. Motionless and absorbed, he had his nose buried in a journal.

"Professor Beaupierre," Madame Lacouture began.

Beaupierre looked up vacantly, focused with some effort, and smiled. "Hello, Gideon, what are you doing here?"

"We had an appointment."

"Today?"

"I'm afraid so. We made it at yesterday's staff meeting, but if it's not convenient..."

"No, of course it's convenient. I'm at your service. *Merci, Madame Lacouture.*"

"Next time," she told him in French, "please try to remember to inform me of your schedule." It was something she told him a lot, Gideon guessed.

"Sit down, sit down," Beaupierre said. "Just give me a moment, a single, er, moment... Extremely interesting... *Bulletin de la Société Préhistorique Française*... want to see..." He returned to his journal while Gideon took the armchair beside the desk. At his elbow was a holder with two photographs, one of Madame Beaupierre, a svelte, glossily handsome woman whom Gideon had once met, and the other of Beaupierre's two grown daughters, women who had been cruelly tricked by their genes in that it was their dough-faced, sausage-shaped father they took after.

"How very interesting," Beaupierre said, pulling off his glasses and looking up from the journal at about the time Gideon was wondering if the director had forgotten he was there. "Were you aware that Révillion has conclusively demonstrated that the blade cores from Seclin have a closer relationship, volumetrically speaking, to Upper Paleolithic than Middle Paleolithic forms?"

"Ah...no, as a matter of fact I wasn't."

"You must admit it raises a number of intriguing issues."

"It certainly does." For starters: who was Révillion, where was Seclin, and what the hell was "volumetrically speaking"? "Jacques, do you suppose we could get on to Tayac? We only have half an hour."

"Of course, of course." Beaupierre closed the journal, pushed it to one side, and made a visible effort to concentrate on his guest, peering at him as if through misted glass. His open, friendly face was all concentration. "How can I help you?"

"How about starting by giving me an overview of the whole affair in your own words? Just to make sure I have it straight."

Beaupierre nodded gravely, crossed one knee over the other, steepled his stubby fingers in

front of his mouth, and proceeded, in a relatively coherent fashion, to tell Gideon the familiar story: how Carpenter had been working the
Tayac site on his own; how he had jubilantly
proclaimed his great find of four perforated
bones; how an anonymous letter to *Paris-Match*
had soon charged that they had actually come
not from a Paleolithic *abri* but from the collection
of a small, out-of-the-way museum where
they'd been stored for upward of forty years.

Gideon teetered on the edge of asking Jacques's
opinion on whether or not Jean Bousquet had
been the writer of that anonymous letter, but he
couldn't quite talk himself into the conviction
that to do so would not be crossing the forbid-
den line between legitimate research and "playing detective," something he'd promised both
Joly and Julie not to do. Reluctantly, he set it
aside for the time being. Maybe later he'd figure
out a way of talking himself into doing it. That,
or renegotiate.

"What museum did the bones come from,
Jacques?" he asked instead. "It's near here somewhere, isn't it? I'd like to go and see the bones
for myself."

"What? Oh, it was...yes, not too far...." He
snapped his fingers ineffectually. "The name es-
capes me, mm..." He rolled his eyes upward
but apparently found no clue on the ceiling and
went on with his recounting of the hoax: how
the shocking accusation of fraud had been sub-

stantiated, and how a wretched, repudiated Carpenter had had to resign in disgrace.

"Such a terrible, terrible end for him," he finished with a sigh. "Would you care for some coffee? It should be...I can ask Madame Lacouture to, mm, ah..."

"I sure w— no, thanks," Gideon said, remembering barely in time the pot of black, gluey matter on the warmer. "Jacques, what do you honestly think Carpenter's part in all this was? I know you've thought about it a lot. Could he have planted those bones himself, or—"

Beaupierre nearly came out of his chair. "Certainly not!" he exclaimed, shocked. "What a thought! Ely Carpenter was the very model of integrity."

"I'm only asking the question; I'm not suggesting anything," Gideon said placatingly.

"Ha, you'd better not ask such a question of Michel. He'll throw you out the door. Ely was like a son to him—not in age, of course, but otherwise—and the idea that...that...well, the very idea that Ely himself would..."

"Well, who then?" He didn't like upsetting Jacques, but this was one of the questions that had brought him to France in the first place. And now he had more reason than ever to ask it.

"I'm sure I—I have no idea."

"Come on, Jacques. You must have thought about it."

"Thought about it? Oh, well, of course,

thought about it…but…to what purpose… mm…" His fingers crept longingly across his desk toward the journal, his eyes toward the printed page.

That seemed to be that; for Beaupierre, after all, it had been a pretty long attention span. Gideon got to his feet.

"Well, thanks, Jacques. I'm off to see Pru. Which way's her office?…Jacques…?"

CHAPTER
12

"So tell me, what else is going to be in this book besides the Old Fart of Tayac?" Pru McGinnis asked. "Piltdown, I suppose?"

Her chair creaked under her considerable weight as she leaned back, ran her fingers through her already disordered red hair, clasped her fingernail-chewed hands behind her head, and propped her snakeskin-booted feet on an open drawer, one over the other, *clunk, clunk.* After getting her doctorate from Northern California State, she had taught for four years at the University of Missouri, from which she'd emerged with a country-western drawl and a style of dress to match—jeans, boots, belt buckles the size of dinner plates. The accent had soon gone, but the Western garb remained.

"Piltdown, of course," Gideon said. "The Abominable Snowman, the yeti, the Tasaday hoax, the Formosan Psalmanazar story—"

"Ah, good old Psalmanazar. Well, I'll give

145

you one I bet you don't have. What do you know about the Lost Hippopotamus of Lake Mendota?"

"I never heard of it."

"Aha. See, that's because we kept it a secret till now. The world was not yet ready. But today...today at last, I break my silence."

Gideon put down his notepad and settled back. If Pru was in the mood to tell one of her fish stories, the only thing to do was relax and enjoy it, because he didn't know any way to stop her. The Old Man of Tayac would have to wait.

"What are you putting your pen down for? Are you crazy?" she asked. "This'll be the best part of your book. This'll make it a best-seller."

"I figure I'll just memorize it. That way I'll get every word."

"Sure, I can see how that makes sense. Okay, this happened when I was an undergrad at the University of Wisconsin. You went there too, didn't you?"

"A long time before you," Gideon said.

"Not that much. Anyway, my roommate, Gloria Kakonis—she was track and field too—had this old umbrella stand that she got somewhere that was made from this humongous, moth-eaten old hippopotamus foot, you know? Gross. So late one night, in the middle of January, right after a snowstorm, we drop a couple of heavy books inside it, hook up twenty feet of clothesline to either side, and take it outside, up to the campus, right out in front of Bascom Hall. Then

Gloria grabs hold of one rope, and I get hold of the other rope, and we start carrying this thing down the hill suspended between us, okay? Only every couple of feet we set it down in the snow so it looks like a footprint. But *our* footprints are so far away nobody connects them.... What? What are you grinning at?"

"It's a funny story, Pru. I'm just imagining it."

"Wait, it gets better. We carried that thing for an hour, till our arms were practically coming out of our sockets and we couldn't feel our toes anymore from the cold. Then we go back home and wait for the next morning."

"When everybody discovers to their astonishment that there was a hippopotamus loose on campus the night before," Gideon said.

"Not exactly. Actually, they didn't know what the tracks were, so they brought in a couple of professors from the zoology department. They look at the tracks, they look at each other, and go, like, 'Egad, Farquelhar, damned if it isn't the greater four-toed *Hippopotamus amphibius!*' And off they trot, following the tracks, and by now there's a whole crowd with them, including some reporters. So. Down the hill they go, through town, and right out onto Lake Mendota, which is frozen, of course, under all the snow—and which also happens to be the water supply for Madison, if you remember. Out they all go on the lake, a hundred yards, two hundred yards...and suddenly the tracks stop."

"Stop?"

"Stop. End. In a big hippopotamus-sized hole."

Gideon burst out laughing.

Pru threw her head back and cackled along with him. "Nobody wanted to drink the town water for a year—and even then everybody said it tasted like hippopotamus!"

When they finished chortling, Pru wiped her eyes and said: "Are you going to put that in your book?"

"Nope."

"Why, you don't believe me?"

"Not for a minute. Okay, can we get serious now?"

"I'm always serious. When am I not serious?"

"Okay, seriously then, put me in the picture. I know what the Tayac hoax was about and how it turned out and all, but I don't have any feel for the way it *was*."

"It was crappy."

"Yeah, okay, I understand that, but what happened, exactly? How did it start? You were there—did Ely bring everybody out to the site to see those four bones? Did he come running into the office one day waving them over his head and yelling? What?"

Pru took her hands from behind her head, crossed her arms on her chest, and brooded silently for a few moments.

"It was a dark and stormy night," she said.

Gideon sighed.

"No, really. Well, a dark and rainy late afternoon and we were all at the café—all of us but Ely—having one of those edifying, useful debates that we love so much over a carafe of *vin de la maison*. I think at the moment, appropriately enough, the issue of contention was our favorite: Neanderthal artistic behavior or the lack thereof. You know the drill, I think?"

Gideon nodded. "Did the Neanderthals ever produce anything that could reasonably be called 'art'? And by extension, were they therefore capable of understanding and practicing symbolic behavior? Or did true symbolic behavior arise only with the coming of the Cro-Magnons? Or was there a more diffuse—"

"You got it," Pru said. "So there we were, going at each other hot and heavy—we must have been on the second carafe by then—when in comes Ely, dripping wet. He walks up to us without a word and just stands there. He looks at us. We look at him. We all know something's up, but what?" She paused, seeing that Gideon had begun jotting notes.

"Would you rather I didn't write this down?" he asked.

She began to say something but changed her mind. "No, go ahead, I guess. It's not as if it's a secret. So where was I? Right, Ely stands there looking at us. He says exactly five words—this is a quote, not a paraphrase—'I've just come from Tayac.' Then he puts this knotted bandanna on the table in front of us and starts untying it, but it was soaked, so he has to get a knife and saw it open, which he does, while in the meantime we're dying of suspense because of this weird look on his face. And then he gets it open and there on the table are those four little bones with the little holes in them." She slowly shook her head, remembering. "Knocked our knee socks off."

"I can imagine," Gideon said, and so he could. "But didn't anyone express any doubts? I mean, *you* must have wondered—"

"If only," Pru said wistfully. "Maybe things wouldn't have turned out the way they did. But, you know, at the time nobody dreamt—I mean it never crossed our minds—I mean, now it's obvious, of course, but *then* even the *suggestion* that they were faked would have been so, so—"

"I know," Gideon said. "I'm doing a whole book on the problem, and I'm not finding any shortage of material." He finished making a notation, taking care to write legibly so that he'd be able to read his notes later, something that wasn't always doable. "So when did the first suspicions arise?"

"Pretty soon, actually, as soon as we got over the shock, but it was that letter that really brought the whole thing tumbling down. You know about the letter, don't you?"

"The anonymous letter to *Paris-Match*?"

"Yeah." Pru took her feet off the drawer and rolled her chair back a few inches. "It said the bones actually came from this little museum, which was easy enough to check out. They did, all right, and that did it. Everybody in the world had to accept them as a fraud. Except Ely."

"What did he do?"

"At first he wouldn't acknowledge the evidence, just kept defending his find, which really isolated him. And made him look more and more ridiculous, poor guy."

"It must have been really hard on him. From what I've heard, he got a little paranoid."

"More than a little. You know, even after it got through to him that he'd been had, he never really recovered. He got terribly suspicious of everyone—blamed everybody but himself for what'd happened to him. He spent all his time— twelve, fourteen hours a day—digging a couple of sites in the woods, working them all by himself or maybe with a single workman to help. The institute pretty much had to run itself for a while there."

"What was he after?" Gideon asked. "Or was it just a kind of escape for him?"

Pru shook her head. "No, I think he still believed in his own theories and he was determined that if he just kept going he'd come up with something—anything—to confirm them. I guess that makes him obsessive as well as paranoid. Or is it compulsive?"

"Either way," Gideon said with genuine sympathy, "it sounds as if he went over the edge."

"I think that's fair to say, yes. He came up with nothing, of course."

"And even if he had, who would have taken it seriously?"

"You got a point there, partner. And so in the end he pretty much self-destructed and had to resign." Her gaze shifted over Gideon's shoulder to the cubicle's single small window, and for a few seconds she stared through it without speaking. "And then," she said in a faraway voice, "he climbed into his little toy plane, pointed it toward Brittany, took off into the wild blue yonder...and thank you and good-bye, Ely Carpenter."

Gideon looked hard at her. "You make it sound as if...do you think he committed suicide?"

"Do you happen to know what his last words were?" she asked him.

"No, of course not." And then after a moment: "Does anybody?"

"Oh, yes. It was in the papers. He was on the radio to the local air traffic control when he went down, and the very last thing he said was '*Dites-leur que je suis desolé.*'"

"'Tell them I'm sorry,'" Gideon murmured. "So you think it *was* suicide?"

"Sort of."

"Sort of? How do you sort of commit suicide?"

"Oh, you know what I mean. He'd radioed for help, so you can't call it suicide in the usual sense, but I think it was a lot closer to self-destruction than to an accident. I think Ely just plain self-destructed."

"'*Dites-leur que je suis desolé,*'" he repeated thoughtfully. "Pru, isn't it possible that was a kind of confession, that he was admitting to having faked those bones himself?"

"No, I don't," she said stiffly.

"So what was he apologizing for?"

"It could have been for a lot of things, Gideon. How much do you know about his life? He had a retarded grown daughter that he left in an institution back in the States, did you know about that? He always felt guilty about her. He had a divorced wife back there too. Who knows what else? But I think he was just saying he was sorry for getting himself and the institute involved in the whole damn mess, that's all."

"That's certainly possible, but isn't it also possible he was admitting—"

"No, it isn't." She straightened up in her chair and squared her shoulders. "It wasn't Ely, Gideon, definitely not Ely."

"Why 'definitely not'?"

"Gideon," she said, leaning forward, "I am not going to get into it, okay? Don't push me, okay? Just take my word for it, he wouldn't have done it. Ely Carpenter was a really, really neat guy until this happened to him."

"Sorry," Gideon said meekly.

Pru sat back, suddenly sheepish. Her jaw muscles, which had bunched up, relaxed. "Yeah, me too. I didn't mean to come on so strong, but I

really had a lot of respect for the man." She fal-
tered, then went on, "In fact, there was a time—
oh, hell, you'll find this out anyway—when the
two of us...when I came that close to marrying
Ely, or did you already know that?"

"No, I didn't know it."

Not that he could claim to be bowled over at
the news. Pru's cheerful, brawny amiability had
always been attractive to men, and it seemed to
work the other way around too, but never for
very long. Ever since he'd known her she'd been
in and out of affairs, uniformly brief, and rarely
associated with any visible trauma. "Why didn't
you, or am I getting too personal?"

"Oh, I don't know, I don't really remember—
oh, wait a minute, yes I do. He was already married at the time, that must have been it. Later,
after he got divorced, I guess I just never got
around to it again."

"Well, I didn't mean to—"

"Listen, it's not just that I had a thing for him,
trust me. He was a first-rate archaeologist too,
he really was. I hate the way his reputation's
been raked over the coals over that stupid Tayac
thing, I hate it. He'd never in a million years
have pulled a dumb stunt like that."

"But apparently he did fall for it," Gideon
said gently.

Pru puffed her cheeks and blew out a mouthful of air. "Yeah, that he did, he surely did."

"Okay, if not Carpenter, who then?"

She shook her head. "No. Uh-uh. Look,

haven't I given you all kinds of goodies? Isn't that enough? Go bug someone else."

"Pru, help me out, will you? I have to start somewhere. If you say it's a guess, that's what I'll treat it, unless it leads somewhere definitive on its own."

She took her feet off the drawer and leaned forward, looking her onetime professor in the eye, her elbows on the arms of her chair. "Let's say it was the other way around—let's say I was sitting here asking you to rat on one of your colleagues, and all you had to go on was a guess—no proof, no real evidence, just a hunch—would you do it?"

"So it *is* one of your colleagues?" Gideon said.

"God, are you pushy. Look, don't get tricky with me, just answer the question. Would you do it?"

"Yes."

"Bullshit."

"All right, no," Gideon admitted. "I don't suppose I would." But even with Pru's unwillingness to answer, she'd told him something, or he thought she had. *Colleague.* Fellow archaeologist, fellow scholar at the institute. Pru didn't go along with the Bousquet-as-perpetrator idea. She had somebody else in mind.

"Suppose my eye. You *know* you wouldn't." She returned her feet to the drawer and leaned back again. "Okay, then, enough of that. Anything else I can help you with?"

"Yes. Do you happen to know what museum

those four metapodials were taken from? I'd
love to go have a look at them. All I've seen is
photos."

"Sure, but you don't have to go to any museum. They're right here."

"The original cave lynx bones? With the
holes?"

"Yes. What are you so surprised about? The
museum didn't want any more to do with them,
so we hung on to them. They're under lock and
key—important historical artifacts. Ask Jacques
or Michel to show you."

"Will do. I'm off to see Michel next."

"And for your records, the museum they
came from is the Musée Thibault. It's just a hole
in the wall, run by one of the local antiquarian
societies, but it's been around forever. It's in La
Quinze, a few kliks north of here, on the way to
Périgueux."

"Thanks," Gideon said, writing it down.
"Jacques couldn't remember."

"He couldn't *remember*?" Pru laughed. "Jesus,
how does the poor soul make it from one day to
the next?"

"What do you mean?"

"Jacques has been involved with the Thibault
since he was a kid, for God's sake. He's been on
the board of trustees for umpteen years. Ar-
mand Thibault was his mother's brother. You
tell me, how could any normal person not remember its name?"

How indeed, Gideon wondered. Was it possible that Beaupierre—

But Pru was wagging a blunt finger in his face. "No, no, no, no, that's not what I meant. I see what you're thinking, I know how your mind works. You're thinking he was hiding something, he was being devious, am I right?"

"Well, I don't see how I can help it."

"Forget it, Prof, Jacques wouldn't know 'devious' if it walked up to him and said *bonjour*."

"Maybe not, but—"

"Come on, pal, don't make a federal case out of it. You know Jacques pretty well—where his brain is at any given time, nobody can say. The man's not accountable. He's a few peas short of a casserole, shall we say. The receiver's off the hook sixty percent of the time, you know? The elevator usually doesn't go all the way to the top floor, or let me put it this way, the sewing machine ran out of thread a while back, the—"

"Okay, enough," Gideon said, laughing. "I think I get your drift."

More out of courtesy than in hopes of learning anything new, Gideon began his session with Michel Montfort with the same opening question he'd used with Jacques: will you tell me in your own words about the Tayac affair? His account, expectably briefer and more focused than Beaupierre's, was still the same story, and Gideon used the time to study the celebrated archaeologist sitting across the desk from him.

Pru had given him as apt a nutshell description of Montfort as he'd ever heard. "Somewhere along the way," she'd once told him over a glass of wine, "Michel crossed over the line from being a legend in his own time to being a legend in his own mind."

He had known at once what she'd meant; there was a whiff of play-acting in Montfort's famously blunt manner. But not really an unpleasant whiff; in fact, it tended to take the edge off his frequently disagreeable remarks and give him a playful, Papa Bear–like quality. At the same time it could leave you with the feeling that you weren't actually dealing with a snuffly, grousing, basically good-hearted old codger at all but some character actor who had specialized in snuffly, grousing, basically good-hearted old codgers for so long that he couldn't remember how to play anything else. Gabby Hayes with a Ph.D. and a French accent, say.

Not that Montfort could really be called an old codger. He was only in his middle fifties, but he was one of those people who seem to have been around forever. He had already been a great name when Gideon was an undergraduate. And with his old-fashioned taste in clothes—dark suits, usually blue or black, with matching vests, always buttoned—and his bulb-nosed, fleshy, weathered face ("a face like a two-pound loaf of homemade sourdough," Pru had said at the same memorable tête-à-tête), he was like a holdover from another generation, lacking only a black derby to complete the picture of a self-made, rough-and-ready 1920s merchant king.

But he'd changed a lot in the last three years; more than Gideon had realized at the previous morning's staff meeting. Physically, he was much the same: a little older, of course, but still thick and hearty across the chest and shoulders. Yet at the same time he seemed in some intangible way diminished, like a man who has successfully recovered from a serious operation but still, in an indefinable way, is not—and never again will be—the man he was. The Tayac affair had taken a lot out of him, and no wonder. He had put his own considerable reputation on the line backing the "find" and the integrity of the man who had made it; he had—

"Hello there. I've finished," Montfort said.

Gideon blinked. "Excuse me?"

"I said I've finished. Telling it in my own words."

"Oh, of course, I just—"

"Some time ago now. I thought you might not have noticed."

Gideon smiled. "I'm sorry, I'm afraid I was thinking—"

"No matter." Montfort was playing with his blunt-barreled tortoiseshell fountain pen, impatient as always but seemingly not in a bad humor. "Now, if there's anything else you want to know…"

"I'd certainly like to know if you have any idea—any hypothesis, even—as to who was behind the hoax. And why."

Montfort's fleshy chin descended to his chest. "I do not."

"Are you completely satisfied that Ely himself had nothing to do with it?" He braced himself for the explosion Beaupierre had warned him about.

Montfort took his eyes from Gideon's and stared fixedly at the wall beyond, a wall full of framed diplomas and certificates—the same ones, Gideon thought, in the very same places, that had hung there three years ago.

"I am," he said.

Gideon waited for more, but nothing came. It was evident that the archaeologist's relative good humor had taken a turn for the worse. Now he was rhythmically rotating the fountain pen over and over against the desktop, thumping each end: turn...*clack;* turn...*clack*...

"I'm sorry, sir, I felt I had to ask. I hope you understand."

Montfort sat drawn into himself, with his lips compressed, volunteering nothing. The conversation, such as it was, expired. A summer fly, alive beyond its time, buzzed dejectedly on the windowsill.

Turn...*clack;* turn...

Gideon cleared his throat. What he wanted to ask about was Montfort's view on Carpenter's plane crash, but he decided it might be a better idea to change the subject. "Pru just told me that the Tayac metapodials are kept here. Would it be possible for me to see them?"

Montfort shrugged. The pen was flicked onto the desk. "Come with me," he said, rising heavily from his chair and leading the way to Madame Lacouture's immaculate office.

"The key to PN-277," he told her brusquely.

She looked up from her desk, frowning. "To Tayac?"

"Yes, Tayac, that's what I said."

She had that forbiddingly proprietorial look on her face, but if she was thinking about challenging him she changed her mind. "As you wish." Opening the middle desk drawer, she withdrew a key from a built-in key rack and handed it to Montfort. To Gideon she nodded stiffly but respectfully. Apparently, being seen in the company of the great man had raised him in her estimation.

Montfort took Gideon back into the outer room with its homely litter of papers and stone tools, went to a gray metal cabinet with a small pasted-on paper label that read "PN-277"—the "PN" for Périgord Noir, designating the archaeological region, the "277" for the site number assigned to Tayac—and swung open the doors. Inside were a few lidless cartons containing some nondescript and even dubious stone tools (Gideon remembered that the best of the materials had gone to Paris) and a single small cigar-box-size plastic container with a lid. Montfort signaled to Gideon to clear a corner area on one of the tables, placed the container in the resulting space, and, without preamble, lifted the lid.

"There you are, the instruments of disaster themselves. Help yourself."

They didn't look like instruments of disaster. They didn't look like much of anything; four small, flattish, slightly curved, dun-colored bones, thickened at the ends, with an insignificant little hole, not much different from a natural foramen, at one end of each. They lay in a row on a bed of cotton batting, and what they looked like more than anything else was a row of slightly oversized footbones from an ordinary house cat. Which was natural enough, come to think of it. Aside from being a little bit larger and a lot more extinct, *Felis spelaea*, the prehistoric cave lynx, was pretty much the same animal as *Felis catus*, the common domestic cat. But of course these weren't just any old *Felis spelaea* bones, these were the bones that had set Mesolithic archaeology on its collective ear, at least for a while, causing elderly, supereducated men and women to shout insults at each other (and in one celebrated episode, to hurl bones at one another at the annual meeting of the European Society for Archaeological Research at Cambridge University).

And what had brought it all on were those insignificant little ovoid holes, especially the one in the leftmost metapodial, the one that had been drilled only partway through, thus "establishing" that it was not a trade item but a homemade Neanderthal product, caught in-process, so to speak. Gideon picked it up, turned it over, and lightly fingered the perforation.

"No wonder these had everybody going for a while," he said, replacing it in the container. "They're a whole lot more convincing than I thought they'd be. What exactly was it that first made you think they might be fake, do you remember?"

"I'm afraid I can take no credit for that. To be

perfectly honest, it was that letter, that anonymous letter. Without that, I think I might never have allowed myself to believe...to even consider the possibility, the monstrous..."

"What about that letter, Michel? Did you ever come to any conclusion as to who might have written it?"

Montfort shrugged wearily. "Who knows? Bousquet, I suppose. There was...ah, what difference does it make now? The fact is, it was true, and it performed a valuable service to our science, unwelcome though it was."

"But how would someone like Jean Bousquet have known that it wasn't a real find, that the bones came from a museum?"

Montfort glared at him from under ragged eyebrows. "Exactly what are you driving at?"

"I was just—"

Montfort cut him off. "Gideon, I must tell you I'm extremely troubled by your direction. Is this the sort of thing you're looking for for your book? Speculations? Unverified suppositions?"

"Michel, I assure you I'm not going to be printing any unverified suppositions. At this point I'm just hunting for any kind of lead that I can follow up."

That pacified Montfort, but not much. "I see. Well." He closed the container. "Now, if there's nothing else I can help you with, there are a number of matters awaiting my attention."

Gideon gestured at the container. "Well, I was

hoping you'd tell me a little about your own examination of the bones."

"I would have thought," Montfort said coldly, "that you would have taken the trouble to read my monograph in the *Comptes Rendus de l'Académie* before coming here."

"I did, and I thought it was a tremendous piece of detective work," Gideon said hurriedly—and honestly. "It's just that my French wasn't quite good enough to carry me through some of the chemical analysis, and I want to make sure I have it right for the book."

Montfort's scowl eased. The container's lid was raised again. "Of course, I understand. Where would you like me to begin?"

"Could you sort of walk me through the whole thing?"

"Tell you in my own words, you mean?"

"Yes, exactly."

"But this time you'll pay attention?"

Gideon laughed. "On my honor." He held up a ready notebook and pen to prove it.

Watching and listening to Montfort expound was a pleasure. He became a different man. The years dropped away from him as he spoke and gestured, and the old energies, the old enthusiasms of the scientist in his element, visibly rekindled. And the process of inference and deduction he described really was dazzling, involving microscopic study, fluorine tests, crystallographic analysis, spectroscopic examination, and solid reasoning. In the end he had shown conclusively that the museum's identification numbers on the bones had been removed with abrasive and that the holes had been bored with a modern carbide-tipped steel drill bit, then further abraded with a bone awl and smoothed with a rawhide thong to make them look authentically Paleolithic. Afterward, the bones had been soaked in an acid iron sulfate bath to disguise the giveaway light color of the abraded surfaces, then drenched in a dichromate solution to speed the oxidation of the iron salts.

Gideon, whose forte had never been chemistry, wasn't sure that he understood it much better in English than he had in French, but at least now he thought he could make enough sense of the process to describe it for Lester's masses.

When they went back to Madame Lacouture's office to return the key, she was just hanging up her telephone, and she held up one hand to forestall them while she scratched some neat, quick notes in a record book on her desk, talking to herself while she did: "Eleven thirty-five," she murmured in French, "Professor Barbier for Dr. Godwin-Pope...concerning...newly found bison figures at...Les Combarelles."

She pecked the final period with satisfaction, closed the book, and looked up at Montfort. "You're finished with the key?"

"Would I be handing it to you if I weren't? Now then, Gideon—"

"Madame," Gideon said, his eyes never having left the record book, "is that a log of telephone calls?"

She eyed him with misgiving. Apparently his rise in status hadn't necessarily extended to the asking of questions. "Yes," she said suspiciously.

"And do you log in all calls?"

"She does indeed," Montfort answered for her, "with the frightening efficiency of a machine. She always has, and she always will. Someday, God willing, we may even find a use for it."

As far as Gideon was concerned, with any luck that day had arrived. "Would you mind looking to see if you have a record of a call from Jean Bousquet?" he asked. "It would have been roughly three years ago. I'd like to know the date."

Montfort rolled his eyes. "Are we back to that again? *Why* do you keep—" He interrupted himself. "Never mind, I don't want to know. It would have been in October or November," he told Madame Lacouture. "You may remember the call. As I recollect, you said he was somewhat abusive."

A spot on either side of Madame Lacouture's throat turned crimson. "I remember," she said shortly. "I'll get the log."

It took her three seconds to retrieve the appropriate volume from a file cabinet. "Jean Bousquet's call was made at two-fifteen in the afternoon, on the twenty-fourth of November," she said, reading from it with satisfaction. "He was telephoning from Ajaccio. The subject was the provision of a character reference from Director Beaupierre, who was unavailable at the time. I transferred him to Professor Montfort instead."

"Well, there you are then," Montfort said. "The twenty-fourth of November. That would have been, oh, a good two months after the last we saw of him. Are you satisfied?"

"Look, I don't mean to keep hammering on the point—but you're absolutely sure it was Bousquet himself on the line? Positive?"

"That it was Bousquet? Yes, of course I'm positive. One couldn't mistake his offensive manner of speaking. Would you like me to swear to it? To attest to it in writing? In blood, perhaps?"

Madame Lacouture closed the log book with a snap. "Is that what you wanted to know, Professor Oliver?"

"It sure is, thank you," Gideon said, and welcome news it was, because, irrespective of whether those dog-chewed bones had or hadn't been Bousquet's, it established for a fact that he could hardly have been murdered by Ely Carpenter. Not when he was still alive two months after Ely's death.

And as for Joly's suggestion that the story of Bousquet's phone call might have been a concoction in its entirety, that, he thought, was now out of the question. The idea that all five of them—Montfort, Beaupierre, Audrey, Pru, and Émile—had conspired in a lie to protect Carpenter, a man who had yet to be accused, from being implicated in the possible murder of an unidentified victim who might or might not be Bousquet was barely believable as it was. To add to that the now-required assumption that the iron-sided Madame Lacouture was in on the plot, even to the extent of falsifying her telephone log, was beyond credibility.

No, whoever killed Jean Bousquet—if those bones *were* Jean Bousquet's—it wasn't Ely. A hoaxer he might well be; that was yet to be seen. But a murderer—no.

"Speaking of Bousquet," Montfort said as they headed back into the hallway, "how did your examination of the skeleton go in Saint-Cyprien? Did you find your diffuse periosteal rib lesions?"

Gideon weighed his reply. "My examination," he said, "was inconclusive."

Not for the first time, Gideon found himself wondering why the French weren't obese. There were plenty of scientific and pseudoscientific explanations as to why they weren't all lying prostrate on the sidewalk with heart attacks despite all that duck grease and goose liver, but why weren't they *fat*? They deserved to be fat. The croissant Émile was chewing on, one of two on his plate, probably had a quarter pound of butter in it, and it was very likely his second breakfast of the day, a particularly annoying French custom. But like most of his countrymen he was as thin-bellied as a snake. True, you did see occasional genuine tubbies lumbering along the streets, but when you got close enough to hear them, they invariably turned out to be speaking English or German.

Delicately, Émile wiped his chin. "So," he said with what Gideon took for a droll wink, "you would like to know who perpetrated the Tayac hoax. Wouldn't we all?"

"I guess we would at that," Gideon said, perfectly willing to let him be arch if he wanted to. Having struck out three times in a row trying to get Beaupierre, Pru, and Montfort to take even a wild guess, he'd worried that he might be in for more of the same with Émile, but he'd barely sat down in the paleopathologist's cubicle and asked his first question before Émile had put a cautionary finger to his own lips.

"Why don't we go out and talk about it over a decent cup of coffee?" he'd said with a meaning-laden glance (*The walls have ears!*) at the thin partitions.

They had gone not to the Café du Centre, the staff's usual gathering place, but a block in the other direction, to what passed for the downscale end of Les Eyzies, to a small, nameless corner bar ("Bar," said the sign painted on the window) full of stagnant cigarette smoke and blue-frocked, stubble-jawed road workers on their morning break, some drinking coffee, most drinking red wine. There, at a sticky table in the back, they had made clumsy small talk for a few minutes over Gideon's *café au lait* and Émile's *café noir* and his pair of croissants. But now the small talk was over. Émile finished the first croissant, moved the plate aside, straightened his bow tie—drooping orange clocks à la Dalí on a field of sickly green—and leaned forward with his elbows on the table.

"I have no empirical data, you understand.

Only my own suspicions—firmly based, however, on what I trust is a solid framework of logical premises and inductive inference, rigorously applied."

"I understand," Gideon said. Joly's remark about professors and speechmaking came back to him.

"Very well, then." Émile pressed his lips together and worked them in and out like an athlete preparing for a lip-wrestling competition.

Gideon stretched out his legs, settled back in his chair, and moved his coffee within easy reach. This was going to take a while.

"Montfort," Émile said.

Gideon almost tipped over the coffee. "*Montfort!* But Montfort's the one who exposed it. He wrote the definitive paper."

"Correction. Michel did not expose it. An anonymous letter to *Paris-Match* exposed it. Only *after* it was exposed and therefore no longer possible to credibly defend did he write his oh-so-illustrious definitive paper."

"Well, that's a point, I guess, but—well, of all the people to possibly suspect...Ely was his protégé, his—"

"If you've already made up your mind on the matter," Émile said stiffly, "I can't help wondering why you want my opinion."

"No, no, I haven't made up my mind, Émile. I don't even know where to start, and I do want your opinion. You just caught me by surprise, that's all. I'm sorry. Okay, I'm listening. What possible reason would Montfort have for planting those bones?"

"Consider the facts. Whose theory of Neanderthal cultural development did the Tayac bones supposedly prove?"

"Ely Carpenter's."

"Yes, but from whom did Ely get it? Michel— it was his own darling theory, wasn't it? He'd been spouting it for the last twenty-five years, decades before Ely ever appeared on the scene." His nose twitched like a squirrel's. "He's still spouting it, for that matter. Or were you suffering from a temporary hearing loss yesterday?"

"No, I heard him all right, but—"

"Surely you can have no doubt that he'd been hoping all his life for such a find. But since no such find existed—or *could* exist, let me add— does it require a great stretch of the imagination to speculate that his zeal got the better of him and he decided, shall we say, to help his theory along a little? I hate to suggest that your charming belief in the moral sanctity of the scientific community may be less than totally accurate, but such things have been known to happen. I hope I don't astonish you."

Gideon nodded. Émile was right, they happened, and Tayac itself was a prime example. Somebody had faked those bones, and that somebody was almost certainly a scientist, and that scientist was very probably someone connected with the institute. That didn't leave very many possibilities, and the others—Ely, Jacques,

Audrey, Pru...and Émile himself, let's not forget Émile—were all reputable, established scholars too, hardly more likely as tricksters than Montfort.

"Okay, let's say you're right," he said. "Why wouldn't Montfort just 'discover' the bones himself?"

Émile's gray eyes glittered. "Because, despite what you seem to think, the great Michel Montfort is hardly a monument to courage. I believe he was afraid to attempt it on his own for fear of being found out. But if he saw to it that Ely was the one who discovered them, then if anything were to go wrong, it would be blamed on someone else. Which, I remind you, it was."

"But then why—if all that's true—would he put so much time and effort into his monograph? He's the one who *proved* it was a fake, Émile. He showed exactly how it was done, step by step, in detail."

"Why? To salvage his reputation to the extent possible."

"How does that salvage his reputation?"

"I should think it would be obvious. Didn't I hear a certain author say just the other day that Michel was going to be referred to as the 'hero' of the affair in an upcoming book? Or was I mistaken?"

"Well—"

Émile hooted sourly. "And of course he was able to show 'exactly how it was done.' Who better than the person who perpetrated it in the first place?"

Gideon sipped his cooling, milky coffee and pondered, trying his best to look at things with an open mind. "Look, everything you say is certainly possible," he said after a few moments, "but why pick on Montfort? Why assume that it wasn't Ely himself, for example? I'm not saying it was, but wouldn't he be the more obvious choice?"

"There are *three* obvious choices, the three men whose theories of Middle Paleolithic cultural development were ostensibly confirmed by the finding of those worked metapodials—theories, I need hardly point out, on which they had publicly staked their reputations: Ely Carpenter, Jacques Beaupierre, and Michel Montfort. Let's look at them one at a time. Ely was surely not foolish enough to imagine that he could escape exposure for long with such an artifice. Jacques, on the other hand— We speak in confidence, I assume?"

"Of course."

"Jacques, on the other hand—it pains me to say it—hardly possesses the ingenuity and cunning necessary to execute such a scheme." He paused, waiting to see if Gideon would agree or disagree. Gideon, who was undecided on this point, gave him a take-it-any-way-you-like shrug instead.

Émile took it as agreement. "And that," he

176 • Aaron Elkins

concluded with the air of a lawyer wrapping up an airtight case before a bedazzled jury, "leaves us with Michel...Georges...Montfort." *Voilà*.

Things were getting interesting, Gideon thought, watching the Vézère glide by at his feet, slow, and green, and placid, in no hurry to get anywhere. By himself at lunchtime, he had repeated the meal he'd had the day before with Julie—marinated roast beef and sliced tomato on a baguette, with a paper cone of French fries and a bottle of Orangina, all from a streetside crêpe and sandwich stand—and taken them down to the park, to the same riverside bench he'd shared with Julie.

There, on a pleasant lawn among brilliantly green young willow trees, he slowly ate his sandwich, looking at the river and the terraced fields and white limestone cliffs beyond it, watching the boaters trying to steer their rented inflatable pink kayaks, listening to the relaxing clicks and murmurs of the men playing *pétanque* behind him, and mulling over his conversations of the morning.

Émile alone had been willing to voice his suspicions about Tayac, and although his accusation of Montfort did have at least a certain internal logic, it was hard to know how seriously to take it. Did Émile himself really believe what he was saying, or was he venting his dislike of Montfort, a dislike keener than Gideon had realized...or was he simply playing malicious little mind games for the fun of it, something Gideon had no trouble imagining him doing?

Whichever, it was important to remember that, as Émile himself had said, he had no empirical data (otherwise known as hard evidence) to support his views. Still, it was a line of thinking that hadn't previously occurred to Gideon, and, improbable or not, it had now lodged itself under the surface of his mind like a burr.

He was also finding it difficult to make up his mind about Jacques Beaupierre. Was it really possible, given the circumstances, that anyone, even Jacques, could have actually forgotten the name of the Thibault Museum? Pru's defense of him notwithstanding, it hardly seemed believable. And if he hadn't really forgotten, then clearly he had *chosen* not to answer. Why? The obvious reason was that he preferred Gideon not to know just which museum the lynx bones had come from. And the obvious reason for that—the most likely reason, anyway—was that he didn't want Gideon to know that he himself was associated with it. And if you accepted that much, there was only one place to go with it: Beaupierre was afraid that Gideon might leap to the conclusion, the very reasonable conclusion, that Jacques himself, with easy access to the Thibault, had had something to do—something very central to do—with the obtaining of those bones and therefore with the hoax itself.

In other words, that Jacques Beaupierre had been the one behind it.

On its own terms it made as much sense as Émile's theory about Montfort, and in the same way. Had the fraud been successful, it would have confirmed Jacques's long-held, often-stated beliefs about Neanderthal culture. Suppose he'd been driven enough to plan the hoax and pull it off, but afraid to risk the fallout if it was exposed? In that case, why not plant it in Carpenter's private dig? That way, with Ely sure to shout about it from the rooftops, the cause would be advanced. But if it was found out, as it inevitably, necessarily, *was* found out, it would be Carpenter who would—and did—take the vilification. Was the genial, abstracted Beaupierre capable of that?

On the other hand, he reminded himself, this was the same man who'd needed reminding on whether he'd had breakfast the other day, the same man who, in Gideon's presence, had once hemmed and hawed and been unable to put his finger on the exact title of a book he himself had written two years earlier. (It was *L'Archéologie*.) Surely, honestly forgetting the name of the Musée Thibault was within his abilities, as Pru had said. And Émile, who knew the director better than he did, had almost contemptuously dismissed him as the possible perpetrator.

...*as it inevitably, necessarily, was found out*. The words drifted back through his mind, so distinctly and separately that his lips involuntarily shaped them. Had exposure of the fraud truly been inevitable? If so, then yet another possibility had to be considered: what if everyone had been looking at the hoax the wrong way around? What if its purpose had been not to promote the sensitive-Neanderthal school of thought but to *dis*credit it? Looked at that way, it had been a great success: Ely, Montfort, Jacques, and their brothers-and-sisters-in-arms had come out of it bruised and winded, along with their theories. But for the other side, the Neanderthal-as-hopeless-knucklehead side, it had been a great shot in the arm; their theoretical stock had soared.

And looking at it from that angle, Gideon thought, tipping the bottle up to get the last cool, sweet swallow out of it, meant that Audrey, Émile, and Pru might have had the very same motive as anyone else in planting those doctored bones for the luckless Ely to find and to crow about—namely, giving a leg up to *their* side in the theoretical wars when the truth came out.

Wonderful, he thought with a shake of his head and a wry smile, this was real progress. When he'd started off this morning he didn't have a single suspect, beyond Ely himself, on whom to hang the Old Man of Tayac. Now there wasn't anyone who *wasn't* a suspect.

It just went to show what the scientific method could accomplish when properly employed.

Yawning, he reached for the cone of *frites*, saved for his dessert, and stood up. Carpenter was on his mind too as he started back up the path. Pru and Jacques had both jumped defensively, almost angrily, to his support. Ely had been "the very model of integrity," "a really, really neat guy." But had he, really? When Gideon had known him three years before, he'd found him competent and likable, with an entertaining flair for the dramatic, but at the same time there had been something about him—unexpected gaps in his erudition, a surprising unevenness in his knowledge—that had made Gideon wonder. Once, when Gideon had made a passing reference to *Paranthropus robustus*, he'd been shocked to see that Ely had no idea what he was talking about, although he'd done a good job of covering it. Of course, that alone didn't—

"Ah, it's a pleasure to see a man that deep in thought. Dare I interrupt?"

It was Audrey Godwin-Pope, striding stoutly along at his side—all 110 pounds and five feet two of her—in her swaying tweed skirt, gray cardigan, and crepe-soled lace-up shoes, with her sturdy tortoiseshell glasses hanging from a lanyard around her neck and a pencil sticking out of the gray bun at the back of her head (in the past, he'd seen as many as three at a time).

"Oh, hi, Audrey. Sorry I didn't get to you this morning. I ran a little late."

"Not to worry. So what is it that's furrowing that manly brow, or shouldn't I ask?"

"I was thinking about Ely Carpenter, as a matter of fact." He slowed his pace to let her keep up more easily and held out the paper cone. "*Frites?*"

She reared back. "Do you have any idea what they fry those things in around here? Thinking about Ely along what lines?"

"Oh, his background, his education. Wondering what kind of a person he was, really."

"A one of a kind," she said warmly. "A really splendid man. The usual male hang-ups, of course, but in his case—"

"What do you mean, a one of a kind?"

"Just that." She smiled and shook her head. "There'll never be another Ely Carpenter, Gideon. I'm sure you know about his amazing past—grew up out West, parents divorced, got into trouble early, spent a couple of years on a juvenile detention ranch in Montana, learned about cowboying, got onto the professional rodeo circuit at seventeen—"

"No, I had no idea about any of that. Really?"

"Really. And what's more, he was good. I've seen the cups and the ribbons: bull-riding, calf-roping—"

"When did he go into archaeology?"

"Oh, much later. After he got tired of falling off bucking broncos he spent some time in the Air Force as a mechanic, then did the same thing for another dozen or so years with a commercial air transport company. And then, of course, he won the lottery. Well, you know, perhaps I will try one of those *frites*. How much harm can one do?"

"They're all yours," he said, passing her the cone, which she didn't refuse. "Won the lottery in what way?"

"In the real way, the way that counts. State of Connecticut, almost a million dollars. Whereupon he decided that more than anything else in the world he wanted to be an archaeologist. Quit his job, went back to school with a vengeance—here's this forty-six-year-old airplane mechanic, not even a high school graduate, mind you, but in less than five years he had his M.A. Wrote a letter to his hero, Michel Montfort, declaring his passionate interest in the Middle Paleolithic and his admiration for Michel's work, and begging for the chance to study under him. Michel said come ahead, three years later he had his doctorate...and the rest is history."

That explained a lot, it seemed to Gideon. Ely had essentially been a self-made man, starting school in middle age and then immediately plunging into a narrow, obscure, and difficult subject area. It was an admirable course to follow—people had done a lot worse with lottery winnings—and it had a lot of things going for it, but breadth of education and systematic scholarship weren't among them. Certainly it explained the gaps in his knowledge. Possibly it also explained why he'd been so easily taken in over the Tayac hoax—assuming, of course, that he was the victim and not the perpetrator.

"Fantastic story," he murmured. "Actually won the lottery."

"Yes, but, you know, he really had no interest in the money. He had a retarded grown daughter, did you know that?"

They were coming to the turn-off in the path that led up to the *mairie*, the town hall, where Gideon would be filing his report on the previous day's attack, and his mind was turning to that. "Yes, I heard," he said a little absently. "Back in the States."

"Yes, and I think most of it went to take care of her," Audrey continued, lost in recollection. "But then, apart from his airplane, Ely didn't have any use for a lot of money. He wasn't a fancy dresser or a high-liver. He drove an old clunker." She finished the *frites* and absently wiped her fingers on her sweater. "Aside from flying and shooting, archaeology was his whole life. Two or three times a year he'd take a few days to fly off to one of his air-rifle competitions in Lisbon or Barcelona, and that was it. Other than that..." She drifted pensively off.

"Well, I head up this way," Gideon said. "Thanks for—" He stopped in his tracks and stared at her, dumbfounded.

"One of his *what*?"

"Air-rifle competitions," Joly mused with one of his less scrutable expressions. "So Ely Carpenter owned an air rifle." If anything, he seemed pleased.

"Yes, at least one. Audrey said she'd seen his favorite. He showed it off to her when it came. I guess it was something special."

"She wouldn't know what kind it was?"

"No, just that it was made in Korea. She didn't really pay that much attention."

"Well, well." Yes, definitely, Gideon thought; that little tremor at the corners of his mouth was Joly's version of a cat-that-gobbled-the-canary smile.

They were in the snack room of the *mairie*—a modest, utilitarian space with a hulking red Coke machine, an old refrigerator, coffee fixings (a simmering glass pot of water on a warmer and a crusted jar of Nescafé), and three small round plastic tables with two plas-

tic chairs each. Making his statement for the
police had taken only twenty minutes with
Joly's assistance, and doing his best to help put
together a composite sketch of "Roussillot"
hadn't taken much longer. (Unfortunately, the
result, like most composite sketches, had more
in common with composite sketches in general
than it did with any recognizable human
being.)

Afterward, he and Joly had been shown to the
snack room to wait until the statement was
typed up for his signature. Gideon had gotten a
Coke from the machine; Joly had chosen only to
smoke. While they waited, Gideon had started
filling Joly in on the highlights of his interviews.
The inspector had sat quietly, seemingly not
very attentive, and not stirring until the rifle was
mentioned.

"You don't sound all that surprised about it,"
Gideon said.

"No. I've been devoting quite a bit of thought
to Professor Carpenter, as a matter of fact."

"You don't mean as a murder suspect?"

Joly gave one of his whole-body shrugs.

"Lucien, the fact that he owned an air rifle
doesn't mean it was the same one that killed that
guy. Other people own air rifles."

"I have the report from ballistics" was Joly's
answer. "Listen." He removed a slim wallet
from the inside pocket of his suit coat, slipped a
folded sheet of paper from it, set a pair of reading glasses on the prominent, angular bridge of

his nose, shook out the paper, and read aloud, translating into English as he went.

"'The projectile, though deformed, is identifiable as a wasp-waisted twenty-two-caliber, thirty-four-grain ultra-magnum lead-alloy air-rifle pellet. This projectile, which is among the world's heaviest commercially available twenty-two-caliber lead pellets, is manufactured especially for the South Korean–produced'"—a ponderously meaningful look at Gideon—"'Cobra Magnum F-16 five-shot repeating air rifle, an expensive, compressed-air-powered, high-velocity sporting/hunting weapon charged with pre-compressed air from a standard three-thousand-psi diving tank and capable of generating a muzzle velocity of almost four hundred meters per second when used in conjunction with this pellet. It is the opinion of the examiner that such a projectile, fired within a range of five meters, could well have caused the injuries previously described.'"

Joly removed his glasses—he wouldn't wear them a fraction of a second longer than he absolutely had to—and slipped the report back into his wallet. "Now, it may be that I'm leaping to conclusions," he said. "It may be that there are many expensive, high-velocity Cobra Magnum F-16 air rifles firing wasp-waisted thirty-four-grain magnum rounds here in Les Eyzies to choose from—one in every stone cottage, for all we know."

"Well…okay," Gideon said, "but even if it is

the same rifle, that hardly means it was Carpenter who did the killing. Look, what if you found a window broken with a Mesolithic hand chopper—would that mean it had to have been a Neanderthal that did it?"

Joly studied him. "Am I mistaken, or are we a little defensive this afternoon?"

"No, it's just that—Lucien, are you actually, seriously considering the possibility that Ely Carpenter himself committed that murder?"

"Why should I not?"

"Well, because..."

Because what? What was he supposed to say, that distinguished archaeologists, directors of respected scholarly institutions, didn't go around bumping off people who annoyed them? Maybe they didn't, but they also didn't go around getting themselves involved right up to their eyeballs in outrageous frauds either, did they? So where did that leave him? Of course it might have been Ely. Joly had every right to consider the possibility.

He had, when it came right down to it, more than he knew. "There's something else you need to know," Gideon said reluctantly. "I just hated to...oh, hell, it's just that..."

Joly watched him attentively, his eyes narrowed against the cigarette smoke curling from both nostrils and drifting up his cheeks.

"Remember when I told you Ely had gotten pretty paranoid after the hoax broke? Well, it was worse than I realized. Audrey told me he took to keeping a weapon near him whenever he was off in the boondocks working on one of his sites."

"Oh?" said Joly, his interest quickening.

"And the weapon she remembered seeing was...well..."

"His favorite Korean air rifle."

Gideon nodded.

"So," said Joly with evident satisfaction, and then, after a pause: "I have a little news for you too. I've been in touch with the aviation authorities about Carpenter's death." He looked levelly at Gideon. "It seems there are some rather dubious aspects to it."

Gideon frowned. "I don't follow you."

"Frankly, I'm not convinced Carpenter's dead."

"*What?*" The Coke can smacked down on the table, spattering Gideon's hand with fizz. "That's crazy."

"Consider the hard facts," said Joly. "Or rather the lack of them: no corpse, no wreckage—"

"*What?* But I thought—"

"So did I...because that is what you told me." He smiled sweetly. "But the plane, having apparently gone down not on land but in several hundred meters of water—"

"*What?* But—"

Joly exhaled twin jets of smoke. "Gideon, are you going to permit me—"

"But he *did* go down over land," Gideon said

hotly. "Over Brittany. That's what everybody said."

But if that was what everybody said, then everybody was wrong. Carpenter's plane, a single-engine Cessna 185, had gone down *off* Brittany, or so the authorities had concluded. He had taken off at night from the small airport at Bassilac, near Périgueux, heading north along the French coast to Brest, some 320 miles away. Not long afterward, however, he put in an emergency call to the air route traffic control center at Lorient, saying that his engine was faltering, his gauges were malfunctioning, and he was rapidly losing altitude over the Bay of Biscay. A brief, hurried communication, cut off in midsentence, ensued, and Ely Carpenter was never seen or heard from again. A search for his plane produced no results. The reasonable inference— and the official verdict—was that he had plunged into the great bay in darkness, somewhere near the sparsely inhabited Îles de Glénan, about 60 miles short of his destination.

"...reasonable inference..." Gideon echoed. "I had no idea...I was sure..."

"So you can see," Joly said, "there's plenty of room for doubt. How can we know that he didn't merely pretend to crash his airplane into the sea and then continue, in darkness, to some isolated farmer's field along the coast at which, with a little advance preparation, he might easily have landed so small a craft in secret?"

Gideon got up and went thoughtfully to the window, leaning on the sill and looking over the town square and the main street, directly on the other side of which the cliffs loomed in the slanting sunlight, white and pocked with shadowed *abris* for the first few hundred feet, then darkening to gray-brown and curving outward into their picturesque, protective overhang. Little wonder all those Neanderthals and Cro-Magnons had found this temperate valley such a comfortable place to live.

"Now wait a minute, Lucien. I don't know anything about flying airplanes, but even I know that if they're within range of air traffic control, they're on somebody's radar screen. There's a gizmo on the plane that sends out some kind of identifying signal—"

"A transponder, yes," said Joly, grinding out his cigarette while he arranged his thoughts. "Imagine this. Carpenter leaves the Bassilac airfield fully in accordance with a previously filed flight plan. Then, once out over the sea, he begins to descend and, in apparent distress, informs the air traffic control center at Lorient that he is inexplicably losing altitude. Their radar confirms that this is so. Carpenter continues his descent, utters his heart-rending 'last' words: *'Dites-leur—'*"

"*'—que je suis desolé,'*" said Gideon.

Joly looked at him. Gideon shrugged. "Pru McGinnis told me. This morning."

"Utters his last words," Joly continued, "drops to thirty or forty meters above the water, and turns off his transponder. The radar signal disappears, contact is lost. To all appearances, the worst has occurred, the airplane and its pilot are no more."

"But in reality he just keeps going?" said Gideon, who was beginning to think Joly was making a pretty good case.

"Precisely. He continues flying at this low altitude and lands his craft at some prearranged site he has chosen. Even if he *were* to be detected in flight again, his Cessna would be so low and so small that it would appear as no more than a fleeting image for one or two sweeps of the radar antenna—and in any case, with the transponder deactivated it could not be identified. You understand?"

Gideon turned back from the window, impressed. "You've really been looking into this, haven't you?"

"Is it so preposterous to wonder," Joly continued, "whether this was his way of escaping from his difficulties, his way of leaving his troubles behind and starting a new life?"

"Well—"

"And remember this: Carpenter's 'tragic' communication with the air traffic control tower was recorded on the night of September twenty-fifth. Less than seventy-two hours later, on September twenty-eighth, Madame Renouard made her report to the police asserting that Bousquet had not been seen for several days. Doesn't this bring us back to the possibility—"

"No, it doesn't. You keep harping on that, but on that score you're off base, Lucien. Ely didn't kill him. It's impossible. He—"

Joly held up a finger. "Do you recall telling me that when Carpenter was working in these boondocks of yours—these remote, isolated boondocks, with the rifle so very close at hand— he sometimes had an assistant, a single assistant, working with him?"

"Sure."

"Do you know who that assistant was?"

"I have no—you're not going to tell me it was Bousquet?"

"But I am. Bousquet was frequently with him, serving as a manual laborer and paid from Carpenter's own pocket."

Gideon, surprised, slowly shook his head. "But they hated each other. Why would Ely hire him?"

"Apparently he had little choice. Jean Bousquet was the only worker available with some experience of archaeological sites."

"Well, all right, so they were working together. That doesn't mean anything. Remember, he was still alive two months after Carpenter left. He called."

"Yes, so say the fellows of the institute. But it has yet to be independently confirmed."

"It's been confirmed, all right. Madame Lacouture, Beaupierre's secretary, remembered it too. She had it in her logbook. I saw it. Sorry to spoil your theory, Lucien."

Joly digested this. "Secretaries say whatever they're told to say. It's their job."

Gideon laughed. "You haven't met Madame Lacouture. I'd be surprised if anybody tells her what to say."

"She sounds something like my secretary, now that I think of it," Joly said with a slow smile.

"And anyway, even if you're right, which I don't believe, what would Carpenter be escaping from? Let's say he actually killed whoever the bones belonged to. The body was safely buried, nobody knew about it—why would he want to disappear?"

"And what about his humiliation over the Old Man of Tayac, or have you forgotten that?"

"Oh, that, right," said Gideon, who had in fact forgotten for the moment.

"Imagine further his state of mind," the inspector said, removing a stray shred of tobacco from his tongue with the tip of his finger and discarding it in an ashtray after careful study. "He would have felt that the world was closing in, that his life was incapable of reconstruction. He was an intelligent, resourceful man—would a new identity have been so terrible a prospect?"

Gideon returned to his chair and lowered himself thoughtfully into it. Joly's doubts were getting through to him. "Maybe it wouldn't, at that. From what we've been finding out about him, he'd had several lives before."

He drained the lukewarm remainder of his Coke, crumpled the can in his fist, and tossed it into a wastebasket already brimming with cans and paper cups. "Ely Carpenter still out there somewhere," he said slowly. "Well, I grant you, it's an intriguing thought."

"Yes," Joly said, "but what are we to do with it? Where do we begin to search for him? It's a cold trail we have in front of us."

"It's worse than a cold trail, Lucien, it's a dead end—two dead ends. Not just Carpenter, but the body in the cave too. Remember, we have no way of proving that he was or wasn't Bousquet, and with the bones gone, we're never going to have any."

"Well, there you have—" Joly glanced up at the entrance of a blue-uniformed policeman, blond, blue-eyed, and ridiculously young-looking, who had deferentially approached their table. Joly's visage stiffened to that of an *inspecteur principal*.

"Que vous désirez, Noyon?"

"I'm very sorry to interrupt, Inspector," the officer said in French, "but Prefect Marielle wanted me to ask you...what do you wish done with the bones?"

There was a moment's silence, and then:

"Bones?" said Joly.

"Bones?" said Gideon.

* * *

"Yes, the bones," Noyon repeated. "The dog's bones."

Joly smacked his forehead—harder than he'd intended, judging from the wince that followed. "The *dog's* bones! I forgot completely. Where is my brain? Gideon, we do have some skeletal material for you to look at."

Gideon stared at him. "Did I miss something there, Lucien? I mean, sure, I'll be happy to look at your dog bones if you want me to, but I don't quite see—"

"No, no," Joly said, laughing, "not the '*dog* bones,' the '*dog's bones*.' Toutou's bones."

"Umm...Toutou's bones..."

"Toutou!" Joly said impatiently. "The Peyrauds' dog, the animal that first discovered the remains in the cave and brought home some of the bones. Marielle collected them—"

"Well, why didn't you say so?" Gideon said, jumping to his feet. "You expect me to know the damn dog's name? Where are they? Let's go."

Joly rose more slowly, looking at his watch. "I believe I'll leave them to you, my friend. I have other things to pursue. I'll come back in an hour?"

"Fine," said Gideon, who preferred working without an audience for a lot of reasons, not least among them that he liked to talk to himself. "Maybe I'll be able to tell you something by then."

"I hope so, but I wouldn't get my hopes up.

I've seen these bones, and they don't look like very much."

"Well, we'll see." Turning to Noyon, Gideon spoke in French: "Okay, Officer Noyon, lead on. Where are they?"

"They are in the evidence room, sir," said Noyon. "If you would care to follow me?"

In police parlance, "evidence room" usually meant a secure area—perhaps a steel-barred cage or a locked room with a stout metal door—in which labeled bags and boxes were neatly ranged on shelves along with carefully tagged larger items of material evidence relating to crimes, such as rifles, axes, and ball-peen hammers. In the case of the Les Eyzies municipal police department, however, the evidence room was a paper-supply cubicle attached to the office of its prefect, Auguste Marielle.

Marielle, a bulgy man in a blue-and-white uniform, emerged from the cubicle with a thick red folder, the old-fashioned expandable kind with accordion sides, held closed by a string wound around a couple of cardboard grommets. "I'm afraid you won't find much of use in these, Professor."

He placed the folder on his handsome teak desk and undid the string. "Of course, one can see at once," he said in French, "that, except for a few mouse bones, they are human. There's little doubt about that much. Beyond that, however, I feel safe in saying no more than—" he cleared his throat: *hm-hm-hhhmmm*—"that, ah, they are clearly male, and most likely adult—yes, yes, clearly adult, and, ah...so forth. Would you agree, Professor?"

"I would, yes, but it'd probably be worth going over them again."

"As you wish, although in my opinion there is little further helpful information to be gotten from them. You might like to know, incidentally, that Professor Émile Grize, a most eminent and well-regarded expert—perhaps you know him?— agreed with my conclusions entirely."

"I see," Gideon said. "All the same, it couldn't hurt to have another look. Speaking as a trained forensic anthropologist."

The only place in the *mairie* where a relatively private, unclaimed space could be found for Gideon was in the snack area, and it was there, where he and Joly had sat earlier, that he laid the bones out, this time with a pale cup of instant coffee beside him. One of the other tables was occupied by a pair of clerks from the treasurer's office who were gobbling down a late lunch, but when they saw what was being spread out four feet away from them they rewrapped their sandwiches in waxed paper, picked up their soft-drink cans, and silently departed.

On the table in front of Gideon, and taking up very little of the tabletop at that, were eleven human bones—the tiny rodent bones had been discarded—or rather what was left of eleven bones after Toutou had worked them over. All were from the right side: the femur and fibula from the leg, six assorted hand and wrist bones, two partial ribs, and the ulna, the larger of the two forearm bones. As he'd expected, they were in awful shape. The femur, fibula, and ulna were no more than sticks, their ends completely chewed away, and everything bore the deep, parallel scores and furrows of prolonged, happy canine gnawing.

They don't look like very much, Joly had told him. "Pathetic is what they look like," Gideon said aloud now, looking at the worn shards and slivers. Chances were, Émile had probably said all there was to say about them: they were human, they were male, and they were adult.

Even the ribs, which had offered the most hope, weren't of any use. Gideon had reached for them first, hunting for signs of the periostitis that would point—against all odds, he now believed—to their being Bousquet's. There weren't any such signs, but even that meant nothing, because they weren't the ribs he needed. Not only were they from the wrong side, but they were the bottom two, the eleventh and twelfth, the "floating" ribs, below the lungs themselves and thus lower than where the tubercular lesions would have shown up if they'd been there. So their absence told him nothing at all one way or the other.

"Not one blessed thing," he grumbled. Maybe this person had had TB, maybe he hadn't.

Maybe he was Bousquet, maybe he wasn't. Human, male, and adult; that was it. "Damn."

He poked at the sorry fragments without much optimism, but came to a sudden halt when he reached the forearm bone, the ulna. "Hey, no callus formation," he said, moving his thumb over the surface. "What do you know about that? No thickening, no inflammation!"

A woman carrying a box with knitting needles and wool walked into the snack room, then turned on her heel and walked out again when she saw the large male sitting at a table in earnest conversation with a bone. In English. Gideon smiled absently in her direction, seeing her but too lost in thought to quite register her. The absence of inflammation on the ulna, as far as he knew, was of no conceivable help in identifying the remains, but it had engaged his attention as a physical anthropologist, for whom the chief challenge and the chief interest of bones was always the reconstruction of the living human being from them—and the more fragmentary and incomplete the skeleton, the greater the challenge.

What was absorbing him at the moment was a mental comparison with the skeleton's other ulna, the one he'd seen when he'd examined it in the *abri*. That one, as he'd told Joly, had been markedly enlarged and inflamed. He'd assumed at the time that it had probably been the result of some kind of systemic disease, but if that was true, he'd expect it to show up bilaterally—not necessarily, of course, but more likely than not. Yet this one, the right one, the one in his hand, was perfectly healthy. That made him wonder if the inflammation on the other one had possibly been caused by some kind of trauma.

But not your usual trauma. Not a single blow, for example—the bone hadn't been broken, or chipped, or cracked. Its condition might conceivably have been the result of a localized infection, possibly one that had ulcerated, but he didn't think so. He dearly wished he could have it in front of him now, but he remembered it pretty well as it was, and what he remembered told him it had come from some kind of repeated punishment over time—years, maybe. Some kind of friction, pressure, pounding...

With his fingers he outlined on his own forearm the region that would have been affected: the part just below the elbow; not the "back" or "front" of the forearm so much, but the "outside" of it—the pinky side, the part protected by the volar antebrachial muscles. "Now what the heck would cause something like that?" he asked the ulna. "What kind of work, what kind of activity...hobby...?"

He stared at it, brushing his fingers over the roughened areas, for a long time without getting anywhere. "Ah, the hell with it," he said finally, putting it aside for the time being and beginning to sift through the hand and wrist bones.

The bones from the wrist were hopeless, the capitate, trapezium, and hamate gnawed to barely recognizable nubs; surprising, really, that they hadn't been consumed altogether, small as they were. Those from the hand—the first three metacarpals—were in slightly better shape but didn't promise much, metacarpals being among the less informative bones of the body. But the moment he picked one up—even before he picked it up—something leaped out at him, something important enough to make him sit up with a start. And abruptly, his heart was in his mouth. In a single instant, out of nowhere, a whole series of isolated, disconnected details, meaningless until now, had suddenly spun about and clicked unexpectedly together into a recognizable—an unmistakable—whole. He was on to something at last, but it seemed so impossible, so fanciful—

What he was staring at was the first metacarpal bone, the one that forms the base of the thumb, the part hidden in the palm of the hand. And running down the middle of this short, stout bone was something that should have jumped out at him the second he opened the folder: a sort of miniature canyon with high, craggy walls that stood out like a tiny mountain range. This, he knew, was the end product of a fracture that had healed without having been properly set. The roughened area was a dense extrusion of bone, two strong, rugged wings of lamellar bone that had formed around the break to repair and strengthen it. It wasn't one of nature's prettier healing techniques, but it was enormously effective, making the bone stronger than it had been in the first place.

What made this particular break so unusual, so *significant*, was its direction; the bone hadn't snapped crosswise, as bones usually broke, but had cracked down its length, so that the healed cleavage ran in a slight spiral from one end to the other. And the two ends of the bone themselves had rotated a few millimeters in relation to one another and then remained there as the injury healed.

It was, in other words, a torsion fracture, the kind of thing that happened as a result of irresistible twisting pressure. Most commonly, you saw such fractures in skiing accidents, when the body spun during a fall but the foot stayed put, being enclosed in a rigidly fixed boot. When that happened, something had to give, and that something, when it wasn't the ligaments of the knee, tended to be one of the bones of the ankle or the leg.

But thumbs—thumbs were a different story. Unless you stuck your thumb firmly in a hole in the wall, like the little Dutch boy, and then tried a backflip, there weren't many ways you could wreck your first metacarpal in quite this manner. In fact, in all his experience, Gideon had encountered one way and one way only.

"My God," he whispered.

CHAPTER
16

It was the first time Gideon had ever seen Joly's jaw drop, a sight made even more memorable by the unlit cigarette pasted to his upper lip. He shook out the match he'd just lit. "What did you say?"

"I said," Gideon replied, "that these bones aren't Jean Bousquet's, they're Ely Carpenter's."

"Not..." Irritably, Joly plucked the jiggling cigarette from his lip, gestured with it at the paltry assemblage on the table, and stared indignantly at Gideon. "From *these*? But, really, how can you expect me...how can you...?"

Gideon picked up the fractured thumb bone and showed it to Joly. It was this that had cinched it, he said, shamelessly taking his own sweet time. (This was another one of those all-too-rare moments, another rabbit out of the hat, and it would have taken a stronger man than Gideon to keep from milking the situation at least a little.) A fracture of that particular kind, on that particular bone, a longitudinal torsion fracture of the first metacarpal, was so closely linked to one particular cause that it had a name: anthropologists called it "cowboy thumb."

A better name might have been "rodeo thumb," Gideon pointed out, because these days it didn't usually happen out on the range but during saddle-bronc-riding competitions at rodeos, when contestants instinctively grabbed for the saddle horn while they were in the process of being ejected from their saddles. And although hanging on for dear life to a relatively fixed point while the rest of the body was flying head over heels ten feet above the ground probably saved a good many heads, ribs, arms, and legs, it was unlikely to do a thumb any good. All too often, unlucky countestants wound up with ugly longitudinal torsion fractures of the first metacarpal.

"Just like this one," he concluded, handing it to Joly. "You were right about Ely's not going down in that plane, Lucien. The plane crash was a sham, all right, but it wasn't Carpenter who pulled it off. He was right here—he never left. That's his left thumb you're holding."

"Mm." Joly gave it barely a glance, and a doubtful one at that, before putting it on the table.

"You don't buy it?" Gideon asked, a little deflated in spite of himself.

Silently, Joly rolled the unlit cigarette back and forth between his thumb and forefinger.

"It's not that I doubt you, Gideon—not necessarily—but there are others I have to convince, and to take such a leap—*such* a leap—on the basis of a single small bone..."

"What difference does it make how big it is? Would you be more comfortable with it if it was some kind of skull fracture?"

Joly shrugged.

"The point is, it's almost certainly a rodeo injury, so unless you think there might be any other former rodeo cowboys around—*missing* rodeo cowboys, that is—that just about has to mean it's Ely Carpenter."

"We don't have rodeos in France," a grumpy Joly said. "Not your kind of barbaric rodeos, riding wild bulls and such things."

"Well, then—" He blinked. "What did you just say?"

Joly looked at him. "I merely said we don't—"

"Of course!" Gideon exclaimed, his mind racing. "Why didn't I—" He reached excitedly for the right ulna. "That does it!"

Joly took the bone from him and turned it uncomprehendingly from one side to the other. "And what's wrong with this one?"

"Nothing. That's the point."

Ordinarily it would have been another golden opportunity for showboating, but Gideon, taking his cue from a low warning rumble somewhere in Joly's chest, explained succinctly what it was that he himself had only just realized. It was Joly's mention of wild bulls that had done it. Gideon had been to a couple of rodeos in Arizona, and he remembered that in bull-riding competition, bareback-riding rules allowed only one hand to come in contact with the rigging that was cinched to the bull. The other had to wave free. That meant that one forearm, and one forearm only, suffered hard, repeated pounding, rodeo after rodeo, against the bull's spine and the cowboy's thighs and pelvis.

"And that," he told Joly, "was more than enough to account for the inflammation in the left ulna but not the right."

Joly squinted at him. "And you're positive nothing else could account for it?"

"No, of course I'm not positive—how could I be positive of that?—but I sure can't think of anything else that makes sense under the circumstances, can you?"

"Nothing comes immediately to mind," Joly allowed, apparently on the edge of being persuaded.

"All right, then. That makes *two* rodeo-related injuries found in a body buried here in rural southwest France—where there aren't any rodeos—approximately three years ago. And if we take into account the fact that Ely Carpenter, former rodeo competitor, disappeared from sight, from this very area, three years ago and his body was never found, what would you say the odds are against its being anybody but him? A thousand to one? A million to one?"

Joly picked up the metacarpal and studied it again, silently shaking his head.

"I hope you'll put that someplace safer than Marielle's back room," Gideon said. "Safer than the Saint-Cyprien morgue too."

Joly nodded. "These will go to Périgueux with me this afternoon." He wrapped the metacarpal in a paper napkin, put it carefully in the folder with the rest of the fragments, and rewound the string around the grommets, then continued to sit there, motionless and contemplative. "So then, what happened to the plane?" he murmured at last.

"What do you mean, what happened to it?"

"Where is it?"

"Well—what you said. The pilot probably landed it on some farmer's field in the dark."

"And then what? Where is it now?"

"Who knows? Gotten rid of some way or another. Maybe it really was ditched in the ocean to get rid of it."

"A one-hundred-and-fifty-thousand-dollar airplane? I think not."

"All right, the black market, then. What difference does it make?"

"Perhaps none. Still…" He sank into another long, heavy silence, emerging to mutter: "Did we have it backward then? Was it Bousquet who killed Carpenter, and not the other way around?"

"Maybe, but I don't see why you want to limit it to Bousquet."

"Yes, you're right about that," Joly agreed. "All right, whom would you suggest?"

"Well, remember, this thing happened while feelings about the Tayac hoax were still running pretty high. There was a lot of tension in the air, a lot of anger and recrimination."

With his eyebrows lifted, Joly studied him. "You think he was killed over the hoax, then."

"No, not necessarily *over* it. I'm just suggesting that there's a link between the two."

"And your basis?"

"Look, murders and hoaxes aren't exactly everyday occurrences, and here they are happening at the same time, in the same little town, involving the same people. The probability of their being two completely separate, completely unrelated incidents seems pretty remote to me. There has to be a connection."

The unlit cigarette that Joly had been playing with finally came apart in his fingers. He made an annoyed clicking sound, tongue against teeth, and scooped the tobacco into an ashtray, automatically taking another Gitane from the pack, but not lighting that one either.

"*Non sunt multiplicanda entia praeter necessitatem,*" he intoned in bishoplike cadence.

Gideon couldn't help laughing. *Entities should not be multiplied unnecessarily.* In other words, always choose the simplest explanation that fits the facts. Occam's razor, the law of parsimony. What made it funny was that he knew exactly where Joly had gotten it—from Gideon himself at the forensic seminar he'd conducted in Saint-Malo.

"Well, what do I know, Lucien," he said good-naturedly. "I'm just the guy who looks at the bones."

"The bones," Joly repeated, shaking his head slowly back and forth. "Cowboy thumb," he muttered, his tone somewhere between wonder and reproach. "The things you tell me."

CHAPTER
17

Situated in a pleasant, wooded valley lined by low cliffs, Préhistoparc wasn't nearly as bad as Gideon had feared, neither seedy nor phony-baloney, although there was a definite Disney World feel to it. One paid an admission fee and then walked along a footpath that meandered through the natural forest, where two dozen life-size, extensively labeled groupings of Neanderthal and Cro-Magnon men and women going about their lives were artfully placed. The Neanderthals were perhaps a little exaggeratedly brutish-looking and the Cro-Magnons were maybe a tad overclean and refined for people who lived in muddy rock shelters and wore animal skins, but on the whole the displays were interesting and within the bounds of scientific knowledge.

"So what's *your* opinion, Gideon?" Julie asked after he had filled her in on the day's bizarre developments while they strolled between the exhibits. "*Did* we all have it backward? Was it Bousquet who killed Carpenter and not the other way around?"

"Maybe, but there are other possibilities." He stepped aside to let a couple of French kids waving rubber "Neanderthal" axes bought in the gift shop romp by hooting Plains Indian war whoops out of North Dakota by way of Warner Brothers.

"All we know for certain," he said, getting back on the path, "is that it's Ely Carpenter, not Bousquet, who's dead. But who killed him—that's anybody's guess. Just because he had problems with Bousquet doesn't mean he didn't have them with somebody else."

"Somebody else at the institute, you mean."

"Well...yes. I didn't want to think so at first, but there's sure something funny going on. It's not just that everybody's playing it so cagey and close to the vest—well, everyone except Émile, who may just have his own ax to grind. There's also the theft of the bones from the morgue in Saint-Cyprien, what about that? We assumed it was to keep me from identifying the skeleton as Bousquet's—which might conceivably have implicated Ely—but now we know it *wasn't* Bousquet's skeleton, it was Ely's, so what was that all about?"

"Oh, that," said Julie. "I already explained that."

"You did? When? Where was I?"

"It was right after we got back from the hospital, and you were right there. You brushed it off at the time. I can even give you your exact words: you said no way, impossible, uh-uh, couldn't be, you knew these people, they thought like scientists, and so forth. You went on for quite a while. If I'm not mistaken there was even a 'whereas' and a 'therefore' in there somewhere. It was quite impressive."

"Oh, gosh, did I really do that? I'm sorry, it must have been the concussion. Um, what was it you said again?"

"It wasn't the concussion, it was just you being professorial and smarter-than-thou," she said pleasantly. "You can't help it—I'm used to it. Anyway, what I said was that the bones might not have been Bousquet's at all—and *that* was exactly what someone didn't want anybody to know."

"I have to admit, that has a familiar ring," Gideon said. "It's also starting to make sense, given what we know now." They paused briefly to take in the next scene, a messy but probably fairly accurate rendition of "Dismembering the Reindeer with Stone Implements."

"And," he continued as they moved on, "the more I think about it, the more sense it makes. Somebody—one of those five people at the institute—didn't want it known that the body in the cave was Ely's, that he hadn't gone down in the plane, or even left Les Eyzies—that he'd been murdered right there and the plane crash never happened." He took her hand as they walked. "You had it right, Julie. You were way out ahead of Joly and me. We should have paid attention."

"Apology accepted," Julie said, "if that's what that was."

"It was," Gideon said. "And abjectly offered."

"You think Carpenter found out who was behind the hoax and threatened to expose him, and that's why he was killed?" She frowned, wrinkling her nose and looking askance at him in a way that never failed to make him laugh. "What, is that too melodramatic?"

"It's melodramatic, all right, but that doesn't mean it couldn't be true. You notice I've learned my lesson. I'm not brushing off your ideas anymore—no matter how far-fetched they are."

Julie didn't bother to respond, and they continued companionably along the path, stopping to admire "Pursuing the Woolly Rhinoceros," "Harpoon Fishing During the Magdalenian Era," and "Prehistoric Artists at Work."

"I do have a question, though," Julie said as they walked on. "I understand Lucien's theory of how Carpenter could have gotten away with a fake crash, but this *wasn't* Carpenter. So who was in the plane? Did it go down, or didn't it go down?"

"Joly thinks the whole thing was a setup, that the crash was faked just the way he thought before, except, of course, that it wasn't Ely at the controls. With Ely supposedly dead in a plane wreck, nobody was going to get suspicious and start looking into his disappearance in Les Eyzies—the killer was off the hook. As to who was piloting it, that's anybody's guess. Not Ely, that's all we can say for sure."

"And the 'Tell them I'm sorry'—what would have been the point of that?"

"Probably just a little added fillip to give it credibility."

"Pretty ambiguous, though," Julie said. "It could mean so many things."

"Yeah, I imagine the idea was to not overdo it by making everything too cut-and-dried. This way it seems more natural, more real. I'm guessing, you understand."

"Yes, but it makes sense—except don't pilots have to file a log or a flight plan or something? Could someone really get away with pretending to be someone else."

"Apparently yes. According to Joly, you can file your flight plan over the phone, just by calling ahead. If you have all the details on the plane right—tail number, air speed, probable route, fuel, that kind of stuff—no one's going to question who you say you are."

"It must have taken a lot of planning," Julie said.

"True, but Joly thinks that came later, that the murder itself wasn't premeditated—and I think he's probably right."

"Not premeditated? How do you come up with that?"

"Well, apparently he was shot with his own rifle."

"So?"

"People who have murder on their minds generally bring their own weapons. They don't rely on whatever happens to be at hand—and especially not an exotic Korean air rifle."

"I see. Yes, that makes sense."

They had stopped at "A Magdalenian Hunting Scene," with a spear-holding, loincloth-clad man and a tawny, crouching, cougarlike animal staring at each other across the face of a low ridge.

"Who's hunting who?" Julie said. "Whom."

"Hey, you know who that is?" Gideon gestured at the feline. "That's *Felis spelaea* herself— the cave lynx. That's the animal those four perforated bones at Tayac came from."

"Oh, that's interesting," Julie said. But she didn't quite manage to stifle a yawn; after almost two hours she'd had her fill of Paleolithic daily life.

So had Gideon, if he was going to be honest about it. "Want to go?"

She nodded. "Seeing all this activity's worn me out: killing mammoths, hunting bears, painting caves, picking berries, fighting tigers...do you suppose these people ever had time to just sit around?"

"And do what? Read books? Watch TV?"

"Sure, what's the matter, you never saw *The Flintstones*?"

"Well, that's a point," Gideon said, laughing and throwing an arm around her shoulders. "Come on, it's getting a little chilly. Let's head back. I'm ready for a drink and some dinner."

The short drive back to Les Eyzies took them first through the tiny village of Tursac, clumped at the base of its massive, forbidding Romanesque church, and then along the valley of the Vézère, through a landscape of willows, poplars, and occasional stone houses, rimmed by low, white, mineral-streaked cliffs, and always threaded by the green, slow-flowing river. It was the same route they had taken to get to Préhistoparc only a couple of hours earlier, but then Gideon had been so absorbed in telling her about Carpenter, and Julie so engrossed in listening, that they'd hardly noticed the scenery. Now, with Julie driving (she was both the better driver and the jumpier passenger; they had discovered long ago that they both tended to be happier when she was the one behind the wheel), they took advantage of having largely talked themselves out to take in the sunny, fresh, agreeable countryside.

She had pulled the Peugeot into a parking slot in front of the hotel and turned off the engine before they returned to the subject of murder.

"Gideon, does Lucien think there's a connection between the Tayac hoax and Carpenter's death?"

"No. Or at least he prefers not to consider it yet. He actually quoted the law of parsimony to me. In Latin yet."

"And what about you?"

"Sure there's a connection," Gideon said as they climbed out of the car. "I don't know what it is, but I'd bet twenty bucks it's there."

"So would I," Julie said with vigor, "unless somebody's decided to repeal Goldstein's Law."

At that they both smiled. Abe Goldstein had been Gideon's professor at the University of Wisconsin, a brilliant, eccentric Russian Jew, and the only person on whom Gideon was whole-heartedly willing to confer the title of mentor. Later, as an old man, he had become a close friend, of Julie's as well as Gideon's, and his loss was still deeply felt.

His Law of Interconnected Monkey Business—so named by Abe himself—was simply that when a lot of unusual or suspicious incidents occurred in the same place, at the same time, to the same people, the odds were that a relationship existed between them. And in Gideon's opinion, a string of events involving an elaborate archaeological hoax, the murder of the director of the archaeological institute that was involved in it, and his burial in one of that same institute's sites qualified as sufficiently unusual, suspicious, and connected to bring Goldstein's Law into play.

In Abe's own words: "In real life—I'm not

talking about theory construction, but real life—
interconnected monkey business trumps parsimony. Every time."

But later on, in the wood-beamed hotel dining
room, as they sat digesting a relatively simple
(for France) à la carte dinner of pumpkin soup,
medallions of veal, and green salad with warmed
goat cheese, Gideon had second thoughts.

"You know," he said over coffee, "I wonder if
we've been just a little too quick to invoke Interconnected Monkey Business. I've been thinking:
there might be other reasons—other things besides the Old Man of Tayac—for somebody's
wanting to kill Ely."

Julie looked up from the log fire into which
she'd been contentedly and a little sleepily staring. "Mmm?"

"Did I ever mention to you that when he got
the directorship he wasn't the only one in the
running?"

"Yes, you said the board was considering
Jacques and Audrey too."

He nodded soberly. "That's right."

She came fully awake. "Oh, wait a minute!
You're not seriously telling me somebody killed
him over the promotion, are you? That's crazy,
why? Academic jealousy? Gideon, if you people
went around murdering each other over that,
there wouldn't be a department head left standing in America."

"Well, that's true enough," Gideon said. "All the same, I keep thinking about Jacques—I keep coming back to him."

"Jacques Beaupierre," Julie said, laughing. "Now there's a vicious, bloodthirsty killer if I ever saw one."

"I know, but the thing is—"

"Yes, you told me: he couldn't think of the name of the museum the bones came from. Sorry, I don't think that would hold up as evidence of foul play—not with anyone who actually knew anything about him...." She trailed off, peering into his eyes. "Why, you *are* serious, aren't you?"

"Well...not in the sense of accusing him of murder, no, I suppose not, but as something to think about, or rather for Joly to know about...." He stared down into his demitasse cup, rotating it on its saucer. "Julie, this whole thing is pretty painful to me. I mean, sitting here saying, 'Let's see, which one of my old friends, people that I know—and like, for the most part—which one of them would I want to help Joly catch for murder and put away for the next thirty years?' But somebody *did* do it, somebody blew apart Ely Carpenter's heart with that gun of his, and covered his body with dirt in the cave, and faked that crash to cover it—and I think it's going to turn out to be one of them. I wish to hell it wouldn't, but..."

She covered his hand with hers. "I know.

You're right. I think so too." She shook her head. "It just seems so...impossible."

"Jacques was the most senior member of the institute, you see, and Ely was the most junior and kind of a loose cannon besides, a firebrand, the sort of guy who attracted controversy without trying."

"Then why *was* he appointed? And come to think of it, why wasn't Montfort in the running? You'd think he'd be the obvious choice."

"He was. It was offered to him more than once. He turned it down—just not interested in that end of things. As for why Ely got it—" Gideon hunched his shoulders. "I'm not sure. Could be because he was an American, and it'd been a while since there'd been an American director. Whatever the reason, he's the one who got it, even though most people figured it was bound to go to Jacques as a matter of course."

"And so you think...?"

"I think that with Ely gone...it did."

"Oh." It was Julie's turn to begin toying with her cup.

"What is it?" Gideon said.

"Nothing, but as long as we're rat-finking on our friends, I might as well get into the act too." She sighed; her mouth turned down at the corners. "Lucien might want to give some thought to Pru as well. She had a possible reason for wanting Ely dead. She told me at lunch."

"Their affair, you mean. Yes, I suppose that's always—"

"Affair, what affair? No, I mean, about his firing her."

"Firing her? Ely fired Pru? She never told me that."

"Well, laid her off. Practically as soon as he was in the director's chair."

"It could have been on account of their affair," Gideon mused. "To get rid of her, if he was tired of it."

"*What* affair, dammit? I don't know about any affair. All I know is they needed to make some financial cuts, some position had to be eliminated, and Pru was the one who got the ax."

"Well, she would have been the least senior."

"After Carpenter himself, you mean. Anyway, if he was trying to get her out of his hair, it didn't work, because she hung around Les Eyzies and supported herself as a cave guide until Jacques rehired her."

"And when was that?"

"Right off the bat. I guess he had more pull with the foundation, or maybe they found some more money somewhere, because the very first week he was on the job he not only put Pru back on the payroll, he brought on a full-time hotshot secretary from Paris instead of the student part-timer they'd had before."

"Madame Lacouture," Gideon said with a smile. "And his life has never been the same since." He gestured inquiringly at the empty coffee cups, and at Julie's nod he signaled Madame Leyssales for more.

"Altogether I think Pru was out three or four months in all." Julie twisted uncomfortably in her chair. "Look, Gideon, the only reason I'm bringing this up is that it would be stupid to *avoid* mentioning it to Lucien, but not for a single minute do I think there's anything to it. There was absolutely no sign of resentment there—none. We were just telling each other our life stories—abridged versions, obviously—and she happened to mention it, that's all."

"But what you might not know is that everybody *but* Pru has a permanent outside appointment for the seven months a year the institute's not in session. Pru's never latched on to a tenured university position, and as near as I can tell she spends the off-season traveling—Europe, Africa, Japan—on the cheap. I mean *pensiones*, B-and-B's, ryokans, that kind of thing. Sometimes she latches on to a temporary job at a dig somewhere, but those are few and far between."

"So?"

"So Pru, unlike everybody else at the institute, *depends* on her institute stipend to keep body and soul together. Unless, of course, she has some independent income, about which I wouldn't know—but if she doesn't, then getting laid off would have had to be a serious blow."

"And you're suggesting she might have been so upset that she killed him over it?"

"Don't sound so incredulous. I'm just saying pretty much the same thing I was saying about Jacques, namely that when Carpenter was ap-

pointed she lost something important to her...
but when he was killed she got it back. It's
worth keeping in mind, that's all. Hey, aren't
you the one who brought this up?"

The coffees came. Julie added a little cream to
hers, bringing a discreet sniff of disapproval
from Madame Leyssales—except for their morning *cafés au lait,* the French held to the belief that
coffee should be taken black.

"Yes, but the more I think about it," Julie said,
"the less likely it gets. Why would she be crazy
enough to mention getting laid off to me if
she'd murdered him over it, or if it even crossed
her mind that someone might eventually think
she had?"

To create precisely the impression of inno-
cence she had, in the event that Carpenter's
murder was eventually discovered, thought
Gideon, but there was such a thing as getting too
rococo, and he had the feeling that they'd just
about reached that point, or perhaps passed it a
while back. Besides, although he'd managed to
hold off the after-effects of his concussion all
day, his head had begun to ache—all this heavy
thinking—and he was beginning to sorely feel
the need to lie down.

"You're right about that," he agreed, swigging
down the two tablespoons or so of coffee in the
tiny cup and wishing he'd remembered to ask
for decaf instead. "We'll pass all this on to Lucien—he'll probably laugh—but I vote that we
return to our previous hypothesis."

"Agreed," said Julie. "The Theory of Interconnected Monkey Business is hereby officially reinvoked." She stood up. "Let's get you to bed before you fall out of your chair."

"Still awake?" she asked.

"Uh-huh," Gideon said, not sure if he was or not. He'd been lying on his back, not his usual position for sleeping, and staring at the occasional reflections of headlights shimmering across the dark ceiling.

"Can I ask you a question?"

"As long as it doesn't require actual thought."

"Why didn't you tell me that Pru had an affair with Carpenter?"

"I didn't see that it had any connection to the murder. Anyway, I only found out about it myself this morning."

"That's right, this morning. And we spent most of the afternoon walking around Préhistoparc, and then got all the way through dinner before you mentioned it, and even then it was accidental."

Gideon yawned. "Well, it didn't seem pertinent to anything, so why talk about it?"

"Boy," Julie said wonderingly, turning onto her side and away from him, so that Gideon automatically nestled snugly in behind her, fitting himself to her, his arm across her waist.

"Boy, what?" he breathed into her hair.

"Boy, men are sure different from women."

CHAPTER
18

For Lucien Anatole Joly, the next morning got off to a bad start. When he went downstairs, slippered and sleepy, to his front door for the breakfast delivery, he found in the bakery sack four puny marzipan cookies instead of his customary robust brioche and two croissants. This after six and a half years—two thousand mornings!—of receiving exactly one brioche and two croissants, no more, no less, day in, day out, every morning of the week but Sunday.

Then, over this dismal meal (was it possible that some deranged person had actually ordered marzipan cookies for breakfast? Was he even now looking with shocked displeasure at Joly's brioche and croissants?), his wife, Josette, told him that her insufferable younger brother, Bernard (he of the semiconductor empire), along with his wife, Rosamond (she of the most piercing laugh known to humanity), and their unspeakably precious twin girls would be spending

Christmas week with them yet again. Five days, four nights, God help him.

And when he reported briefly to his office at Police Nationale headquarters in Périgueux, Madame Fossier had even worse news: the *juge d'instruction* appointed to oversee—i.e., hinder, impede, and generally foul up—his investigation of the Carpenter case was Chauzat, the ignorant, interfering busybody Chauzat, from whom getting a simple search warrant was like pulling six teeth.

Thus, by the time he arrived at Marielle's office in the Les Eyzies *mairie* he was in no mood for further annoyances, but annoyances there were. It was in the prefect's office, which Marielle had grumblingly turned over to him for the day, that he was to meet with the professional staff of the Institut de Préhistoire, preparatory to interviewing them individually. His original intention had been to interrogate them in their own offices, but he had decided the walls of the cubicles were too flimsy for confidential conversation. Instead, he'd requested the director, Jacques Beaupierre, to ask them to report to the *mairie*, two blocks away, at nine o'-clock in the morning.

At five to nine, therefore, Joly was seated behind Marielle's handsome teak desk in Marielle's high-backed, creamy leather chair (both of them annoyingly superior to the standard Police Nationale issue in his own office), waiting. But nine o'clock came and went, as did five minutes past and ten minutes past, while Joly fumed, illogically refusing to telephone Beaupierre, preferring to wait and see just how tardy they would be. When they at last arrived *en masse*, it was to a frigid welcome.

"It's twenty minutes past nine," he said quietly but pointedly, his clean, thin, long-fingered hands folded on Marielle's spotless blotter.

"Well, ha, ha, but you know how it is, Inspector," Beaupierre replied as they took the chairs that waited for them in a semicircle before the desk. "You must understand, there was some difficulty in informing everyone, and besides, we are all quite busy at this time of year, oh, extremely busy, and there are so many things that call for our, mm..." He cleared his throat and fell silent, apparently fascinated by the laminated certificate that hung on the wall behind Marielle's desk: a commendation from the communal hotel association for his unstinting cooperation in the temporary traffic rerouting of 1994.

"May I also point out, sir, that we are unaccustomed to being *summoned* in this manner?" The speaker, seated beside Beaupierre, was a thick-bodied, rumble-voiced man in his middle years who made no effort to hide his displeasure.

Joly turned a fishlike eye on him. "Ah. And who would you be, please?"

"Who would—!" The man's neck swelled. "My name is Michel Georges Montfort," he said, drawing himself up in his chair, "doctor of archaeology, professor at the University of the

Dordogne, and diplomate of the National Academy of Sciences."

"I see. Thank you."

Joly, of course, knew perfectly well who he was—Gideon had given him lively descriptions of them all—but this was the wrong day to trifle with him, even if the trifler happened to be a diplomate of the National Academy. Besides, Joly had learned long ago that in dealings such as these it was necessary to establish early and firmly who had the upper hand and who didn't.

"It's hardly something to be upset about, Michel," said one of the others, a waspish creature who reminded him of his brother-in-law except that Bernard was unlikely to be seen in public in a bow tie featuring what appeared to be a depiction of egg yolks exploding in a microwave oven. "No doubt the inspector is simply eager for edification on the recent changes in thinking regarding late Quaternary palynological stratification."

Émile Grize, Joly thought, feeling a dangerous tightening of his jaw muscles; Gideon had told him about him too.

"I should be happy for edification on any subject," he said politely.

Grize looked at him uncertainly.

"However impractical," Joly concluded, scolding himself before the words were out of his mouth. He wasn't starting out on the right foot, and if he kept it up, he would shortly have a roomful of enemies.

In general, Inspector Joly had never been much taken with scientists. Most of them, he believed, could be accurately grouped into three classifications: superior and disparaging, like Grize; pompous and self-inflated, like Montfort; and (the largest class by far) well-meaning but muddle-headed, like Beaupierre. There were exceptions, of course—Gideon, for example, at least most of the time—but not many in his experience.

He sat eyeing them with his hands folded for a few moments more before speaking again. "I am Inspector Joly. The officer seated behind you is Sergeant Peyrol, who will take notes. Later, I shall be interviewing each of you individually, so be good enough to keep yourselves available."

He stopped, anticipating objection, but they had suddenly become as docile as lambs, hanging on his next words. They sensed by now that something important was up, and they were off-balance. Joly began feeling a little more benevolent. "I hope this will not inconvenience you," he offered by way of a small olive branch. "I shall try to disturb your daily activities as little as possible."

"Exactly what is this about, Inspector?" demanded Montfort, but now his tone was merely grumpy, not openly rude; presumably a matter more of constitution than intention. "Does it relate to Jean Bousquet?"

"It very well may," said Joly. "Dr. Oliver has

now completed his analysis of the bones from the *abri* and reached his conclusions. I'm sorry to inform you that they are the remains of Dr. Carpenter."

It was as if someone had seized one end of the carpet on which their chairs rested and given it a snap. Everyone started. There were ejaculations of surprise, snorts of disbelief, gasps of incredulity; in Beaupierre's case, all of them from the same mouth.

"That can't be!" Audrey Godwin-Pope exclaimed. "His plane...he died in a plane crash. Everybody knows that."

"Yes, yes," others cried, "that's true."

"Not so," said Joly.

"How horrible!" Beaupierre said into the abrupt silence, staring first at Joly, then around the circle of his colleagues, and then, every bit as fixedly, at empty air. "How *horrible*! I—"

His lips had gone dead white; he seemed to be having trouble catching his breath. Joly, afraid he might be on the verge of a stroke, rose. "Monsieur—"

But Montfort cut in. "Jacques, get hold of yourself, for God's sake," he muttered, although he too looked a little gray.

To Joly's surprise it did the trick. Beaupierre nodded, drew in a long, shuddering breath through his mouth, and quieted down, one hand lifted to his closed eyes. The others began to talk excitedly among themselves, so that Joly had to rap on the desk for quiet.

"That is all I wish to say at this point. You are welcome to return to your offices for the present. Sergeant Peyrol will inform you when I wish to see you. We will—"

"Bousquet, it must have been Bousquet," Prudence McGinnis said to no one in particular. "Jean hated him."

"Which of us didn't he hate?" asked Montfort. "He might have murdered all of us in our beds."

"He didn't hate *me*," Grize said. "I had nothing against him, and he had nothing—"

But Joly didn't want a discussion of the subject at this time. "We will start in three-quarters of an hour, at ten-thirty," he resumed firmly. "I hope we can be finished by midafternoon. I think it would be best to begin with the director. Professor Beaupierre, is that acceptable to you?"

"What?" Blinking, Beaupierre floated back into this world. "Yes, of course—well, I...that is...yes, all right."

"Very good, ten-thirty, then. Mesdames, gentlemen, thank you."

They were slow in getting up—Joly could almost hear the gears spinning and grinding in their heads—and Prudence McGinnis paused at his desk on her way out.

"It *was* Bousquet, wasn't it?"

"We'll talk about it later, madame," replied Joly.

She stood her ground. "Well, who else could it have been?"

"Later, madame."

* * *

The interval before his first interview was put to good use. Sergeant Peyrol, having heard at length about his superior's wretched breakfast, went out and returned with two excellent croissants, a passable brioche, and a double *café noir* from the Café de la Mairie across the street, so that by ten minutes after ten Joly was once again feeling human.

"Thank you, Peyrol," he said, concluding his meal. He wrapped the remains in the newspaper on which he'd eaten so as not to sully Marielle's gorgeous desk and placed all in a wastepaper basket. The excellent Peyrol—not the most quick-witted sergeant he'd ever had, but an honest fellow—had even brought him a foil-wrapped towelette to wipe his hands and lips, which he did with satisfaction.

"Now then, Peyrol: what did you think of our cast of characters? Do you have any observations?" When he could, Joly liked to tutor his subordinates, generally employing the methods of Aristotle.

"Well, I know who *didn't* do it," Peyrol said. "The director, Beaupierre. He was shocked, all right. I thought he was going to drop dead in front of us."

"Shocked, yes," Joly said, "but at what?"

Peyrol was stumped. "Why...at the news of Carpenter's death, what else?"

"Might he not have been shocked only at the news that it had been found out?"

Once it sank in, Peyrol's simple face glowed

with comprehension. "You mean he himself was the—"

"Now, Peyrol, I offer it only as a possibility, one of many to be explored. You must learn—"

When the telephone sounded, Joly snatched it up on the first chirp. "Yes?"

"Inspector? It's Beaupierre. I...I'm not feeling very well, not well at all. I have a stomach condition...this has been a terrible, terrible shock, you have no idea..."

"I'm very sorry to hear it."

"Would it be possible...would you mind if I didn't come in until later? I need to lie down, to, to calm my system. I'm afraid I'm not really up to, to—"

"Of course," Joly said soothingly. "Go and rest. I won't bother you for a while."

Joly had no doubt about Beaupierre's being genuinely agitated, and postponing the interrogation was fine with him. His policeman's instinct told him—shouted at him—that while the director might not have murdered anyone, he wasn't being candid either. Joly smelled something—guilty knowledge, self-recrimination, remorse, pangs of conscience?—and letting Beaupierre simmer in his own juices for a few hours wouldn't be the worst thing in the world.

"Peyrol," he said, hanging up, "go and ask Dr. Montfort if he would be good enough to join me. Oh, and Peyrol?"

"Sir?"

"With my compliments," said Joly.

CHAPTER
19

Enter at your own peril the bizarre, startling-but-true world of man-apes, cannibalistic rites, and long-lost primitive tribes, where a host of fascinating questions awaits the adventurous reader.

- *Does the fearsome and enigmatic giant yeti, an object of terror for two millennia, lie in wait for unwary travelers to the Himalayas even today?*
- *Who—WHAT—was the Cardiff Giant, and why have scientists continued to deny this strange, frightening being's existence for more than 100 years?*
- *What is the shocking true story of the Stone Age tribe discovered living deep in the Philippine jungles in 1972? What is behind their total, mysterious disappearance without a trace?*
- *Does the legendary, elusive Abominable Snowman still stalk the misty forests of the*

> *Pacific Northwest? What is the true nature of
> the gruesome new evidence?*
> *Find the answers to these and other mystifying puz-*
> *zles of science in this revealing exploration by the*
> *man known to millions as the Skeleton Detec—*

"Oh, lordy." Gideon put the sheet down, shaking his head.

"Hm?" Julie said from her wicker lawn chair a few feet away. "Did you say something?"

"No, that was only a muffled cry of anguish. I was looking over Lester's suggestions for flap copy."

She lowered the Patrick O'Brian paperback she was reading and looked sympathetically at him. "Not all that great, huh?"

They were in the side garden of the hotel, having come back an hour earlier from an after-lunch stroll along the river and a pause for coffee and pastry on the terrace of the Café du Centre. (With Joly interrogating the institute personnel, Gideon's interviews were necessarily on hold and they were in tourist mode again.)

"Aside from the fact that they're a tad on the sensational side," he said, "that they're just plain stupid, and that they don't have anything to do with what I'm trying to do in the book, they're fine. I just wish I hadn't been dumb enough to give him our fax number. I could have been carrying on in happy ignorance."

"Poor baby. I don't think writing for the masses agrees with you."

"The masses are great, I don't have any problem with the masses. It's Lester that scares me."

"Dr. Oliver—I didn't realize you had returned." It was Monsieur Leyssales, the hotel's bearded proprietor, calling from the doorway. "There were two telephone calls for you a while ago. I believe messages were left."

"Joly, maybe?" Julie said to Gideon. "Something may have turned up."

"I'll go see," he said, standing. He gestured at the faxed sheets. "Whatever it is, it has to be better than dealing with this." He turned. "If it's Lester, I can always say I never got the message."

Beneath its rustic exterior the Hôtel Cro-Magnon was a thoroughly up-to-date establishment, boasting not only a fax machine but an elaborate voice-mail system, getting through the intricacies of which took Gideon several minutes. When he finally pressed the right sequence of buttons, he was surprised to hear the more-distracted-than-usual distracted voice of Jacques Beaupierre.

"Gideon, I must talk to you...I thought perhaps, as a friend...may I speak with you confidentially?" Jacques could hardly be heard; Gideon pressed the telephone closer to his ear. "Now? It's extremely important, I assure you, or I wouldn't...I haven't been completely truthful in the past, I'm afraid, and now I don't know how to...I'll wait for you here."

Click.

Vintage Beaupierre. Talk about what? Where was "here"? At least he knew when "now" was, but that was no thanks to Jacques; according to the voice-mail system, the call had come in at 11:50 A.M., about two hours before.

The second message was also from Jacques, a marginally more coherent postscript. "No, not here at the institute," he whispered. "I don't know what I was thinking of. No, I'll meet you at...the Musée Thibault."

"Ah, you remember the name after all," Gideon said to the recording.

"Yes, that's better, the Thibault. You know where it is, yes? In La Quinze? I'll go there now, this moment. You'll come, won't you? I'll wait for you. Gideon, there's been a...a misunderstanding....I have a dreadful confession...that is to say, mm, ah..."

La Quinze was less than eight miles from Les Eyzies, but it might have been on a different continent, a gray sprawl of nondescript buildings with mildewed, stuccoed walls clumped alongside the road. Unlike Les Eyzies—or Saint-Cyprien, or most of the other villages of the Dordogne, for that matter—La Quinze had no flower boxes, no colorful awnings over the shops, no decorations, no trees, nothing at all to brighten the tired streets. Once upon a time the fortified church at its hub must have been imposing if not handsome, but it was sagging and decrepit now, with its roof partially caved in. Altogether, the place looked more like southern Sicily than southern France.

It was two-fifteen by the time he located the museum, situated as it was at the rear of a building housing the village bakery. There he mounted two shaky wooden steps to a plain wooden door with a cardboard sign thumbtacked to it, identifying it as a *musée d'histoire naturelle de la Dordogne* and indicating that the regular hours were 10 A.M. to noon on the second and fourth Wednesdays of the month, but that if the door were to be found locked at other times, the key could be obtained from M. Chatelard in the *boulangerie* out front.

It was a Thursday, but the door was unlocked. Gideon pushed it open to find himself in a room about thirty feet by twenty, crowded with the simple artifacts of Paleolithic men and the bony remnants of third interglacial and Würm glaciation fauna, housed in appropriately dusty glass display cases and scrupulously arranged in row after row after row, to illustrate patterns and progressions, developments and deviations, each item with its own lovingly handwritten label beneath it, in Latin and in French, most of them penned in faded brown script and curling with age.

It was, as a matter of fact, just the kind of good old-fashioned no-nonsense museum he liked: no buttons to push, no moving parts, no dumbed-down interactive frippery to get in the way of all that information, and as he closed the door behind him he drew a deep breath for the pleasure of taking in the clean, dry smells of stone dust, bone dust, and wood polish.

And stopped with his hand still on the door handle, apprehensive without knowing why. He sniffed again. There was the smell of stone dust and wood polish, all right, but of something else as well, something that didn't belong. The fragrance of roasted almonds from the bakery at the front of the building? He breathed it in. Yes, that was there too, but—

"Jacques?" he said, directing his voice toward the open door of what appeared to be a workshop-storeroom off the exhibit area, dimly lit by a couple of long, narrow windows near the ceiling.

No answer.

He called again, although no one in the adjoining room could have missed hearing him the first time. "Jacques? It's—"

He stopped, almost against his will placing the alien odor for what it was. Gamy, musky, sickish, his years of forensic work had made it unhappily familiar to him: the mingled smells of blood, of sphincters suddenly relaxed, of fluids and tissues that belonged by rights inside, not outside, the human body's fragile envelope of skin. He went to the open door. The grim smell grew worse, but all he could see was an empty room with unmatched storage cabinets along the walls and, drawn together in the center, two work tables strewn with stone implements and taking up almost all the floor space. A column of dust motes, caught in a shaft of sunlight, rotated slowly above the tables.

But the moment he stepped through the doorway he saw something more: there on the floor, at the back, partly hidden by the rear table, a blackish, viscous blotch soaking into the soft, splintery old floor.

With his stomach turning over, wishing himself anywhere but there, Gideon walked toward it, jumping when something crunched under his heel. Jerking his foot back, he saw a pair of twisted, broken spectacles with heavy black 1950s-style frames.

Beaupierre's.

Steeling himself, knowing now what must lie on the floor, wedged into the space between the far side of the table and the wall cabinet but hoping against hope that he was wrong, he went toward it, heavy-hearted and unwilling.

Blinking in the sunlight, Joly emerged from the doorway of the Musée Thibault and avidly, gratefully lit up another Gitane, getting it out of the pack, into his mouth, and alight with what seemed one motion.

"How's it going in there?" Gideon asked.

Joly flapped his hand: *Wait, let me get in one good puff first.*

Gideon obliged. He'd already been waiting for over an hour as it was. When Joly had first arrived in response to his telephone call, along with Roussillot—the real Dr. Fernand Roussillot, deputy medical examiner of the regional directorate of judicial police—and three plainclothes investigators, they had wasted little time in unceremoniously hustling him out from underfoot. He had walked around the block, had stopped at a mean little bar for an espresso, had drunk it while the bristle-chinned regulars eyed him with mute, open suspicion, and had then returned to the museum, leaning against the well-equipped crime lab van from Périgueux that was parked in the alley beside it.

After a while Joly had come out for his first smoke and to ask for more details about Jacques's telephone messages. Gideon had told him everything he remembered. Unfortunately, he'd also had to tell him that he'd erased them without giving it a thought. And what did he suppose might have been the nature of Beaupierre's "terrible confession"? Joly had asked. Gideon had had to shake his head and say he just didn't know.

Joly had listened silently, with his head bowed, until Gideon had finished—or maybe until he'd finished his cigarette—and then had gone back inside without comment. Gideon had returned to leaning against the van and waiting some more. Waiting and thinking, or rather trying to think, but although his thoughts turned and turned, sifting over and over through the same dark, troubled catalog of events, every time he seemed to come close to making sense of them the pattern fractured; his mind would shy and skitter away like a nervous horse.

Having gotten in his one good puff and followed it with a second, Joly was now ready to reply to Gideon's question. "Roussillot says the cause of death was a blow, or possibly more than one blow, to the left rear portion of the head," he announced, gushing smoke from mouth and nostrils.

Gideon grimaced. That much he'd been able to tell on his own.

"The blood-spatter pattern makes it clear that he was struck down right there, where you found him. There are some signs of what may turn out to have been a struggle, but nothing much—no overturned chairs or broken glass. That suggests it may have been someone he knew and trusted."

"Struggle? You met Jacques. He was in his seventies, and not exactly what you'd call a fighting machine in any case. How much struggle could he have put up?"

"Yes, that's so." Joly took another pull, so hard that the cigarette sparked, and then handed Gideon a plastic envelope. Inside was a man's gold ring set with a square blue-gray opal inlaid with a gold horse's head in low relief—or more likely an imitation opal and fake gold, since the band showed blue-green deposits on its inner surface and in the crevices of the setting. "Have you ever seen this before?"

"I don't think so."

"It didn't belong to Professor Beaupierre?"

Gideon shook his head. "Not as far as I know. He certainly hasn't been wearing it."

"It's not familiar to you at all? No one at the institute wears such a ring?"

"No, not that I noticed—and I think I would have noticed. Did you find it in there?"

"Under the table, less than a meter from the body."

"You think it might have come from the murderer, then—gotten wrenched off in whatever struggle there was?"

"I do. It was in plain sight, not the sort of thing that would have lain there unseen for days." He slipped the envelope into an inside pocket. "We'll see." He took another long pull on his Gitane.

They both looked up as the shirtsleeved Dr. Roussillot came out into the alley, wiping his hands on a paper towel. "You wouldn't happen to have another cigarette, would you, Joly? Mine must be in my coat."

When he had it going he expelled a double lungful of smoke, closing his eyes and emitting a deep sigh of simple pleasure. Not only did the French get away with their fatted goose liver and *confit*, they smoked like characters in 1940s movies. And apparently got away with that too.

"Aaahh. Well, then: time of death was between two and four hours ago."

Gideon had been prepared to dislike Dr. Roussillot on sight, partly on account of Joly's earlier description of him ("stiff-necked, fussy, punctilious"), but mostly—illogical as he knew it was—because of the whack on the head he'd taken from the other "Dr. Roussillot" in Saint-Cyprien. But the genuine article had turned out to be a merry, freckled, comfortably overfed man of forty who, while demanding enough in his instructions to his subordinates, seemed anything but stiff-necked. Possibly this had something to do with his being a self-described fan of Gideon's, having read "with great pleasure and enormous profit" his recent series of papers on the assessment of postcranial skeletal trauma in the *Journal of Forensic Sciences*.

And when Gideon had apologized for stepping on Jacques's glasses and otherwise trampling the crime scene, Roussillot had stopped him at once. "It's nothing, nothing at all. Completely understandable under the circumstances. I beg you, don't give it a thought."

An offended Joly had stared at him. "That's not what you say when it's one of my men that does it."

"But none of *your* men," Roussillot had said simply, "is Gideon Oliver." From then on he and Gideon had gotten along fine.

"And that's the best you can do?" Joly asked the pathologist now. "Two to four hours?"

"Ah, well," said Roussillot, seemingly without taking umbrage, "there's laboratory work yet to be done, of course. We've taken serum and vitreous humor samples, and we'll see what the gastric contents have to tell us, and so on, but no, I don't expect to be able to do any better than that."

"But we already knew that much, dammit," muttered Joly. "We knew *more* than that."

They knew because he and Gideon had worked it out by simple arithmetic. Jacques had telephoned Gideon a little before noon. Inasmuch as it would have taken no more than fifteen minutes for him to drive to La Quinze, he might have arrived as early as twelve-fifteen. When Gideon got there a little over two hours later, Beaupierre was dead. Necessarily, then, it was impossible for him to have been murdered before twelve-fifteen or after two-fifteen. And the state of the spilled blood when Gideon had found him—dry where it was thinly spattered, still viscous where it had puddled—indicated that it hadn't happened either much after one forty-five or much before twelve forty-five. A one-hour time span.

"I was hoping you could narrow it down for us a little more," a displeased Joly said.

Roussillot chuckled with real amusement. "Narrow it down to less than an hour? You don't expect very much, do you?" He turned his twinkling gaze on Gideon and switched to English that was almost as fluent as Joly's but more heavily accented. "They think we're magicians, don't they? Alchemists. Where would they be without us, do you suppose?"

"Oh, all right, I apologize, Roussillot, don't get up on your high horse," said Joly. "It's only that I had hopes of eliminating at least one or two of them from suspicion."

"The institute people, you mean?" asked Gideon.

"Yes. After all, I was interrogating them one by one during the very time we're speaking of. But it's not possible, you see. How long would it have taken to come here from Les Eyzies, do this deed, and return? Forty minutes, no more. Less, conceivably. Any one of them would have had ample time to do it—before seeing me, after seeing me—with no one the wiser."

"I see what you mean." Gideon had a sudden thought. "You know, the baker out front might have spotted somebody. You might want to talk to him."

Joly gave him the Gallic equivalent of an are-you-trying-to-teach-your-grandmother-to-suck-eggs scowl, but Gideon was saved from whatever he was going to say by the appearance at the door of one of the investigators, a somewhat elderly plainclothesman named Félix, who was beckoning with a plastic-gloved hand. "We've found something, Inspector. Come have a look."

Gideon followed Joly and Roussillot inside, to a corner of the exhibit area, where a display case had been pulled away from the wall to reveal a rock about the size of a misshapen softball lying on the floor. There was a smear of blood on it and a clump of matted gray hair. Gideon turned away.

But Roussillot bent low to examine it more closely, then straightened up. "Well, I think we may assume we have our murder weapon, gentlemen." He clucked his disapproval. "A rock. Not the most elegant of choices."

"No, not just a rock," Gideon felt compelled to say. "That's an Acheulian cordiform hand ax—Middle Paleolithic."

Joly, Gideon, and Roussillot looked at one another. The same thought crossed all their minds, Gideon knew, but it was left to Roussillot to say it.

"Well, you have to admit," he said, "for an archaeologist it's a hell of a way to go."

•

"Gideon, it wasn't your fault. You're being...
well, morbid is what you're being. Have some
more *kir*."

The *kir*—white wine and black-currant syrup
over ice, the region's warm-weather afternoon
drink of choice—wasn't doing him much good,
but he took another sip anyway and settled farther down in his chair, stretching out his legs
and crossing his ankles. "Yeah, I know. It's just
that...I was sitting right there in the garden
fooling around with Lester's dumb flap copy,
and all the time Jacques's messages were right
there on the machine. If I'd only known he was
trying to get hold of me—oh, hell."

"But how could you possibly know? Be reasonable, you're making it sound as if you went
out of your way to shirk your responsibility.
How could you conceivably imagine anything
like this would happen?"

"I know, but I keep going over and over it in

my mind. There were so many places where I could have kept it from happening. Why didn't I check our telephone messages when we first got back, for instance? I could have been at the museum by twelve-thirty. He wouldn't have been sitting there by himself all that time, waiting for me."

"But you might as well say why did we go out at all, why didn't we just stay in the room, and then he would have gotten you on the phone the first time he called."

"That's true too. Or if we'd come back a couple of hours—"

"Here's Lucien," she said, pointing with relief to the inspector's long, angular figure bent almost double in climbing out of the low-to-the-ground Citroën he'd parked at the curb on the far side of the street. "Finally. Thank God, maybe he can talk some sense into you." She waved to him.

Having straightened up in his stiff, machine-like manner—something like a sofa bed unfolding—Joly peered around, saw Julie's wave, and started toward them, looking worn. Gideon had left him in La Quinze a couple of hours earlier, and Joly had promised to join them when he was through, for an apéritif at the Café du Centre. With the day warmed by golden late-afternoon sun, they'd been waiting for him on the café's patio, a pleasant terrace shaded by striped awnings and situated on one side of the village square, opposite what looked like a steepled country church, belfry and all, but was actually the *mairie*, Prefect Marielle's domain.

"Are those *kirs*?" Joly asked plaintively, dropping into a chair at their table. "I would kill for a *kir*."

"Not necessary," Julie said, signaling to the waiter that a *kir* was wanted for the newly arrived gentleman. She had picked up the French knack for saying a lot with an economy of gesture, Gideon noted admiringly.

"Lucien," she said, "will you please talk some sense into this man? He thinks he's responsible for Jacques's death. He thinks the reason Jacques is dead is because we didn't check our telephone messages."

"I didn't say that," Gideon said grumpily, "I only—"

"Jacques Beaupierre is dead because his murderer wanted him dead," Joly said wearily. "Do you really think that if he hadn't been able to kill him because you arrived on the scene—assuming of course that he didn't decide to kill you as well—he would simply have dropped the idea, and forgotten all about it, and gone away somewhere?"

Gideon shrugged. "Maybe. Maybe he was killed to keep him from telling me what it was he wanted to tell me. If I'd been there for him and he'd already told me, the cat would have been out of the bag and there'd have been no point in killing him."

"It seems to me, Gideon, that you give your-self far too much importance in this. In my opin-ion, Beaupierre would have been murdered all the same, if not this afternoon, then tomorrow. If not tomorrow, then the next day." The *kir* came and Joly drank greedily, the ice cubes clinking in the glass. "Aah, life returns, the tissues rejuve-nate. Now, I grant you," he said with a pale smile, "it might not have been with an Acheu-lian cordiform hand ax of the Early Paleolithic variety—"

"Middle Paleolithic."

"—but murdered he would have been. Be-sides, if he *was* killed to keep him from making his 'dreadful confession,' then why not hold me responsible too? If I hadn't permitted him to put off the time of his interrogation, he might never have called you at all, or gone to La Quinze. And yet I assure you I do not hold myself responsi-ble."

Gideon puffed out his cheeks and blew out a stream of air. "Yes, okay, you're both right," he said, beginning to come around—in his head if not in his gut. "I guess I'm not making much sense."

"*Thank* you, Lucien," said Julie, raising her glass to him.

"Now then," Joly said, setting down his *kir* after another grateful sip, "to other matters. You remember the ring?" He turned civilly to Julie. "Perhaps Gideon hasn't yet mentioned this?"

"The opal ring? No, he told me about it. You found it near Jacques's body at the Musée Thibault."

"Exactly. And this ring preyed upon my mind. I felt sure I had come across some reference to a similar ring not long before. And at last, at *long* last, it came to me. Now listen to this." He took a sheet of paper from his jacket pocket, unfolded it, and set his reading glasses on his nose. "I translate," he said with a polite nod to Julie. It took him a moment to find his place. "Here we are. '...brown eyes, brown hair. When last seen, was wearing—' No, never mind that.... Ah, here, here. Now listen to this. 'He also wore...'" Joly looked up to make sure he had the full attention of his audience and went on, emphasizing every syllable. "'...also wore on the little finger of his right hand an embossed, heavy gold ring with a stone of opal or sapphire with a horse's or dog's head embedded in it.'" He whipped off the wire-frame glasses, put them in their hard black case, and clicked it closed.

"But what are you reading from?" said Gideon after a moment's startled silence. "Who's it talking about?"

"This," Joly said triumphantly, "is the report on Jean Bousquet that was filed at the time of his disappearance, presumably with the cameo brooch of Madame Renouard's grandmother."

"Bousquet!" the other two exclaimed.

"None other," said Joly, sitting back and radiating satisfaction. "Apparently he has found reason to revisit the Périgord after all."

"And you think he's the one who killed Jacques?" Julie asked.

"It's hard to imagine another explanation. Rings do not generally fall off fingers on their own."

"Bousquet," Gideon said again, mostly to himself. It was amazing how the name of this drifter who had spent only three months in Les Eyzies and hadn't been heard of for the last three years kept cropping up. First it was Bousquet who'd been murdered and buried in the *abri*, possibly by Ely. Then that was switched: it was Bousquet who had murdered Ely. Now it was Bousquet who had killed Jacques. Well, this time at least, they might have it right. The ring was hard to argue with; it was something you could hold in your hand, something tangible, not just another airy conjecture based on a rickety structure of hypothetical premises.

"Gideon," Julie said excitedly, "do you suppose that man in Saint-Cyprien, the one who hit you with that fibula—"

"Femur, not fibula. I wish he'd hit me with a fibula."

"All right, femur—could that have been Bousquet too?"

"I don't know, it never occurred to me. You know, you might be right."

"He had such a ring?" Joly asked.

"If he did I didn't see it. But he did have brown eyes and brown hair."

Joly smiled. "So does everyone else in France. In any case, with Marielle's assistance we have mounted a search for him. There is unfortunately no photograph of him available, and the physical description tells us little, but many people in Les Eyzies have reason to remember him, including some on Marielle's staff. If he's still in the area, I should be surprised if we fail to find him. Of course, having achieved his end, he may already have left again."

"But what end?" Julie asked. "Why would he want to come back and kill Jacques?"

"Ah, yes, as to that—"

"Inspector? They...they told me I might find you here." It was Audrey, strangely unsure of herself. "Is it true that Jacques has been...that Jacques is dead?"

Joly rose. "Yes, madame, I'm sorry." He placed a hand on her elbow. "Will you sit down?"

She appeared not to hear him. "There are... there are some things I should tell you that may be relevant...." She looked indecisively at Gideon and Julie.

"It's all right, madame," Joly said, "you can speak. But if you prefer, we can go—"

"No, what does it matter?" She nodded vaguely in their direction—almost like Beaupierre himself, as if since she was going to be his replacement as director she intended to replace him in manner as well—and took the chair Joly was holding out for her.

In Gideon's mind, Audrey Godwin-Pope had always served as a model of calm, invincible self-certainty, and it was shocking to see her so rattled. Her thin, old-lady cardigan sweater had been misbuttoned. Her chignon, always before a neat, business-like bun, had loosened so that straggling gray tendrils floated free at the nape of her neck. And to make the picture complete, somewhere along the way she'd broken the nosepiece of her tortoiseshell glasses, inexpertly sticking them back together with a twist of Scotch tape. It was as if she'd changed overnight from the rock-solid Audrey he knew to somebody's hunch-shouldered, slightly dotty old hermit aunt who lived in the attic bedroom.

"Audrey, would you like something to drink?" he asked softly.

"What? Yes, all right, whatever you're having. No, a vodka. With ice." But she'd never taken her eyes from Joly, and it was to him she spoke: "Inspector, I haven't told you before—I should have told you this morning…."

Joly waited, encouraging her with a friendly dip of his chin.

"You see…about a week before Ely left…that is, before he was killed…he told me that he knew…that he thought he knew who was behind the hoax, the Tayac hoax."

"Jean Bousquet!" Julie couldn't keep from whispering.

"Jean Bousquet?" Audrey said, glancing dully at her. "No, not Bousquet. I mean, yes, he thought Jean might have written the letter—the letter to *Paris-Match*—out of spite, but no more than that. Jean would have been incapable of more." Nervously, she appealed to Joly. "I did tell you that, Inspector. You remember." The waiter placed her drink on the table; she didn't notice.

Joly nodded patiently, his graceful hands folded on the table.

"But as to who was *behind* it," Audrey said, "that was different. Ely thought it might be— he had no proof, you understand, but still he was sure that it was—or almost sure that it was—"

"Jacques Beaupierre," said Joly.

"Yes," she said, stopping short with surprise. "Jacques."

"And why didn't you tell me *this* earlier?" he asked without reproach.

Audrey discovered her vodka and drained it in a few absentminded gulps. "You...you have to understand, Inspector," she said defensively, "by that time Ely wasn't the same person anymore. He was like a wild man—vengeful, suspicious. I couldn't take what he said seriously. I mean, it was preposterous to think even for a minute that Jacques...surely you see that it would have been irresponsible—*wrong*—for me to go around repeating it?"

Her pleading look took in Julie and Gideon, and, indeed, Gideon could see it, could see why she hadn't mentioned Ely's suspicion to Joly, or to him, or to anyone else, in all this time. In her place, he'd probably have done the same. But now, with the sudden knowledge—Audrey had found it out only this morning—that Ely had been a victim of homicide and not of a plane crash, and with Jacques's death following only a couple of hours later, things were terribly different. What would have been unthinkable three years ago had come to pass; what would have seemed merely "preposterous" was now just one more not-so-unreasonable possibility. The question was...

Joly was looking at him. "You wanted to ask something, Gideon?"

"Yes, I do. Audrey, what made him think it was Jacques, do you know? You said he didn't have any proof."

Ely had worked it out, she explained disjointedly, by a process of elimination. There were only three people whose theories and reputations hung on the Tayac find: his own, Michel Montfort's, and Jacques's. Since he knew he hadn't done the faking, that left Michel and Jacques. Michel, he had reasoned, was extremely unlikely to have done it, having long ago proved himself a serious and objective scholar; moreover, unlike Jacques and Ely himself, his preeminence in the field was acknowl-

258 • Aaron Elkins

edged—he didn't *need* Tayac. And that left Jacques.

Gideon couldn't help smiling a little. It was very nearly the same line of reasoning that Émile Grize had employed, only Émile had used it to eliminate Jacques and Ely and to finger Michel Montfort.

"Oh, and I'm forgetting the four metapodials," Audrey added. "That was the crucial point. They were from the Musée Thibault. Jacques was on the board there. He would have had easy access."

Gideon nodded. Jacques's access to the bones carried more weight with him than Ely's process of elimination.

"Madame," Joly said casually, "when was the last time you saw Jean Bousquet?"

She stiffened. "Jean! Why—it was years ago. When he disappeared, when he left."

"Have you heard anything to suggest that he might be back in this area?"

"Back? You mean now? No, why do you ask? You don't mean you think—" She goggled at him, a disturbingly un-Audrey-like action, and tugged distractedly at her hair; more gray hairs came loose from the bun. "But why—but—"

"Thank you so much for your help, madame. Are you quite all right? Would you like me to have someone drive you home?"

"What I find myself wondering about," Joly mused after their second round of drinks had been delivered—Joly himself, who would be driving home to Périgueux for dinner, had switched to mineral water—"is the frequency with which she seems to have access to information possessed by no one else."

"I don't follow you," Gideon said.

"Consider. It was from Professor Godwin-Pope that we learned that Carpenter possessed an air rifle—and that he had even proudly showed it to her; it was from her that we learned he had taken to keeping it at hand when he was excavating; it is from her that we now hear that Carpenter had fixed Beaupierre in his mind as the villain of the Tayac debacle. Now why do you suppose Carpenter would choose to divulge these things to her, and only to her?"

"Why wouldn't he?" Gideon asked. "They were good friends. Audrey was the only other American on the staff aside from Pru, and I guess by that time the Ely-Pru thing was on the wane and maybe a little awkward. He probably just felt most comfortable with Audrey."

"Yes, perhaps," Joly said.

"Besides," said Julie, "you can't really conclude that she was the only one he told, can you? For all we know, maybe he told everybody else too, but Audrey's the only one who's come forward."

"Yes, that's so. It might be that I'm making something from nothing."

At their feet was an elderly, limping, white-muzzled dog that had been scratching steadily behind its ear for the last few minutes. It had been brought by a customer at another table but had found itself neglected once its owner started on his apéritif and opened his newspaper. Looking for company, it had wandered over to sit by the three of them instead, lolling its tongue, watching them talk, and occasionally giving a halfhearted wag of its tail between scratches. Now, apparently tired out by the effort, it stopped, looking up at Joly, who absently reached down to continue its scratching for it.

"What do you think," he said after half a minute or so of this obviously mutually agreeable activity, "of the following as a working hypothesis? Assume first that Carpenter was correct in his suspicion that Beaupierre was behind the fraud. He confronts him with it. Beaupierre, terrified at the prospect of exposure, murders him—or rather pays or otherwise convinces the willing Bousquet to do it and to help him with the concealment of the body. The deceptive flight of the airplane is arranged through parties unknown at present. And Bousquet, very likely with some financial assistance from Beaupierre, takes himself far, far away and settles in Corsica to make himself a new life."

Gideon noticed that Julie, who had laughed at the notion of Beaupierre as a murderer the previous afternoon, wasn't laughing now.

Neither was he. "You know," he said thoughtfully, "that could explain why he had the nerve to call the institute for a job reference a few months later. He knew Jacques wasn't about to turn him down. But of course Jacques wasn't in and it was Montfort he wound up talking to."

Joly inclined his head. "Yes, that might be so. Now...where was I?"

"He settles in Corsica," Julie said.

"Yes, thank you, he settles in Corsica and the incident fades away. Three years pass, we arrive at the present. Carpenter's murder comes to light." Joly continued scratching rhythmically away at the dog while he spoke. "Beaupierre becomes anxious, he becomes conscience-stricken, the urge to confess seizes him, as his telephone calls to you suggest. And Bousquet, understandably fearing that he is about to give everything away, silences him in the most direct and certain way possible." He looked down at the dog. "So, what do you think of my theory, *chien*? Does it strike you as an idea worth pursuing?" The dog gazed back up at him with rheumy eyes. "Yes, I believe you do," Joly said.

"Well, I'm not so sure I agree with him," Gideon said. "I can see where you're coming from, but how could Bousquet possibly know whether or not Jacques was getting faint-hearted? In fact, how could he know so quickly that we'd ID'd Carpenter? It just happened yesterday. And nobody else knew about it until you told them this morning at, what—ten o'clock? And by two, maybe by one, Jacques was already dead. Pretty fast work for someone who hasn't been in the neighborhood for three years."

Joly brushed this aside. "We've had telephones in France for some time now, you know. Someone could easily have been in touch with him, perhaps Beaupierre himself."

"What for? To inform him he was getting cold feet and was about to go and confess everything?"

"Now wait a minute, Gideon," Julie said. "That's not as ridiculous as it sounds. I didn't know Jacques very well, but, yes, he struck me as the kind of person who might very well have wanted to give Bousquet a chance to confess on his own before implicating him."

Gideon nodded. "Okay, I'll give you that much, but—sorry to be the one who's always saying it—aren't we making a lot of assumptions here? All we know for sure is that Jacques is dead."

"No," Joly said, "we know that he was *murdered*. And we have good reason for concluding it was Bousquet who did it. And we also know that Carpenter was murdered. And we know that someone went to considerable effort to keep you from examining his remains. And we know that at the time he was killed there was considerable bad feeling between him and Bousquet. And we know, or believe we know, that he suspected Beaupierre of having implemented the fraud that had caused him so much grief. That's a great deal to know. Well, you ingrate," he said as the dog heaved itself up at its master's whistle and limped off without a backward glance.

He wiped his fingers on a napkin, carefully and one at a time, like someone polishing silverware, before picking up his glass again. "I'm sure you can see," he said, having swallowed, "that all these things cannot possibly be unrelated."

"You're sure *I* can see?" Gideon said, smiling. "What happened to *Non sunt multiplicanda*?"

"I've concluded that I was wrong," Joly said generously, "and you were right."

"Interconnected Monkey Business triumphs again," Julie said, producing a curious stare from Joly.

"Oh, yes—you were right about something else too," said the inspector as they walked across the square with him to his car. "Julie, do you remember suggesting the other day that the single tooth left behind in the Saint-Cyprien morgue might be used for dental identification?"

"Sure, but we didn't know what dentist to contact because we didn't know Jean Bousquet's dentist, or even if he had a dentist—" She stopped. "Wait a minute...of course...it wasn't Bousquet, was it? It turned out to be Carpenter, and—"

"And Carpenter did have a dentist, and his dentist has positively identified the work as his own and the tooth as his patient's lower-right first bicuspid. So we may say at last that the remains from the *abri* have been positively identified. They are Ely Carpenter's."

"But we already knew that," Julie said. "Gideon identified them yesterday."

"But not positively."

"Of course, positively. He said so."

"I really appreciate that, honey," Gideon said, unexpectedly touched, "but unfortunately judges and juries—and especially defense counsels—tend to be more skeptical than you are, and I'm not sure that a lecture on cowboy's thumb would've convinced them. A deposition from Carpenter's dentist will."

"And you'll also be interested in this," Joly said when they reached the Citroën. He reached into the ever-productive inside pocket of his suit coat and brought out a single sheet of paper. "It's a photocopy of his dental chart."

Gideon scanned it. "What am I supposed to be looking for?"

With his pen Joly pointed to the upper-right first molar, through which an X had been drawn—dental shorthand for a missing tooth. "The very first day you were here, in the *abri*, you predicted, from the jawbone, that this tooth would be missing. I confess, with shame in my heart, that I doubted you."

"You mean I was *right*?" Gideon cried impulsively. "Hey, how about that!" Quickly, he recollected himself. "I mean," he said with a modest shrug, "there really wasn't anything to it."

But he couldn't keep a straight face, and they all burst out laughing. It had been a long time since they'd had anything to laugh about, and as they saw Joly off the three of them were still chuckling.

CHAPTER
21

The next morning Audrey was appointed acting director. Her first formal action was to declare the institute closed until the following Monday out of respect for Jacques—and, Gideon thought, to give herself a three-day weekend to pull herself back together before taking over the director's chair. The break suited Gideon and Julie, who agreed over breakfast that they could both stand some time off from bones, murders, hoaxes, and Paleolithic prehistory—all of which were placed off-limits for the long weekend. Gideon didn't quite see why Paleolithic prehistory had to be included, but he was game to go along anyway.

They rented one of the plastic kayaks lined up at the foot of the bridge and paddled happily on the Vézère, going nowhere, until midafternoon, when the unusual humidity and a developing warming trend strengthened to the extent that any form of physical effort lost its appeal. Afterward, when the darkness cooled things down and revived their appetites, they ended the day feasting again at the restaurant Au Vieux Moulin, where they'd eaten with Joly that first night.

The following day, Saturday, was largely taken up with Jacques's funeral, held a bare twelve hours after his body was released by the police (Madame Beaupierre, who seemed more consumed with embarrassment than with grief over her husband's murder, wanted it over with as quickly as possible), and with a stilted, uncomfortable funeral buffet at the Beaupierres' house near the Font de Gaume cave. Although Jacques's colleagues, along with the Olivers, had been invited to both functions, they were treated with icy reserve by the widow.

After these strained and uncomfortable events, Gideon, who was feeling the lingering effects of the concussion more than he wanted to admit, slept away the afternoon while Julie drove a few miles up the Vézère to tour the celebrated Grotte du Grand Roc with its stalagmites, stalactites, and other natural grotesqueries.

On Sunday a huge, black thundercloud began to build up in great, roiling columns a little after dawn. They took one look at it from bed, closed their eyes again and slept late, not awakening until nine, when Audrey telephoned to tell them that the dedication of the institute's new quarters, which had originally been scheduled for the next day but had been tentatively postponed upon news of Jacques's death, would take place as scheduled after all. It had been decided that the new building was to be designated the Centre Préhistorique Beaupierre in honor of its fallen director. Dignitaries from the Université du Périgord and the Horizon Foundation would be in attendance, and Gideon and Julie were cordially invited to the ceremonies.

Gideon cordially accepted for both of them, after which they went downstairs for a satisfying "English" breakfast of bacon and eggs, then set themselves up in the Cro-Magnon's downstairs lounge, a cozy, overstuffed room that looked as if it should have had Charles Dickens—or more appropriately, Gustave Flaubert—seated at the writing desk, lost in reflection and chewing pensively on his quill.

Instead it was Julie who took over the desk to work on a quarterly report on park security problems that she'd brought with her, while Gideon worked on his laptop, polishing his chapter on the bizarre case of "George Psalmanazar," the eighteenth-century "Formosan" who had flummoxed the British scientific world of his day by inventing not only himself but an entire, highly detailed *Historical and Geographical Description of Formosa*, complete with imaginary customs, language, clothing, and religion. (They lived to be over a hundred, they drank snake blood, they sacrificed eighteen thousand children a year to their gods, they beheaded and ate wives who committed adultery.)

It had been swallowed hook, line, and sinker; "Psalmanazar"—nobody ever learned his real name—became a respected friend of Samuel Johnson's and was given an appointment to Oxford as—what else?—a lecturer on Formosan history.

With the lounge all to themselves, rain thrumming on the windows, a pot of hot coffee on a nearby sideboard, and a mantel clock ticking lazily away, they looked forward to passing a quiet and companionable Sunday.

For the Greater Cincinnati Elderhostel's "Footloose in France" tour group, Sunday was day nine of a twelve-day hike through the French countryside, and with a hundred dusty miles on towpaths and country lanes behind them, they were a tanned, fit, seasoned crew of twelve. Still, with the morning temperature approaching eighty, with a median age of sixty-nine, and with all of them still damp and steaming from the rain shower they'd passed through an hour earlier, no one objected when Yvette, the French tour leader (looking cute as a button in her leather hiking shorts and mountaineer's boots), signaled that the midmorning break was at hand.

"This place, how you like to stop here?" she asked in her delightfully mangled English. (Only the resolutely negative Mrs. Winkelman—at eighty-three it was allowable—contended that Yvette's accent was put on.) "The coffee and the juice, they wait themselves in the van, and also some nice French snacks. If you like, we go and sit beside the river, where there is a most nice view of Les Eyzies, the place of lunch for today. Then I tell you some of the facts of this most charming village."

But practiced open-country hikers that they were, they first split into two groups, the men making for the copse of stunted oaks on the left, the women for the one on the right. Five minutes later, perceptibly more relaxed and expansive, they lined up at the supply van, which had gotten there before them and had their juice, coffee, and pastries ready and waiting.

"Joe." Merle Nichols put her hand on the arm of her new friend Joe Pfeiffer, recently widowed, recently retired from the Dayton police department. "Is that a person down there?"

"Down where?"

"Nah, it's just a bundle of clothes or something," somebody said. "It probably washed up from somewhere."

Someone else thought it might be a drunk, someone else a hiker taking a nap. But no one moved any farther down the gentle slope. They all stood there holding their cups and pastries, looking doubtfully at Joe, their expert in such matters.

"I'll go see," he said with a sigh. He had sighted it now, down by the riverbank under the willows, and it wasn't any bundle of clothes; the fourteen years he'd spent in homicide told him that much. And he was betting it wasn't a drunk or a sleeper either.

"Hey, buddy?" he called from fifteen feet away, although he would have been surprised to get an answer. "You okay?...Hey, monsieur?"

He stood there for a moment longer, resisting the urge—an urge more deeply ingrained than he'd realized—to have a closer look, to take over, then turned on his heel and walked back up to his silent, wide-eyed companions.

"Yvette, you better call the cops, the gendarmes. That guy's been dead awhile."

"Oh, for the love of Mike," said Mrs. Winkelman to her neighbor. "Does this mean we don't get to have our tea?"

The crime scene investigators grumbled at having to park the crime lab van alongside the highway and carry their equipment down to the riverbank (which meant they'd have to carry it back up afterward), but once there they got quickly and efficiently to work.

A twenty-by-twenty-meter area was cordoned off with tape, and the nosy gaggle of American grannies and grandpas was helped on their way after a brief interrogation. A panning videotape of the overall scene was made, and a diagrammatic sketch. The position of the body was measured and photographed. The cordoned-off area was then divided into five-by-five-meter sections and each of them meticulously searched by investigators working two at a time, one shuffling along with his eyes to the ground and the other taking notes. Two fairly distinct heel prints from a man's shoe—both probably from the same shoe—were photographed and cast in plaster of paris by the third member of the team. Various objects were diligently recorded, photographed, labeled, and bagged: several different kinds of cigarette stubs, including one with lipstick on it, a cigar wrapper, three ring tabs from beer or soft-drink cans, burned paper matches, a wadded-up facial tissue, two flattened cardboard drinking cups, odd bits of plastic and aluminum foil, a woman's imitation leather belt, worn-out and cheap, two rubber bands, a used adhesive strip decorated with Minnie Mouse pictures and with a little dried blood on it.

None of it was very promising; it was the typical detritus of a place that was an attractive spot for a riverbank picnic and also happened to lie within flinging distance of a highway. The one object of real interest—the investigators were practically slavering to get their hands on it—was a rifle, the wooden stock of which could be seen sticking out from under the right thigh of the corpse. But Joly and Roussillot were just getting started on the body, and until the two of them were through there was no hope of getting at it. And that wasn't going to be for a while; they were both sticklers for the rule book, as slow as boiled honey.

"Georges," Joly called to the lead investigator, "you've finished with the victim? We can shift him now?"

"Absolutely, Inspector, everything by the book."

"We might as well turn him over then," Roussillot said.

The body, fully clothed, lay on its front between them at the foot of a knee-high rock. The face was turned to the left, the arms caught underneath the torso, one leg extended and the other bent-kneed and drawn up to the side. It was plain to both men that the body had been there for some time. Maggots wriggled in the nostrils, the eyes, the mouth, the ears. What skin could be seen was a pasty, greasy, coppery color, mottled with greenish veins. The clothes, still moist from the passing showers, looked as if they'd been out in the rain more than once. Joly, smothering a grimace, instinctively held his breath and squatted to take hold of the shoulders, while Roussillot took the legs.

Between them they rolled the flaccid body carefully and deliberately onto its back. They had both rolled over enough cadavers not to be surprised at the strange, heavy inertia of the dead, the seeming chill that seeped through the clothing.

"Ah," said Roussillot, "what do we have here?" He pointed with his chin at the black, ragged hole, almost certainly a bullet hole, in the center of the man's chest, with a knot of maggots squirming about in it. The surrounding denim of his shirt was stained a rusty brown, with a few spatters and spots as far away as his sleeves. Not much blood, really, considering the size of the hole.

The rifle, which had been underneath him, had remained where it was, lying now a few inches away on the flattened, yellowing grass.

"Well, what do you think?" Joly asked, straightening up and brushing off the knees of his trousers, although he'd never quite let them come in contact with the earth.

"What do I think?" Roussillot paused to light a cigarette for Joly and one for himself and blew out a stream of smoke while he studied the corpse. "I think I see before me a reasonably well-nourished man in his forties, apparently a suicide, who's been dead anywhere from...let us say two days to a week. I think—"

Joly looked at him. "*Two days*, did you say? I should have said a week at a minimum."

Roussillot smiled tolerantly—a good way to get under Joly's skin, although it was no doubt meant kindly. "My dear Joly, these things are not as clear-cut as you people like to imagine. You could well be right—it might be a week. Or it might be only two days. That is precisely why I said—"

"But look at the maggots, at the *skin*. It's already begun to slip in places."

"Yes, very true, but on the other hand, do you see any bloating of the abdomen, any copious discharge of fluids from the natural orifices? No. In fact, there has been little if any distension of the gut. That, in my opinion, is far more significant, more reliable, and it sounds more like two days than seven, wouldn't you say? And surely you've noticed that the smell, while hardly agreeable, is by no means the overpowering odor one would expect from a corpse that's been lying out in the warm sun for a week."

"No, now that you mention it," Joly said thoughtfully, "it isn't." He was obscurely annoyed with Roussillot for pointing out something that he himself should have noticed.

"You have to understand, Joly, the variables of postmortem change—or taphonomic progression, as we refer to it in my profession—are highly inconstant and rarely in agreement. That is the reason we offer our findings in terms of ranges and not of fixed times. In this case it may be that the warmth of the last several days has accelerated some decompositional processes, but not others. On the other hand, the location of the body in this relatively cool spot by the river may have contributed—"

"Yes, yes, I see," said Joly, whose supply of patience for being lectured, even in Roussillot's good-natured and inoffensive manner, was not especially large. "I presume you're willing to risk a more definitive determination of the cause of death, however?" With his cigarette he gestured at the dead man's chest.

"That hole?" Roussillot shrugged. "On the

contrary, I wouldn't want to commit myself until the autopsy. However, I'd be willing to go on record to the effect that it probably did nothing for his health."

That made them both laugh—for men working around corpses it never took much—and cleared the air, and for a few minutes they both went about their tasks, smoking and pursuing their own thoughts, Roussillot kneeling beside the body (without regard for his trouser knees) and gently probing with a finger here and there, Joly bending over the rifle with great interest, but not touching it.

"Joly, wait!" Roussillot said suddenly, reaching out to grasp Joly's shoulder. "What's the matter with me? This is no suicide. Look at the wound, the gunshot wound."

Joly looked. "Yes?"

"Well, look at it! Wouldn't you assume that a man intent on putting a shotgun blast through his heart would place the muzzle of the weapon against his chest before pulling the trigger?"

"Yes, I suppose I would."

"Of course you would. But do you see any charring of the material, any soot, any residue at all that would mark it as a contact wound?"

"No, I don't."

"No. What's more, take a good, close look. Does that look like a shotgun wound to you?"

"No, it doesn't."

"Well, then, it couldn't very well have been made by a shotgun, could it?"

"No. What is your point, Roussillot?"

"What is my...what is my...?" It was gratifying to see, Joly thought, that Roussillot's skin could be gotten under as well. "My point, Inspector Joly," he said in a strained voice, "is that *this* wound...here...could not have been made by *that* shotgun...there."

"But this isn't a shotgun."

"Not a...not a..."

"Shotgun. I believe you've been misled by the barrels, which have a superficial resemblance to the arrangement of certain double-barreled shotguns—an over-and-under pattern, as we refer to it in my profession. If you look more closely, however, you'll see that there are actually *three* barrels. Only the top one is, in fact, a barrel—that is, the cylinder down which the projectile is propelled. The others"—he tapped them with a pencil—"are air reservoirs."

"Air reservoirs?" Roussillot said, squinting through the smoke at him. "What kind of—"

"We see before us," said Joly, "a Cobra Magnum F-16 high-velocity air rifle."

Roussillot stared at it, and then at Joly. "The weapon used to kill the other one, Carpenter."

"Yes, three years ago."

"But how very curious." He grunted as he pushed himself to his feet. "Ah, when did my joints get to be older than I am?" He took a final drag on his cigarette, put the butt into an airtight metal case he carried with him, and continued to emit smoke for two more breaths while looking down at the body. "An air rifle," he said at length. "Of course. No primer, no gunpowder, no explosion, nothing to burn. That would explain the lack of soot, wouldn't you say?"

"I should think so, yes."

"So we're back to suicide. Félix!" he called. "Are you or are you not intending to bag the hands at some point?"

"And how was I supposed to bag them?" said the aggrieved Félix. "He had them under him, didn't he? And then I didn't want to interrupt you and the inspector."

Muttering, he knelt by the body's right hand, shook out a paper bag, produced a length of cord, and was beginning to slide the bag around the hand when Joly intervened.

"One moment, Félix." He dropped to his knees beside the investigator, so intent on the yellowed, upturned hand that for once he gave no thought to grass stains. "Roussillot, what would this be?"

He was pointing at the base of the little finger, which was encircled by a sort of furrow, as if a tightly wound rubber band had been removed only a little while ago.

"Well, now..." Roussillot said, bending attentively over the hand. "Yes. You notice that the skin here is not only indented, but has a dry, withered appearance, quite different from the greasiness of the rest of the hand. As to its cause—"

"Could he have worn a ring there recently?" Joly asked impatiently.

"A ring? Why, yes," Roussillot said. "It could very well be that. It probably *is* that. The compression of the tissue would have...my God, Joly, you don't think—?"

CHAPTER

22

Gideon had started to nod peacefully off over Psalmanazar for the third time when Monsieur Leyssales knocked discreetly on the wall beside the open door. There was a telephone call for the professor. If he liked he could take it on the desk telephone in the lobby.

"Gideon, we have Bousquet" were Joly's first words.

"Congratulations, Lucien. When did you find him? Where?"

"This morning, on the riverbank a few miles below Les Eyzies, where he'd been for the last several days."

In Gideon's drowsy state of mind it took a few seconds to penetrate. "He's dead?"

"A suicide, it seems."

"It seems?"

"A figure of speech. There's not much doubt. He shot himself—with the same rifle that killed Carpenter."

"The same rifle that—why would he—what would he—"

"I have no idea."

"Where was the gun, Lucien?"

"Where you'd expect. Underneath the body. He had collapsed forward onto it."

"His fingerprints were on it?"

"They were. Faint, smudged...but ultimately identifiable."

"Huh. So you think...what? That he killed Jacques and then he went out and killed himself?"

"I should be surprised if it were the other way around," said Joly dryly. "And apparently a single day elapsed between the two. Roussillot, after endless equivocation, has finally concluded that he's been dead about two days. Beaupierre was killed three days ago, as you know....Are you there?" he asked when there was no response from Gideon.

"Lucien, I have to tell you, I have a funny feeling about all this. Why would Bousquet kill himself?"

"Remorse?"

"You're not serious."

"I'm simply—Gideon, if you're free, why don't you come to the morgue here in Périgueux? It would be easier to talk. And Roussillot especially asked me to say he would be happy to delay the autopsy until you arrived."

"Please, not on my account. I'm not that keen on autopsies. I like my corpses ten thousand

years old. Not," he added, "that I don't appreciate the gesture."

"He'll be disappointed. He was hoping you'd
be there."

"What for? He's the pathologist, not me."

"I think he wants to show off a little for you.
He doesn't often get so distinguished an audience, you know."

"I'm flattered, but—"

"And the truth is, I would be more comfortable as well. Not that Roussillot isn't perfectly
competent, of course, but all the same...well,
you know how it is, and inasmuch as you're
here in any event—"

"Okay, sure. I doubt if I'll be any help, but tell
me how to get there."

He used the pen chained to the reception desk
to jot down the instructions. "Thanks, I'll see
you in a little while. Oh, and please—will you
tell Roussillot to feel perfectly free to get started
without me? In fact, encourage him to." Watching that first big "Y" incision—clavicles to
pubis—was something he could easily live
without.

"Who was it?" Julie asked, looking up a moment later. "Anything important?"

"Joly," Gideon said. "They found Bousquet.
He killed himself, apparently right after murdering Jacques. He used the same rifle that
killed Ely."

"Really!" She put down her pen. "So that's

that," she said thoughtfully after a few moments. "All the loose ends have been tied up."

"Yeah. That's what's bothering me about it."

Julie looked at him with her head cocked. "Why should tying up the loose ends bother you?"

"Because *every* loose end is tied up. Every question is answered. Who faked the Tayac find? Jacques. Who murdered Ely? Jacques and Bousquet together. Who murdered Jacques? Bousquet. Who killed Bousquet? Bousquet killed himself. End of story, case closed. No more questions to ask, and nobody to ask them of if we did have them."

"But it happens that way sometimes, doesn't it? Murderers do kill themselves. I still don't see the problem."

"Look, Julie, one of the things I've learned about people murdering each other is that it's never neat, it's never cut-and-dried. It's always messy, there are *always* loose ends, ambiguities, things that don't add up. But this package is too...too tidy, that's all."

"Gideon, didn't you tell me the other day that I was getting too melodramatic? Well, to tell you the truth—"

"All right, think about the air rifle for a minute. Why would Bousquet have hung on to it for three years? Did he take it with him to Corsica? And especially—why would he bring it back here?"

"Well, presumably he did show up with murder on his mind."

"But why bring the Cobra? An air rifle, even a super-high-powered one like this one, still makes a lousy weapon. Even your cheapo Saturday-night special would beat it for killing power. Besides that, it's awkward. It's big, and hard to hide, and I think you need air from a diving tank or something to charge it...and anyway, he didn't shoot Jacques, he hit him with a hand ax. I'm telling you, something's off. We're being had."

"I remember when I first met you, before you were the Skeleton Detective," Julie said wistfully, "you were such a nice, innocent, mild-mannered professor. You trusted everyone, you didn't see trickery and deception everywhere you looked."

"You're right. That was before I learned the First Rule of Forensic Analysis."

"Which is?"

"When in doubt, think dirty," he said, laughing. "Look, I'd better get going. They want me in Périgueux, at the morgue. For the autopsy, I'm sorry to say. I should be back in three or four hours."

"Lucky you," Julie said, getting up. "Well, I'll drive you. It's starting to rain again."

"No, don't bother. I'm fine, really."

"No, you're not fine."

"Yes, I am fine. Anyway, I want to think this stuff through on the way."

"That, my darling absentminded professor, is what I'm worried about. I've seen you drive while you were thinking something through, and it's a terrifying sight—no one on the road is safe. I'll drive, you think. And anyway," she added, reaching into the leather purse on the floor beside her, "I have the keys."

Once in Périgueux, with the rain tapering off and the sun beginning to peek through, they left the car in a parking garage near the Arènes, the public gardens on the site of the Gallo-Roman arena, and found a sidewalk café overlooking some of the ancient tumbled blocks of stone, where they agreed to meet again in two hours. In the meantime, Gideon suggested, it might be nice to have an afternoon espresso, and perhaps even a bite, before he reported to the police commissariat.

"Not that I don't enjoy your company," Julie said, stirring sugar into her coffee at an awninged table, "but I thought you were in a hurry. Aren't they waiting for you?"

"Oh, I don't think another half hour's going to make any difference. Besides, the longer I take to get there, the farther along Roussillot's going to be on the autopsy, which suits me fine."

"It does? I would have thought that the farther it goes the worse it gets."

"Not to me it doesn't. The longer the cutting goes on, the less the thing on the table resembles a human being. It's just a pile—well, separate piles, really—of intestines, liver, spleen—the lungs and heart come out early, you see—"

"Whup-whup." Julie held up her hand, traffic-cop-style. "I get the idea. Thank you *so* much for explaining. Here, you're welcome to my tart, if you like. I can't imagine what happened to my appetite."

"I'm sorry, honey," he said sincerely, then sighed. "Well, I've probably procrastinated about as much as I can get away with. I'd better be on my way." He tossed off the last of his coffee, stood up, and bent to kiss her. "See you in a couple of hours. Have fun."

She gave him a sympathetic smile. "You have fun too."

At the commissariat, he was met at the front desk by Joly, who led him downstairs to the autopsy room. (Like most autopsy rooms, it was in the basement, where there were no windows to distract the technicians on the inside or to spoil the day of any innocents who might happen to look in from the outside.)

On the way, he succinctly filled Gideon in on what had been learned so far. That the corpse was Bousquet's had been confirmed with visual identifications, by his landlady, by Émile Grize, and by Audrey Godwin-Pope. That the weapon found under his body was the same one that had killed Ely Carpenter had also been established: the ballistics section had compared the rifling of the Cobra's barrel to the rifling marks on the pellet found under Carpenter's body in the *abri* and determined that they matched.

"What about Bousquet?" Gideon asked. "Did you find the bullet—I mean, the pellet?"

"It's still in his body, unless Roussillot has removed it in the last few minutes. But X-rays have been taken, and it shows up quite clearly—a wasp-waisted pellet of the same approximate size as the one that killed Carpenter. We'll know for certain later, but I think that for now we can assume that the same weapon was used in both cases."

"Lucien," Gideon asked, stopping him on the landing between floors, "how positive are you that it *is* a suicide?"

Joly looked down his long nose at him. "Do you doubt it?"

"I'm just asking."

Joly shrugged. "Well...fairly positive, I'd say. No, quite positive, but I'll leave it to Roussillot to explain the medical details to you. As you'll see, the trajectory of the projectile, the nature of the wound itself—oh, all sorts of things point to suicide, along with certain psychological tendencies.... You seem a little doubtful, Gideon, or am I mistaken?"

"Frankly, *you* seem a little doubtful, Lucien."

"I? No, not at all," Joly said doubtfully. "Roussillot makes an excellent case."

"Then what's bothering you?"

"Nothing is bothering me." Irritably, he produced and lit a cigarette. "All right, to tell you the truth, it's only that everything...all these events...they come together so, so—"

"Neatly?"

"Yes, precisely!" Joly said, jabbing with the cigarette for emphasis. "There is no Carpenter to question, no Beaupierre to question, and now no Bousquet to question. Nobody! The snake begins at its own tail, swallows itself, and disappears entirely, and we are left with no choice but to take things as they appear. Has that occurred to you?"

"You know, now that you mention it, I think it *has* crossed my mind. Come on, we might as well see what Roussillot's come up with."

The autopsy room was small but up-to-date: a square, unsettlingly antiseptic room with walls of glazed white brick, harsh fluorescent ceiling lights, stainless-steel sinks, and two doors, one a swinging hospital-type door from the corridor, through which Joly and Gideon entered, the other a massive stainless-steel affair leading to the refrigerated storage area beyond.

In the center was a single zinc autopsy table fitted out with its own double sink, hoses, and drains at one end to flush away the many sorts of gunk that needed flushing away, and above it a microphone for in-process dictation, a couple of spotlights on tracks, and a hanging meat-market-type scale (an appropriate device, Gideon reflected) with a basin for weighing various body parts.

Roussillot, clad in a clean white lab coat, was waiting for them beside the table, on which lay the nude, hairy, supine body of a man, his head propped up on a curved plastic neck rest, his hair stiff and wild. A black hole in almost the exact center of his chest, at the sternal notch marking the midpoint of the border between thorax and abdomen, stood out starkly against the putty-colored skin, which had by now begun to slough off here and there. Other marks of decay were unpleasantly evident as well, but Gideon was relieved to see that the corpse had been washed, which had gotten rid of the maggots, and that there wasn't much smell; he had steeled himself for a gagging stench, considering that the dead man had been lying outdoors for several days in warm, humid weather.

That was the good news. The bad news was that the body was untouched by the knife. Despite Gideon's cowardly dawdling at the café, Roussillot had kept his word and waited for him.

He made himself take a hard look at the face. Discoloration, insect activity, and bloating had had their usual disagreeable effects, but it was still possible to get some idea of the living man's appearance.

"Well, it's not 'Dr. Roussillot,'" he said to Joly. "I can tell you that much."

Roussillot was understandably startled, but Joly quickly explained, to the pathologist's loud amusement.

"Well, Dr. Oliver," Roussillot said, his blue

eyes bright, "I look forward enormously to working with you. As you see"—he pointed hospitably to a wheeled side table with an assortment of shining instruments on it: scalpels, scissors, forceps, probes, saws—"we are all ready for you. Enough for two, and I think we'd better get started. There's a coat for you on the rack; gloves in the box."

"Uh, thanks, but can we hold off for just a minute? Lucien's been telling me that you're pretty certain it's a suicide."

"No, no, you'll never catch me saying 'certain,' not in this business. But the probability is extremely high, as I'm sure you can see for yourself."

"I'm a little out of my element here, Doctor. Perhaps you could show me?"

Roussillot gave him a grateful look. "With pleasure. Now then." He was practically rubbing his hands with professorial joy. "First of all..."

First of all there was the nature of the external wound to be considered. As Professor Oliver had no doubt observed, the crater in Bousquet's chest, now so clean and bloodless, was obviously a contact wound. Although there had been no charring of the flesh, no powder-stippling, no soot—the professor was aware that an air rifle's charge, being no more than compressed air, would leave no such residue?—it was still eminently clear that the muzzle had been placed directly against the chest. This could be definitively shown by bringing the suicide weapon itself into contact with the wound. Here Roussillot, reaching behind him, grasped a sleek, modernistic-looking rifle with unblued stainless-steel barrels, a gleaming walnut stock, and a green tag dangling from the trigger guard. Holding it above his head with both hands, he slowly lowered it, only a little theatrically, until the muzzle rested directly on the wound, neatly covering it.

As Professor Oliver could plainly see, the faint purple-brown bruises around the wound were neither more nor less than a muzzle stamp from this weapon; this very weapon and no other. The precise imprint of the muzzle itself could clearly be made out, as well as the end of the front sight immediately above it, and even the rim of one of the two air-reservoir cylinders just below it. In fact, an examination by lens would show that an imperfection in the steel of the air reservoir was exactly reproduced in the skin.

It was all as he said, and Gideon nodded his agreement—as far as it went. "I can't argue with that, Doctor, but after all, a contact wound doesn't necessarily mean a suicide."

"Necessarily, no," said Roussillot. "Usually, yes."

"You are speaking of a rifle, of course, and not a handgun, Roussillot," Joly said. "And so it is, Gideon. How many murderers equipped with a rifle would choose to walk up to their victims in order to place the muzzle of their weapons conveniently against their chests before firing?"

"Yes, well, I guess that's true enough."

"There are other considerations," said Roussillot, "all of which must be taken together. For example, there are no indications of struggle, and—although the laboratory has not finished its work—there seems to be nothing suggestive under the fingernails."

"Mmm."

"Let us turn to the mind, the psychological conditions. Now, I don't claim to be a psychiatrist, but I've made a small study of the pathology of behavior as well as that of the bodily processes, and it seems to me that everything we know about this man's history points to his having a reactive-depressive personality with an inclination toward violent, sociopathic, and self-destructive behavior."

It was clear that something more than "mm" was expected of him, and Gideon did his best to be tactful. "Yes, well, I can certainly see what you mean, but I'm afraid you're really out of my line now."

"If you combine these traits with a repressed—"

Gideon headed him off as politely as he could. "And what about the trajectory of the pellet?"

"Ah, the trajectory, yes. Let us see what we have."

He took an eight-inch probe from the table

and delicately slipped it, rounded handle side down, into the hole in Bousquet's chest, as much as possible letting it slide in of its own weight, down the tunnel that the pellet had torn through flesh and muscle, nerve and blood vessel. It went in about four inches and stopped—the dull *clink* when it hit the pellet was audible—and when Roussillot let go of it it remained in place, held by the tunnel's collapsed walls.

The pathologist, after respectfully waiting to see if Gideon now chose to assume the lecturer's mantle, happily took it back on his own shoulders.

"As you know, Professor, we cannot assume that we are seeing a *precise* representation of the angle traveled by the pellet, because we have no way of allowing for the movement of the thorax and its contents during life as a result of breathing, or of the possible distension of the viscera by food or liquid, or even of the effects of gravity, inasmuch as the body is now on its back rather than upright, as it presumably—but not necessarily—was at the time of the shooting. Nevertheless, we do have before us a reliable, if approximate, indication of the pellet's path. And as we see, it flew straight back, never deviating from the medial plane, but inclining slightly upward, that is to say, in a dorso-superior—"

"Roussillot, will you never get to the point?" Joly said. "And can a man smoke a cigarette in here?"

"No, he may not," said Roussillot. "Now, to

continue—and I apologize for stating what I know must be obvious to you, Professor—a man intent on killing himself with a rifle is likely to do it in a seated position with the butt of the rifle propped on the ground—and with good reason. Shooting oneself while on one's feet would be awkward in the extreme. Holding it out without support would put a strain on the arms. It would produce unsteadiness. Would you agree?"

He waited for a reply, but Gideon had largely stopped listening. He was silent, working things out for himself, staring at the angled probe, barely hearing Roussillot. Still, a part of him sensed that he'd been asked a question. "Hmm," he said vaguely.

"All right, then," said the easily satisfied Roussillot. "He sits—and by the way, allow me to point out that the body was found at the base of a boulder which would have made a suitable chair—he sits, enabling him to rest the stock of the weapon near his feet. If he has chosen, as in this case, not to blow out his brains but to explode his heart, he places the muzzle firmly against the center of his chest, where he believes his heart to be, and where indeed it is. He takes a breath, he makes his good-byes, he quiets the welling panic, the doubts that rise in his breast like swirling—"

"Roussillot, for God's sake," Joly snarled.

"Ah, the man, like others of his kind, has no sense of drama, of romance," said Roussillot with a good-natured sigh. "In any case, our subject eventually pulls the trigger. The path of the projectile is naturally front to back and upward through the body." He gestured at the probe, still in the wound. "As indeed it is with our friend Bousquet. And there is my argument. Death by his own hand. Would you agree, Professor?"

"What?" said Gideon, surfacing.

"Do you agree with Roussillot's reconstruction?" Joly asked, eyeing him closely.

"No," Gideon said, "I don't."

CHAPTER
23

"You *don't*?" Roussillot cried, his voice breaking.

"Well, what I meant," Gideon stammered, thinking that he'd been too blunt, that he'd stung Roussillot's professional pride, "was only that—"

But he'd misread the pathologist. Roussillot was delighted. "You see?" he crowed to Joly. "Didn't I promise you he'd find something?" And to Gideon with every sign of genuine and unselfish enthusiasm: "All right, colleague, tell us, where has my reasoning gone wrong? What was my fatal mistake?"

It wasn't his reasoning that had gone wrong, Gideon told him gently, but his method. Roussillot had made a mistake that many a forensic pathologist—many a forensic anthropologist, for that matter—had made before him: he had thought the matter through, he had analyzed it piece by piece and step by step...but he hadn't gone one step further and physically reconstructed it, he hadn't tried to go through the actual motions to make sure that what had worked out so neatly in his mind would work out equally well in the real world.

"Why don't we run it through for ourselves and see what we come up with?" Gideon said.

"One moment," Roussillot said. A pale green sheet lay furled at Bousquet's feet. He pulled it up and decorously covered the body with it, an act that Gideon appreciated. "Now then," he said, glowing with anticipation.

Gideon pointed at the rifle, propped in its corner. "Can I demonstrate with that?"

Joly nodded. "Ballistics has finished with it."

Gideon reached for it. "We're positive this thing isn't loaded, right?"

"Neither loaded nor charged," said Joly. "It's perfectly safe."

"Okay," Gideon said. "As you rightly said, Dr. Roussillot, if I want to kill myself with this, the chances are I'm going to sit down to do it, so..." He pulled a folding chair out from its place along the wall and set it down in an open space on the floor. "Now..." He was seized with a sudden inspiration. "Would you mind being our victim?" he asked, offering both the chair and the weapon to the pathologist.

"Certainly," a beaming Roussillot said, taking the Cobra. "What would you like me to do?"

"Just sit down and...shoot yourself."

"Delighted."

"Lucien, you wouldn't happen to know

whether Bousquet was right- or left-handed, would you?" Gideon asked.

"As it happens, I would. We have some examples of his handwriting—receipts and the like—and they all show a backward-leaning slant, quite characteristic and unmistakable."

"Backward-leaning—so he was left-handed?"

"Yes."

"I'm right-handed," Roussillot said. "Shall I use my left hand to pull the trigger?"

"No, just do it the most natural way," Gideon said. "We'll extrapolate."

Roussillot, openly enjoying himself, settled his rounded form in the chair, rested the butt of the rifle on the floor in front of him, found that it was too close to allow him to set the other end against his chest, and moved it out another foot. "Like this? Which finger shall I use to pull the trigger?"

Gideon shrugged. "Just do what comes naturally."

Roussillot readjusted the rifle and leaned forward to reach the trigger.

"Wait!" said the keenly watching Joly. "It's upside down."

"Well, yes," Roussillot said defensively. "It's only that it seems more natural that way. The rifle balances itself more comfortably. Also it makes it easier to pull—that is, to push—the trigger—" Abruptly, he realized what Joly was driving at. "The muzzle stamp on his chest—it's

not upside down, it's right side up—the gun-
sight is *above* the muzzle!"

"That's right," Gideon said, having scored his
first point. "People who shoot other people do it
that way, right side up; that's why the sight is
where it is. But people who shoot themselves do
it this way, the way you're doing it. It's possible
to do it the other way, but the odds are against
it."

"The odds?" said Joly. "Gideon, if that's what
you're basing—"

"Give me a chance to finish," Gideon said.
"Would you continue, Dr. Roussillot?"

"Continue what?" said Roussillot, who had
begun to get up, thinking the demonstration
was done.

"You haven't actually shot yourself yet."

"Yes, please shoot yourself, Roussillot," Joly
said.

The pathologist sat down again, rearranged
the rifle the way it had been before—upside
down, butt on the floor, muzzle against his
chest—and once more leaned forward to get to
the trigger. It was a longer reach than he'd estimated, and he had to shift himself to the front of
the seat and hunch over the barrel to make it.

"I find that the most natural way would be to
do it with my thumb," he observed, "like this. I
place my thumb inside the trigger guard. With
my other hand I keep the muzzle against my
chest. I lean over still a little more and push—"

"Stop," Gideon said. "Hold that position if you can, just like that."

Roussillot froze, except for his eyes, which he screwed up to look at Gideon.

"Okay," Gideon said. "If you fired right now, what path would the pellet take?"

"It's somewhat hard to tell from this position," said Roussillot, "but, frankly, I have no reason to think it would be any different from—"

"No, you're wrong," Joly said excitedly. "I can see. It would enter on a *downward* path, not an upward one! By heaven, Gideon!"

"Downward?" exclaimed a flabbergasted Roussillot. "But how can that be? The butt rests on the floor, the barrel inclines upward—"

"Yes, yes," Joly said, "but *you* incline forward, and your body is hunched, curved, crouched over the weapon. The path through your body would be slightly downward, I assure you." He looked at Gideon, his piercing eyes alight. "This changes everything. It means—"

"May I straighten up now?" asked Roussillot, his voice a little choked from hunching over.

Gideon put a hand on his shoulder. "Hold it just a second longer if you can, Doctor. I want you to see something else. You notice that to reach the trigger you had to rotate—"

"I see!" Joly said, too impatient to let him finish. "By reaching with his right arm he turns his body counterclockwise a few degrees, so that when he pulls the trigger the muzzle is pointing not straight back through his chest at his spine, but slightly right to left—which is therefore the path that the projectile would necessarily follow."

"Why, yes, you're right," Roussillot said with dawning appreciation. "I can see that now—it's quite obvious, really. And in the case of a left-handed man it would be reversed. The projectile would travel from left to right."

"But in Bousquet's case," said Joly, "it did neither—it flew straight back." He had forgotten about Roussillot's no-smoking rule and lighted up. Roussillot, engrossed with trajectories, failed to notice.

"That's right," Gideon said. "Add that to the facts that it was angled up, not down, and that the muzzle stamp was wrong way around. Three separate things, and they all point *away* from suicide."

"And toward homicide," Joly said.

"And so one more lovely theory falls victim to squalid fact," said Roussillot, laughing with satisfaction as he straightened up and propped the rifle back in its corner. "Remarkably done, Professor Oliver."

"Oh, it's not that remarkable, really," said Gideon honestly. "It's just that I happened to be part of a case that was a lot like this a few months ago. The King County medical examiner walked me through it just the way I did with you."

"How wonderful it must be to live in America," Roussillot said. "So many murders, so much to be learned."

Gideon laughed. "That's one way to look at it."

"And now," said Roussillot, slipping on a pair of plastic gloves and picking up a scalpel, "I think we'd better get started, don't you?"

"Good heavens, look at the time," Joly exclaimed, looking at his watch. "Much to be done, much to be done. Well, I'll leave the two of you to it, then," he said, making for the door. "A policeman's time is not his own."

Chuckling, Roussillot watched him go. "Amazing, isn't it, how chicken-livered they can be when it comes to opening someone up."

"Amazing," Gideon agreed, looking enviously after the departing Joly.

Roussillot returned to the autopsy table, adjusted the microphone, folded the sheet back down, and flicked on the spotlight above the head of the table. Bousquet's greasy yellow-gray torso and ruined head jumped into brilliant focus.

"Colleague, would you care to make the first incision?" Roussillot asked with a sweet smile, offering the knife.

"Uh, no, thanks. If it's all the same to you, I'll just watch," Gideon said. "From back here."

"But you said his fingerprints were on the rifle," Julie said, starting up the car.

"They were. But that doesn't mean he was alive at the time."

"It doesn't? Can you do that? Put a dead person's fingerprints on something? And get away with it, I mean?"

"There's no way to tell he was dead, as far as I know, as long as the fingertips have some oil or perspiration on them. Or grease, or blood, or anything else that'll leave a mark, for that matter. This was a setup, Julie, arranged to look like a suicide. I'm sure of it."

"Wow," she said softly. "But doesn't that mean—" She paused and threw a worried glance at him. Gideon was sprawled in his seat, his head tipped back against the headrest and his legs extended to the extent that the Peugeot would allow. "Gideon, you look utterly washed-out."

"I don't like autopsies. I'm not too keen on dead bodies, in general."

"You're sure in a funny line of work, then."

"I sure am. You think maybe Uncle Bert was right? That I'd have been better off in cost-accounting?"

"No, I don't. Look, why don't you put back the seat and take a nap for a while? Just relax. It'll do you good. You think you're all recovered from the other day, but you're not, trust me. Give those neuroaxons a rest. I'll wake you up when we get to Les Eyzies."

"You know, I just might do that." He adjusted the back of the seat to as close to horizontal as it would go and settled back. The clouds had closed in again, and with them had come the rain, a cooler, thinner rain, pattering on the car's roof and running down the windshield in irregular rivulets. He watched them for a while, then closed his eyes to the steady, lulling *whish-whish* of the wipers.

"Doesn't that mean what?" he said, putting up the seat half an hour later and finding that they were on the outskirts of Les Eyzies, just crossing the little bridge over the Vézère.

"Feeling better?"

"A lot better," he said truthfully, the sights, smells, and sounds of the autopsy having receded. "You started to ask me something before: 'Doesn't that mean...?'"

It took her a moment to remember. "Oh, yes, I was thinking that if the suicide was a setup, then how do we know that the business with the ring wasn't a setup too?"

"That's exactly what I believe it was. I don't think it came off during a struggle, I think it was planted there. I don't think Bousquet killed Jacques at all. I don't think he killed anyone."

"But how would they have gotten hold of his ring?"

"Easy. They just took it off his cold, dead finger. You see, I think Bousquet was probably killed before Jacques was—which, may I point out, would have made it particularly hard for him to murder Jacques."

"Come again? I thought you said Bousquet had only been dead a couple of days. And Jacques was killed Thursday—one, two, *three* days ago."

"No, I said *Roussillot* finally came to the conclusion that he's been dead a couple of days. I came to a different one. I think it's been a good three days—more likely four or five."

"But Roussillot's a professional pathologist."

"That's true enough. And I'm just a lousy skeleton detective."

"No, you know what I mean. I'm not surprised that you'd know more about bullet trajectories and so on, but wouldn't he know more about the time-of-death aspect—decomposition, bodily changes—than you do?" She glanced at him. "Or don't you think he's competent?"

"No, he's competent enough."

"So how can you be that far apart? A two- or three-day difference of opinion wouldn't be a lot if you were talking about a corpse that'd been out there for a month, but this is a fresh one. The indicators should still be pretty definitive."

She clapped her hand over her mouth. "Oh, my God, listen to me, I'm actually learning this stuff."

"And you're absolutely right," Gideon said. "The indicators ought to be more definitive. They usually are. But this is just one of those cases where they're all over the map. He's looking at one set, I'm looking at another."

"I don't understand."

"Well, what we found...are you sure you want to hear this?"

"Yes, I do," she said staunchly. "I want to know what's going on too, and if you can stand watching an autopsy, I guess I can stand hearing about one. And better before dinner than during." She pulled the car to the curb near the center of the village, shut off the ignition, and turned attentively toward him, her elbow on the steering wheel. "Proceed. Only no gratuitous repulsiveness, please."

Gideon was no more in favor of gratuitous repulsiveness than Julie was and explained, as nongraphically as he could, that the timetables of the various processes of decay and putrefaction, by which the time of death was usually estimated, were seriously out of whack in Bousquet's case. The withered, puttylike skin and the advanced decomposition of the brain (when the skull had been sawn open there had been little more than gray-brown slush inside, as he didn't bother to tell her) went along with his estimate of four or five days. On the other hand, the relative freshness of the abdominal organs—minimal bloating, color change, or odor—supported Roussillot's estimate of only two days. And that was it, in a nutshell. Roussillot was inclined to go with the insides, Gideon with the outside and with the brain.

"You know, there's something familiar about all that," Julie said. She'd relaxed; apparently she'd been expecting something worse. "Weren't you involved in something similar once?"

"No. I'd remember it if I had."

"Hmm. But it's pretty unusual, isn't it? To have differences like that?"

"Unusual, yes, but it happens. Maybe one part of the body was mostly in the shade and another part in the sun, or some parts, being in contact with the ground, stayed cooler, or maybe the funny weather, hot in the daytime and chilly at night, had something to do with it. Or it could have had something to do with what he'd been eating—all kinds of things come into play. I could easily be wrong, Roussillot could easily be right. We'll just have to wait and see what the lab comes up with."

"Right, good thinking, I'm for that." She plucked the key out of the ignition. "Okay, have we finished talking about people's insides?"

Gideon laughed. "Is it safe to go get something to eat, you mean? I think so, yes."

The rain had slackened off again and the filtered late-afternoon sunshine had brought some life back to the village streets in the form of strollers and shoppers. A few feet from their car, waiters on the sidewalk terrace of the Café de la Mairie were drying chairs and tables, and it was there that they went, neither of them being in the mood for a full-fledged French dinner.

They were halfway through the *spécialité de la maison*—*soupe Périgordine*, a rich, garlicky broth swimming with beans, potatoes, and lettuce, with an egg whipped into it and two round slices of bread floating on top—before the subject of Jean Bousquet came up again.

"Why?" Julie said, thinking out loud. "What would have been the advantage of making it look as if Bousquet killed himself? Wouldn't it have been easier and safer to just leave his body in the woods—maybe bury him—where he'd never be found? Or at least not for years."

"Ah, but then there'd be some of those loose ends left. Or as Lucien might put it, the snake wouldn't have swallowed itself. The police would still be poking into things, trying to find him."

"All right, I can see that, but why in the world use that funny air rifle to do it? Was that supposed to mean something?"

"Good question. Possibly it was to 'help' us make the connection between Bousquet and Ely's death. Maybe to imply that Bousquet was consumed with guilt and self-recrimination over it."

Julie tipped her head to the side. "I don't know, it sounds pretty far-fetched to me."

"Yeah, me too."

She spooned up soup for a few moments, thinking. "We *are* assuming whoever killed Ely also killed Bousquet, right? And Jacques too?

"Sure, Occam's razor *and* the Law of Interconnected Monkey Business tell us that. Whatever's going on, it's all connected."

"I agree. All right, now tell me this: why would the murderer have kept that rifle all this time? He couldn't have known he'd want it again three years later to kill Bousquet."

"That's a *real* good question. And who is 'he'? Who are we talking about? Montfort? Audrey? Émile? Pru?" And as an afterthought: "Madame Lacouture?"

"And *why*?" Julie asked. "Above all, why? Okay, let's say Carpenter was killed over the hoax, one way or another. I can think of several possibilities for that. But why was Jacques killed? And Bousquet?"

"And what was Bousquet doing back here anyway? If he's really been dead four or five days, that means he was here before anybody even knew I'd identified the bones as Ely's. So what brought him? What did he want?"

"Whew, we don't have very many answers, do we?"

"No," Gideon said, "but are we ever doing great on questions."

CHAPTER
24

The "new" home of the Périgord Institute of Prehistory was actually five centuries old, a large, rectangular stone house that had originally been an outbuilding of the medieval cliffside chateau—a granary, perhaps, or a winery, or even a dovecote—but owned for most of the last century by a family with tobacco holdings in the nearby Lot Valley. When the last male scion had died the previous year at the age of 101 and the house had come on the market, it had been bought by the Université du Périgord and sparklingly refurbished for the use of the institute, which would have its own quarters at last, after thirty years of renting space from the foie gras cooperative.

Like the chateau itself, the structure had been erected on a long, level terrace about a third of the way up the cliff, its back wall built into a recess in the cliff face, its front coming out to the very edge of the terrace, so that from the big

windows of the main room, mullioned in the
Baroque style, there was a straight drop of one
hundred feet down to the main street and an un-
obstructed view over the village and across the
green valley of the Vézère.

The light-filled windows, some of which had
been swung open to dissipate the remaining
fumes from the recent painting, made a splendid
backdrop for the speakers, of whom there were
an alarming number. Everybody who was anybody in Les Eyzies was there: the mayor, the
deputy mayor, the nine-member municipal coun-
cil, the administrative magistrate, and, of course,
the prefect of police. Unfortunately, most felt the
need to utter a few words of civic benediction
and of eulogy for Jacques, which made for a
long, long morning.

Conspicuously absent from the table of hon-
ored guests at the front was Jacques's wife, who
had responded to her invitation with a curt reference to other commitments.

"One would think she holds us personally responsible for his death," said Émile Grize, sitting next to Pru McGinnis in the row of folding
chairs immediately behind Julie and Gideon.

"Like maybe," Pru said out of the corner of
her mouth, "it might just have something to do
with the choice of weapon? Duh."

It was meant to relieve the general tedium
and sobriety, and Gideon smiled, but a glance at
Julie showed that they were both thinking the
same thing: Madame Beaupierre was right—one

of them *was* responsible. The possible *whys* behind Jacques's death, and the other murders as well, might still be murky, but the possible *whos* were crystal-clear. When you took everything into consideration, starting back with the hoax itself, you couldn't get away from the conclusion that it had to be somebody from the institute: Audrey, Montfort, Émile, Pru. And as a long shot, Madame Lacouture. That was it, the total list of suspects, all of them right there in the room with them, listening to the obsequies for Jacques, gravely smiling or soberly nodding as the situation required.

The speeches ground on, made more formal and stilted by the fact that the main speaker, the director of the Horizon Foundation, Bob Cram— an administrator better known for his scratch golf than his linguistic skills—felt obliged to deliver his address in French, in keeping with the institute's bilingual tradition. But at last they were over and the fifty or so people in the room rose, to the creaking of many aged and not-so-aged knees, and shuffled gratefully toward the bar that had been set up in front of the windows, where coffee, soft drinks, bottled water, and cordials were available. Audrey's presentation as the new director was yet to come, after which everyone could go home for lunch.

Julie and Gideon got their bottles of Évian and spent most of the break chatting somewhat awkwardly with Audrey, whose eyeglasses were still patched with Scotch tape, but who was otherwise more her old self, although stiff and formal in her unaccustomed black skirt-suit; and with a remote, brusque Michel Montfort, no hand at social amenities even at the best of times.

As they took their seats again, Julie put her hand on Gideon's arm. "Tom Cabell!"

"Pardon?"

"Tom Cabell, your friend from Calgary, the medical examiner, the one with the squinchy little mustache—"

"Julie, I know who Tom Cabell is. What about him?"

"It was when the AAFS convention was in Seattle, remember? And we all went out to dinner in the Space Needle. *That's* when I heard about it."

"I suppose," Gideon said mildly, "that if I wait patiently, you'll eventually let me in on this."

"Gideon, I'm trying to tell you that I remember the case I was trying to think of—the one like Bousquet, where the different indicators didn't match and they had all that trouble coming up with the time of death? I thought it was one of yours, but it was one of his. Don't you remember? He was going on and on about it over the veal scallopine and I was doing my best not to listen, but I couldn't help hearing."

"Julie, I honestly don't—"

It hit him like an electric shock. "I remember!" he said, sitting bolt upright. "You're right! I wasn't thinking of it because it wasn't a murder at all, or even a forensic case, it was just a hiker who got—who got..." He stared at her as the full impact hit him. "Julie, do you realize—"

"*S-s-s-t,*" Émile hissed from behind them. Audrey had begun her address.

Gideon didn't hear two words of it. He was scowling out the windows and into space, not thinking as much as simply sitting there, barely breathing, letting things fall into place as if by gravity. They'd been wrong about everything— everything. It was as if they'd been trying to play some gigantic, frustrating pinball game, only without their being aware of it the game board had been upside down from the beginning. Now, in a single instant, it had been turned right side up, and the little steel balls were rolling merrily about, bumping into flippers, setting off lights and buzzers, and plunking neatly and satisfyingly, one after another, into their cups.

"Christ, could it really be true?" he murmured, bringing an inquisitive arching of her eyebrows from Julie and another reproving *s-s-s-t* from Émile.

Gideon patted Julie's knee and broke from his chair. A few seconds later he was at the telephone in the reception area, calling Joly's office in Périgueux and being told that the inspector had gone to Les Eyzies. A second call to the local *mairie* brought Sergeant Peyrol to the phone to explain that Inspector Joly was conducting an important investigation and couldn't be disturbed.

"Disturb him, Sergeant. He'll thank you, take my word for it," he promised.

"Lucien," he said when Joly picked up the receiver, "we've been on one hell of a wild-goose chase."

"No," said Joly crossly, "you don't tell me."

"Listen, when you read that description of Bousquet to us yesterday, the one that was filed when he disappeared, the one that mentioned the ring—"

"Gideon, I'm in the middle of something. Can't this wait?"

"I don't think so, no. The description—it said what he was wearing, didn't it? What exactly did it say?"

"About what he was wearing three years ago? Why in the name of God do you—"

"Just find it, will you, please? Humor me, okay?"

Joly muttered resignedly into the telephone. Papers were shuffled, probably more noisily than was strictly necessary. "All right, I have it here. 'Green-and-white-plaid shirt with short sleeves, workman's blue trousers, moccasin-type shoes with no stockings.' All right?"

"And what—" He licked dry lips. Here came the crucial question. "What was he wearing when you found him yesterday?"

"Yesterday?" Joly cried incredulously. "What

was he wearing *yesterday*? What possible...
what possible..."

The astonished silence told Gideon he'd
guessed right. His chest expanded with the first
deep, full breath he'd taken in the last five minutes. "He was wearing the same clothes, wasn't
he?" he asked quietly.

"I...yes, that's right, the same clothes, but...
Gideon, what's this about?"

"Things are even weirder than we thought,
Lucien. Look, I'm at the new institute headquar-
ters up on the hill. Could you come on up here?
I think you might be wanting to make an arrest.
I'll meet you out front."

"He was *what*?" Joly exclaimed a few minutes
later, as they stood near the stone parapet that
ran along the edge of the cliffside terrace.

"Frozen," Gideon repeated.

Joly was huffing, as was Sergeant Peyrol, both
of them having tramped up the steep road from
the main street, and while he caught his breath
he glowered at Gideon almost accusingly.
"Frozen," he said again, as if trying out something unappetizing on his tongue.

"Yes, I think so," Gideon said, treading softly;
he was verging on snake-oil territory here. "My
guess is he's been sitting in a freezer somewhere
for the last three years."

Joly reflected for a moment, his lips slightly
pursed. "Dead, we may assume?"

"I'd have to say that's a pretty safe guess, yes."

"Yesterday, if I'm not mistaken, you said he'd been dead three *days*."

"I was a little off," Gideon admitted.

Peyrol, who didn't speak English but could understand some, laughed, converted it to a polite cough, and resumed his stiff military posture.

"Gideon," Joly said, leaning on the parapet and looking out over the trim tile roofs of the village, "how certain of this are you?"

"Pretty positive. I should have realized it right away. I just wasn't thinking along the right track."

It was the peculiar way the body had begun to decompose that should have told him, he explained as concisely as he could. Under ordinary circumstances, large-scale decomposition would begin in the dark, moist interior of the body, with rapid growth of bacteria in the lower intestines, resulting in the all-too-familiar bloating, discharges, and putrid smells. From there, the putrefaction would work its way outward while maggots and the like attacked the outside at a slower rate and worked inward.

But Bousquet's body showed the reverse: the internal organs were fresher than the skin. That was what happened when a body was frozen; the freezing killed off all the intestinal bacteria. But later, when it was unfrozen, it would be the surface that naturally thawed first and was therefore first to be available to new bacteria and other organisms. So decomposition proceeded from outside in—as it had in Bousquet's case. The skin was discolored, withered, sloughing off; the insides of the body had barely begun to break down.

Joly, having lit a Gitane, pondered this, continuing to stare across the Vézère Valley. "Not all of the insides. I looked at Roussillot's report. It says the brain was considerably decomposed."

"The head is smaller than the body. It thaws faster."

"Ah."

"And don't forget the clothes, Lucien—the very same clothes he had on the day he disappeared. How else do you explain that? I'm telling you, the guy's been in cold storage for the last three years, right up until you found him yesterday."

Joly made a decisive movement with his head, turned from the parapet, dropped his cigarette, and ground it out with his heel. He briskly straightened his jacket, buttoned both buttons, and tugged on his cuff-linked sleeves. "Shall we go in? I believe it's time to make that arrest."

"Don't you want to know who did it first?"

It was an uncharacteristically smug remark, and Gideon got what he deserved. "Oh, I know who did it," Joly said casually. "What I didn't know was how."

Inside, most of the crowd were milling about near the reopened bar. Audrey, who had finished her presentation a few moments earlier, was accepting congratulations and good wishes. Montfort was berating a small, miserable-looking man about some abstruse archaeological point. Julie was talking to Pru, Émile to Chris and Lynn Thelan, a couple of big American donors. With a quick glance around the room, Joly spotted his quarry. He strode purposefully over the wooden floor, his thin lips set, and waited until he was recognized.

"Yes?"

Joly drew his feet together and stood even a little straighter than usual. "Michel Georges Montfort, in accord with the provisions of the Code of Criminal Procedure I now place you under temporary detention until a warrant for your formal arrest and confinement on the charge of murder shall be obtained. Will you come with me now?"

It wasn't delivered loudly or even particularly doomfully, and yet it crackled through the room like a rifle shot. Conversations stopped in mid-sentence. Without anyone's having turned in an obvious way to stare, everybody was avidly watching the two men. Gideon had a dreamlike sense of being part of some surreal drawing-room tableau. Cups were balanced on saucers, cigarettes on lips, breathing suspended. The only movement was on the part of the man Montfort had been talking to, who shrank inconspicuously away, or as inconspicuously as possible under the circumstances, his feet sliding noiselessly backward over the floor.

To someone watching the scene from off to the side or from any distance, it would have seemed as if Montfort received Joly's pronouncement with no emotion whatever. Certainly he didn't blanch, or gasp, or flush with outrage or astonishment; his mouth didn't twitch, his body didn't jerk. His one visible reaction was to slowly roll the small cigar he was smoking from one side of his mouth to the other while Joly was speaking. His thumbs, which had been lodged in the pockets of his vest while he had been holding forth, remained there as he studied the equally impassive police inspector and weighed his reply.

But Gideon, standing twenty feet away near the windows, with the light at his back, was looking full into his face and saw an extraordinary series of expressions shoot across it with lightning speed: astonishment, disbelief, calculation, resignation, and finally decision, all in the space of two or three seconds.

"May I get my things?" he asked.

Joly inclined his head.

Montfort removed the cigar from his mouth and placed it in an ashtray on a nearby table, first tapping it to remove the ash. *As you see, I am in no hurry,* he seemed to be saying. *I am under no stress.*

On the wall a few feet from Gideon was a coat rack with a wire shelf above it. Although it hadn't rained since the day before, the skies were mixed, and many attendees had brought raincoats or umbrellas and left them there. Montfort removed a brown raincoat from the rack and a large furled black umbrella from the shelf. His eyes briefly met Gideon's, but now there was nothing at all in them; it was like looking into a statue's eyes. An ice-water chill trickled down Gideon's spine.

With the coat draped over his arm, Montfort turned back to the noiseless room and stood there, coolly appraising the throng of rapt, appalled faces.

Joly had only so much patience. "If you please—" he began tartly.

Gideon must have glanced at Joly as he was speaking, because he never saw the coat coming. He only knew that it had suddenly been thrown over his head, smelling of mildew and plunging him into darkness, and that almost at the same time he took a heavy blow at the junction of his neck and left shoulder. He flung the coat off just in time to see Montfort lashing out again with the umbrella, a heavy, old-fashioned one with steel shaft and spokes. This time, throwing up his arm, Gideon caught it flush on the point of the elbow. Tears of pain jumped to his eyes, but still he managed to catch hold of it as Montfort raised it again.

"Michel, don't be stupid. What—"

Montfort was a heavy man with burly, powerful shoulders, and Gideon had had to pull hard on the umbrella to hold it back. Unexpectedly, Montfort let go. Gideon stumbled backward, tripping over his own feet, almost falling.

Montfort came after him. "Bastard!" he said, trying clumsily to shove him aside and get by.

To the window, Gideon realized almost too late. To the open window, a hundred feet above the street. That's what this was about. Reaching out, he managed to clamp his hand on Montfort's upper arm just as the archaeologist got a grasp on the window frame. Struggling, Montfort balled up his other fist and smashed it into Gideon's face like a man driving nails with a hammer. He felt blood spurt from his nose. The heavy, quivering fist was raised again, and Gideon made a grab for that arm as well, using the thrust of his legs and the weight of his body to spin Montfort around and slam him hard against the wall beside the window.

The jolt seemed to take the fight out of the older man. "Gideon, don't let them do this to me," he whispered. Panting, he cast a terrified glance at the rapidly approaching Peyrol. His once-ruddy face was drained of blood, gray-white below the eyes, sickly blue around the mouth. "How can I face this? I beg you—let me go, let me get it over with." One hand plucked ineffectually at Gideon's hold.

For a moment, Gideon softened—a man of Montfort's stature and accomplishments and very real contributions to endure a trial for murder, to go to prison for the rest of his life!—but only for a moment. He brushed Montfort's hand away. His own hand, which had very nearly loosened, tightened on Montfort's arm.

"You stood behind Jacques and crushed his skull," he said through set teeth. "You killed Ely." *And you damn well cost me a bunch of neuroaxons I can't afford, let's not forget that.* "You—"

"Permit me, monsieur," said Sergeant Peyrol to Gideon. And to Montfort, quite sternly, "This won't do, monsieur. Come with me at once, please."

Montfort, with a final, reproachful look at Gideon and a last, longing look at the open window and the empty space beyond, lowered his head and went with the sergeant.

Julie came up to Gideon as the room began buzzing with excited whispers again. "Are you all right?"

"Sure, I'm fine. I think I'd better go along with them to the *mairie*."

She handed him a packet of tissues. "You might want to wipe your nose first."

CHAPTER
25

"Visitez…l'usine," Julie said, practicing her French by reading aloud from the sign in the window of a pâté shop. She brightened momentarily, having successfully translated it, but her expression changed as the meaning sank in. "Yuck. Why would anyone want to visit a chopped-liver factory?"

Gideon shook his head. "Got me."

"It certainly couldn't be anywhere near as entertaining as what you've just been telling me about intestinal bacteria and decomposing brains."

"Probably not as edifying either."

They were on the main street of the village. When Gideon had returned from the *mairie* an hour before and had begun to fill her in, Julie had interrupted: "How about getting out and taking a walk while you tell me? I could use the fresh air—and it'd help to be rubbing shoulders with real, everyday, normal people who're talking about something besides murder for a change."

Having spent most of the afternoon sitting in on Montfort's interrogation as a sort of interpreter of things scientific, Gideon felt much the same way. Strictly speaking, Montfort hadn't been required to submit to being questioned until Joly got his warrant, but he'd waived his right to silence. With his frustrated attorney there but unable to persuade him to shut up, he had woodenly answered question after question in a listless, unconcerned voice that had made Gideon's skin crawl, the voice of a man no longer part of this world.

The first thing he'd done on getting back to the hotel was to stand under a steaming shower until his skin felt as if it had been wire-brushed. Then he'd put on fresh clothes. After that he'd wanted to be around some everyday people too, and they had strolled the length of the village, first south through the riverside park, where mothers with old-fashioned prams, youngsters on swings, and old men playing *pétanque* had restored their faith in normal—or at least normal-looking—people. Then back along the shop-lined main street with its tourists and shoppers, also reassuringly ordinary-looking.

"All right, I understand about his having been frozen for the last three years," Julie said as they started walking again. "But why Montfort? How did you settle on him?"

"Ah, that followed pretty naturally. It was

something you said a few days ago. Do you remember telling me that it was Jacques who
hired Madame Lacouture?"

"Sure. From Paris, the same time he rehired
Pru, his first week as director."

"Right. And do you remember my telling
you that she was the one who backed up Montfort's story about Bousquet's phoning the institute?"

Julie nodded.

"Well, Montfort and Lacouture were the only
ones who actually talked to him, and they both
made it clear they had no doubt that's who it
was, but—"

"But Lacouture couldn't know that, could
she?" Julie said excitedly. "If she didn't start
until Jacques became the director, she wouldn't
have been with the institute when Bousquet was
working there, so she wouldn't have any idea
what he sounded like. If somebody called and
said he was Jean Bousquet—"

"—and Montfort told her he was too—"

"—then how would she know any better? She
wouldn't—wait, who *did* make that call?"

"I don't know. Somebody Montfort put up to
it. I took off before they got around to that."

"But why would he do that? I mean, if Bousquet was safely stored in a freezer somewhere,
and they'd stopped looking for him, and nobody had any reason to think he was dead, let
alone murdered, why would Montfort want to

fabricate a call from him two months later, out of the blue?"

"Because he got nervous. That was when Bousquet's ex-landlady found some more of her jewelry was missing, and concluded—incorrectly, we now know—that he must have been back in town. The idea of the police reopening a search for him scared Montfort, so he concocted the call to head it off. If Bousquet was in Corsica, how could he be in Les Eyzies?"

Their pace had gradually slowed, and Julie's increasingly perplexed frown indicated that she was having trouble putting everything together, for which he didn't blame her; it had certainly taken him long enough, and he had needed plenty of help too. "But what made Montfort freeze him in the first place?" she asked. "That's downright bizarre, to say the least. And why he—"

"Look, instead of bouncing around all over the place, what do you say we sit down to a cup of coffee and just let me try to tell you what I do know in some kind of logical order."

"I'll vote for that."

They had come abreast of the square, where there were a couple of pleasant, familiar cafés to choose from. "Which'll it be?" Gideon asked. "Café de la Mairie or Café du Centre?"

"Which is the one the institute had its staff meetings in again?"

"The Café du Centre."

"The Café de la Mairie then," Julie said without hesitation.

"I guess the best place to start—" Gideon began.

"How about at the beginning?"

"Sure, if I can figure out where it is."

"Start with the hoax, the Old Man of Tayac. What was that all about?"

"Good idea—everything followed from that. Well, what Montfort did—"

"How about starting with *why*, not *what*?"

"Hey, who's telling this story?"

"Montfort was a great figure in the field, wasn't he? He was already established. What did he need with a clumsy stunt like that? Was it because he—"

"Julie—!"

She flinched. "Sorry, I'll be quiet, I promise. Sir."

"About time too," said Gideon. He paused with his hands encircling a soup-bowl-size cup of *café au lait*. "You know, that was the one thing I asked Montfort about: *why*. I had strict orders from Lucien to speak only if spoken to, but all he was interested in was the murders, not the Old Man of Tayac, and so I finally jumped in on my own and asked him what made him cook up the hoax in the first place."

"And?"

"He said: *'Il a bien fallu que quelqu'un le remette à sa place.'* 'Someone had to put him in his place.'"

"'Him'?" Julie set down her own cup. "Meaning *Ely*? I don't understand. I thought Ely was his protégé."

"Oh, he was, he was. And to Ely, Michel Montfort was a god."

"But...?"

"But protégés and their gods have a way of eventually getting on each other's nerves. Look at it from Montfort's point of view. For twenty years he'd been the leading light of the sensitive-Neanderthal school. He was grooming Ely to be his inheritor, the man to whom he was going to pass the scepter. Only..."

Only he wasn't ready to pass it *yet*. And lately it had been the dynamic, colorful, charismatic Ely, not the gruff Montfort, who'd been getting the speaking invitations and showing up in the journal citations. Montfort saw himself increasingly regarded as pedantic, old-hat, even passé; they'd all heard him before, and now it was Ely they wanted to hear from. It was also Ely who was up for the directorship of the institute, and although Montfort had no designs on the job for himself, the idea of being subordinate to his ambitious, popular star pupil was more than he could bear. The hoax was his way of humbling the upstart in general, and of sinking his chances for the directorship in particular.

"Wait—how could it do that?" Julie asked. "I thought he already *was* the director."

"Yes, by the time he found the bones he was, but you see, Montfort had planted them several months before that, when the competition was just getting started. He meant for him to find them *then*. But various things got in the way— the institute was in kind of a mess, and there was an important congress coming up—and Ely didn't have time to fool around at the Tayac site until later, after he was already in the job."

"So Montfort just left the bones there for him to find later?"

"Right. He couldn't keep Ely from being the director, but at least he could still 'put him in his place.'"

"Incredible," Julie murmured. "It seems so... childish."

"Childish, yes, but it worked. Once Ely dug up the bones and fell for them, Montfort turned around and made sure they were exposed as a fraud by writing that letter to *Paris-Match*—"

"Wait a minute, you mean it wasn't Bousquet who wrote the anonymous letter? That was Montfort's doing too?"

Everything had been Montfort's doing, Gideon told her; Bousquet had been a red herring—a patsy—from beginning to end. And it had worked right up until the very end, when Ely, finally beginning to suspect that his beloved Montfort, not Beaupierre, was the power behind the hoax, had confronted him— and wound up dead.

"And Montfort just sat there and admitted all this?" Julie asked.

"Yes. I thought his lawyer was going to have a

stroke." Gideon slowly shook his head. "It was like watching a corpse talk, Julie. Ask him a question, he tells you the answer: 'Did you kill Jacques Beaupierre?' 'Yes.' 'Did you kill Jean Bousquet?' 'Yes.' 'Did you then keep his body in a freezer for three years?' 'Yes.'" Gideon shivered. "And if you didn't interrupt to ask him something, he'd just go on and on like a robot, in this creepy monotone. Mostly, all Joly had to do was sit back and let him tell his story."

He had told it as if by rote, with barely a glimmer of human feeling. The confrontation with Ely had taken place one morning at one of the remote *abris* at which Ely was still desperately hoping to redeem himself. The more Montfort had denied having anything to do with the fake, the more deeply suspicious Ely had become. Near the end of his emotional rope—he'd submitted his letter of resignation only a little while before—he had grown more and more agitated, and Montfort, horrified at the prospect of exposure, had grabbed the nearby air rifle, pointed it in Ely's direction, and pulled the trigger.

He'd realized at once that the body couldn't stay there. Remote as the site was, any search for Ely was bound to include the *abris* at which he'd been working, so he'd dragged the corpse through the brush to another one, a particularly well-hidden little cave in a nearby gully, and buried it there. Before the day was over, the scheme for the faked airplane crash had been developed and put into play. And by the next morning, Ely Carpenter, actually lying under seven or eight inches of dirt in a little cave less than half a mile from Les Eyzies, had been officially lost at sea in the Bay of Biscay.

"So it was actually Montfort in the plane?" Julie asked. "*He* was a pilot too?"

No, it couldn't have been Montfort himself, Gideon told her, because he was still in Les Eyzies early the next morning, when he opened his door to a knock and found Jean Bousquet on his doorstep. Unknown to Montfort, Bousquet had been helping Ely, working in a clearing twenty yards away, putting dirt through a sifter, when Montfort had shown up. He'd heard the commotion and crept back in time to watch Montfort haul Ely's body off. Then, as he told Montfort, he had gone to his room in Madame Renouard's boardinghouse to think. He had spent the night in thought, and had at last come up with his master plan. Unfortunately for him, clear thinking wasn't his strong suit.

He wanted fifty thousand francs. If Professor Montfort would give him fifty thousand francs he would leave Les Eyzies and go to Marseilles. He would give his solemn word never to say anything to anybody about what he had seen. But if Montfort refused, he would go to the police at once. What was Professor Montfort's reply to be?

Naturally, Montfort shot him. With the only weapon at hand—the air rifle that he'd brought home from the *abri*, not knowing what else to do with it.

"So there he was," Gideon said, "looking down at the second guy he'd murdered in the last twenty-four hours, this one bleeding all over his living-room rug, and he felt as if he simply couldn't face the prospect of burying yet another body in another *abri*."

"So he *froze* him instead?"

"Well, as it happened, he already had a rented freezer in a cold-storage warehouse in Le Bugue—somebody used to give him the occasional haunch of venison or wild boar, and that's where he'd keep it—and the easiest, quickest thing to do seemed to be to drive there, dump Bousquet and the rifle into it, and lock it up tight."

"And then what?"

"And then figure out what to do, I suppose. But apparently he never could bring himself to deal with it, and the more time passed the harder it got. So since nothing was forcing his hand, he just put it out of his mind, tried to pretend it never happened."

Until last week, when things had suddenly changed. With Ely's body identified and Jacques showing clear signs of coming unglued, Montfort had had to get him out of the picture too, and it dawned on him that poor old Bousquet was his ticket for getting away with the whole mess. Out came the body, out came the rifle, and a day or so later, there lay the infamous Jean Bousquet on the banks of the Vézère.

"The conscience-stricken victim of his own hand," Julie said softly, "after having done away with Jacques—and Ely, of course, by implication. The snake swallows itself. Go back a second, though. *Why* did Jacques have to be killed? Did he know something about the hoax?"

He not only knew, Gideon told her, he'd taken part, providing Montfort with the fateful lynx bones from his museum. He'd been competing with Ely for the directorship at the time and knew full well that it would take a minor miracle for him to defeat the popular Carpenter. When Montfort, knowing his man all too well, casually suggested "a small prank" to bring Ely down a notch or two, Jacques thought he'd found his miracle. After a few days of waffling, he'd gone along with it, pilfering the bones from the museum—Montfort promised him the source would never be revealed, a promise he didn't waste any time breaking—turning them over to Montfort, and hurriedly stepping out of the picture. That had been the whole of Jacques's guilt, according to Montfort; the subject of his "dreadful confession."

"So he wasn't involved in Ely's murder," Julie said.

"Nope, he was as much in the dark as anyone. He thought what we all thought—that Ely had gone down in his plane."

"I'm glad. I didn't want Jacques to have anything to do with that."

Gideon smiled. "I know what you mean. Anyway, whether Jacques put two and two together and figured out what the murder was about I don't know, but he surely realized there had to be some connection to the hoax. And he definitely knew Montfort was the one who'd engineered that."

"So Montfort had to get to him," Julie said, slowly shaking her head. "Before he told you or Lucien."

That was about it, Gideon told her. Later that morning, seeing Jacques whispering on the telephone, Montfort had casually wondered aloud within Madame Lacouture's hearing as to whom he might be speaking. When she told him that she had no idea but that the call had been made to the Hôtel Cro-Magnon, Jacques's death sentence was sealed.

Montfort had followed him from the institute and trailed after him to La Quinze, done the deed, and then—

"—got Bousquet out of the freezer."

"Yes, that night; like a three-year-old lamb chop. He thawed him out, more or less, in his bathtub—it couldn't have been an easy job, by the way, because the poor guy was bent like a pretzel from spending all that time in the freezer—and left him by the river, with the rifle under him, to be discovered by whoever happened by. It's really pretty brilliant, when you think about it."

"It's really pretty depressing, when you think about it," Julie said. "Whew." She looked up at the sky. "The sun's over the yardarm, and I could sure stand a glass of wine. How about you?"

"You bet," Gideon said emphatically, and glanced at his watch, "but let's have it at the hotel. Lucien promised to try to stop by at five. I told him we'd be in the upstairs lounge."

CHAPTER
26

By the time Joly had poured his second glass of Bergerac from the carafe on the sideboard, the first was having its mellowing effect. He sipped, rolled the wine luxuriously around his mouth, put down the glass, and smiled benignly at them, a man who had earned his ease.

"I want to thank you—both of you—for your very great assistance."

"Lucien," Gideon said, "I was on the phone to you the minute I figured out it had to be Montfort. You already knew. How?"

In reply, Joly passed him a photograph. "Does this person look familiar, Gideon? The picture's a few years old."

Gideon looked at a murky photocopy of a shirtless, heavyset man sitting in a rowboat and squinting good-humoredly into the sun.

Gideon handed it back. "Nope."

Joly smoothed the photo on his thigh and with a few deft, precise squiggles of his pen outlined a foppish goatee and began to fill it in.

"Roussillot!" Gideon exclaimed, turning the picture toward him. "The *fake* Roussillot, the guy in Saint-Cyprien!"

"Yes," Joly said. "Not," he added pointedly, "that he bears much resemblance to the sketch you provided."

"Well, hell, when did I ever say I was any good at—"

"But who is he?" Julie asked.

"His name is Paul-Marie Navarosse," Joly said, taking back the picture and admiring his artwork.

"How did you find him?"

By means, Joly explained, of dedicated, intelligent police work. As Gideon would remember, he had wondered from the beginning about Carpenter's airplane. What had really happened to it? Where was it now? One of his lines of investigation had involved contacting the aviation authorities for a list of persons who had registered the acquisition of a Cessna 185 in the twelve months following Carpenter's disappearance. There had been four of them, and when one—Navarosse—proved to be a small-time importer, a shady character who had twice been the subject of smuggling investigations (one conviction, overturned), Joly took a long, hard look at him.

What he learned made him suspicious enough to have the plane impounded for examination. And despite a few deceptive alterations and papers by the dozen seemingly proving that it had been bought from a Tunisian clock manufacturer named Sadiq who had owned it for the previous six years, an exacting physical examination proved beyond any doubt that it was Carpenter's old Cessna, the plane that had supposedly been rusting on the muddy bottom of the Bay of Biscay for the last three years.

From there, it was only a small step to wondering if it hadn't been Navarosse in the pilot's seat that night, Navarosse who had made the emergency call to air traffic control, Navarosse—

"But what was his connection to—" began Julie.

Joly, who disliked having his narrative rhythm disturbed once he got it going, frowned, waited for silence, and continued.

Navarosse, it turned out, had had a sister, Angélique, who, until her death six years before, had lived in Les Eyzies, where she had been the wife of a renowned archaeologist named—

Rashly, Julie did it again. "Michel Montfort! They were brothers-in-law!"

Just so, said Joly, giving up on narrative rhythm with a sigh. At that point the connection to Montfort was established. He had been saddled for twenty-five years with a black-sheep brother-in-law whom he had helped out time and time again, not so much from a sense of familial loyalty as from motives of self-preservation. Navarosse, it seemed, had not been above using the distinguished Montfort's aversion to scandal to get himself out of his frequent scrapes. Through the years, Montfort had grudgingly provided him with false alibis and even with false purchase orders and receipts to keep his wife's name (and his own) out of the papers. And of course every "favor" had tightened Navarosse's hold on him for the next one.

"This time, however," Joly said, "it was Montfort who demanded favors in return—first the faked airplane crash and then the retrieval of the bones from Saint-Cyprien."

"The business with the plane was a two-way favor," Gideon pointed out. "Navarosse wound up with an expensive piece of equipment."

And a useful one, said Joly. A longtime pilot, he'd been using the plane, one of three that he owned, in the illegal transportation of everything from liquor and cigars to cashmere sweaters and primitive sculpture. And like most enterprising smugglers, he had a front: an import company in Le Bugue that specialized in exotic game meat from Spain and North Africa, for which, of course, he maintained—

Joly paused fractionally, looking at Julie, who came in on cue.

"A cold-storage warehouse!" she cried. "Freezers!"

Joly nodded, and for a minute or two the three of them sat quietly, mulling it all over. "You know," Gideon finally said thoughtfully, "I think that just about wraps things up."

"Yes," said Joly, "the circle closes. The snake grasps its own tail."

"Only this time it doesn't disappear," Gideon said.

On a shared impulse all three of them clinked glasses and drank.

"Well, then," Joly said, draining his glass. "What next? Where are the Olivers off to?"

"Oxford," said Julie, "for a few days' library research. And a little sightseeing. And a little just plain relaxing."

Joly smiled at Gideon. "What, no bones?"

"No, not this time, I'm afraid."

Julie solemnly shook her head. "Gee, that sure is a shame."

AN ARCHEOLOGIST DIGS UP MURDER IN THE ALAN GRAHAM MYSTERIES BY

MALCOLM SHUMAN

THE MERIWETHER MURDER
0-380-79424-1/$5.99 US/$7.99 Can

ASSASSIN'S BLOOD
0-380-80485-9/$5.99 US/$7.99 Can

PAST DYING
0-380-80486-7/$5.99 US/$7.99 Can